ONE QUIET AFTERNOON . . .

Camelli[illegible] ar, Gerstung a[illegible] was the sun glin[illegible] on that grabbed Camellion's attention—just in time to see four or five men lifting their weapons into firing position.

"Ambush—to the left!" Camellion yelled, his hands streaking inside his coat jacket as he dove to the cobblestone ground.

"Balls!" muttered Gerstung. He too started toward the ground, just as the terrorist with the Israeli UZI machine gun got off the first stream of projectiles. All the hollow-nosed slugs passed over Camellion and Gerstung, both of whom were pulling out auto-pistols. Antoine's luck could not have been worse. Two slugs bored into his left hip. A third struck him in the left rib cage. A fourth and a fifth ripped across his back, one cutting a deep, bloody ditch in the flesh, the last one cutting through his back and severing the spinal cord. One moment Antoine was alive and in the prime of life; the next instant he was a corpse, a nothing even before his body crashed to the hard ground.

Camellion—he had calculated distance and windage while throwing himself to the ground—didn't miss. Two of his .380 PPK/S slugs slammed into the man with the UZI, hitting him high in the chest. The astonished terrorist fell against another man, throwing off the fellow's aim.

The Death Merchant continued to pull the trigger, bullets pulsing outward in a stream of destruction . . .

THE DEATH MERCHANT SERIES:

#1 THE DEATH MERCHANT
#2 OPERATION OVERKILL
#3 THE PSYCHOTRON PLOT
#4 CHINESE CONSPIRACY
#5 SATAN STRIKE
#6 ALBANIAN CONNECTION
#7 THE CASTRO FILE
#8 BILLIONAIRE MISSION
#9 LASER WAR
#10 THE MAINLINE PLOT
#11 MANHATTAN WIPEOUT
#12 THE KGB FRAME
#13 MATO GROSSO HORROR
#14 VENGEANCE: GOLDEN HAWK
#15 THE IRON SWASTIKA PLOT
#16 INVASION OF THE CLONES
#17 ZEMLYA EXPEDITION
#18 NIGHTMARE IN ALGERIA
#19 ARMAGEDDON, USA!
#20 HELL IN HINDU LAND
#21 THE POLE STAR SECRET
#22 THE KONDRASHEV CHASE
#23 THE BUDAPEST ACTION
#24 THE KRONOS PLOT
#25 THE ENIGMA PROJECT
#26 THE MEXICAN HIT
#27 THE SURINAM AFFAIR
#28 NIPPONESE NIGHTMARE
#29 FATAL FORMULA
#30 THE SHAMBHALA STRIKE
#31 OPERATION THUNDERBOLT
#32 DEADLY MANHUNT
#33 ALASKA CONSPIRACY
#34 OPERATION MIND-MURDER
#35 MASSACRE IN ROME
#36 THE COSMIC REALITY KILL
#37 THE BERMUDA TRIANGLE ACTION
#38 THE BURNING BLUE DEATH
#39 THE FOURTH REICH
#40 BLUEPRINT INVISIBILITY
#41 THE SHAMROCK SMASH
#42 HIGH COMMAND MURDER

#42 in the incredible adventures of the

DEATH MERCHANT

HIGH COMMAND MURDER

by Joseph Rosenberger

PINNACLE BOOKS LOS ANGELES

No bastard ever won a war by dying for
his country. Wars are won by making
the other poor bastard die for his
country.

General George S. Patton

The only effective morality comes
from the muzzle of a gun.

Richard J. Camellion

To the best friend humanity
will ever have—the
Cosmic Lord of Death.

DEATH MERCHANT #42: HIGH COMMAND
MURDER

An original Pinnacle Books edition, published for the first time anywhere.

First printing, December 1980

ISBN: 0-523-41020-4

Cover illustration by Dean Cate

Printed in the United States of America

PINNACLE BOOKS, INC.
2029 Century Park East
Los Angeles, California 90067

CHAPTER ONE

His hand firm on the steering wheel of the Citroen, Bernard Jordan glanced at Leonard Kidd, the man in the seat next to him. About forty years old, the same age as Jordan, Kidd was a tall, tanned, well-muscled individual, with a face decorated with a brushy mustache and a small, neatly trimmed beard.

Jordan had known Kidd for only a few days; yet his twelve years' service with the Central Intelligence Agency—seven in the covert section—had taught him more about people than the average man learns in a lifetime. It was this experience that convinced him that Leonard Kidd was not only a master in the dirty-tricks department, but also an expert in the art of wholesale termination; and the fact that Grojean had even given him authority over Hallian, the Company's chief of station in Paris, also indicated that Kidd was something very very special. But this! This going to see Madame Sovey was damned stupid. Why, she wasn't about to tell Kidd anything about her murdered husband. Why should she? Kidd was a complete stranger to her.

Jordan turned the car onto a long curve of the Rue de Rivoli, the thoroughfare that would eventually put them on the road that led to Saint-Villeneuve, the last red rays of the setting sun stealing in through the right side of the car.

"In case I didn't tell you earlier, Sainte-Villeneuve is only six miles south of Paris, or slightly more than nine kilometers," Jordan said conversationally. "It's small, a typical French village. We turn off on a brick road to get to the Sovey farm. The farm is three miles east of the village."

Richard Camellion gave a slight nod. "I know," he responded. "I did a recon of the entire area this afternoon, including the Sovey farm."

Jordan's eyebrows raised. "I wondered where you had gotten off to. I didn't think you were scouting the farm. I didn't know you were that acquainted with Paris. Personally I like Paris and the French. What are your feelings toward the French?"

"The same as yours," Camellion replied. "In Paris one can feel at ease with his soul and his surroundings. You get the feeling that Parisians have their priorities in the right order."

"I like to say that Paris is made for people," mused Jordan, "just as New York is a city made for money and power, and modern Moscow has been turned into one made for trucks."

Camellion had not exaggerated about his feelings for Paris and the French. Although Paris was large, sprawling and with more than 8 million people, counting the suburbs, it was never overpowering or impersonal. With some modern exceptions, it was a city of buildings, seven and eight stories high, practically all of them made with blocks of warm, cream-colored limestone—which underlies the Parisian basin, for the city stands precariously over the honeycomb of its own ancient quarries—and decorated with the black wrought iron whose working is a minor French art.

And the roofs. They alone make a fascinating study. The only drawback to roof-gazing is the irritating tendency to march upon a dog's *besoin*—dogs are not curbed in Paris—but even this hazard has its bright side: According to French folklore, it is a guarantee that good luck will follow soon. Of course, that applies only when stepped on with the left foot. The right foot offers no such compensation.

It's the buildings of Paris that will fool you. They often conceal behind their façades a marvelous medieval vestige—the inner courtyard. The faces of the buildings may be blank stone, but once you push the buzzer at one of the front doors, another world appears when the doors swing open—a world complete with trees and flowers and lawns.

In his reverie about Paris, it occurred to the Death Merchant that the variety of courtyards was more than matched by the unpredictable jumble of streets. Some streets were descended from Roman vias, and some from footpaths of the Middle Ages. But most of the straight and wide streets dated from the nineteenth century, when city planners first began to make an impact. Many still had names that were reminders of a time beyond living memory when they served purposes other than crossing points for cars—Rue des Mauvais Garçons ("Bad Boys' Street"), Rue de la Grande Truanderie ("Great Knavery Street"—opposite, incidentally, "Little Knavery Street"), Rue des Quatre Vents ("Street of the Four Winds"), Rue du Four (Oven Street), or Rue Montorgueil ("Prideful Mountain Street"—an example of early Parisian humor, since the "mountain" was a medieval garbage heap).

But we Americans didn't have any Middle Ages, thought Camellion. *This is why we have such trite street names* as *First, Second, Third, Walnut, Oak, Maple . . .*

The ride continued in silence, Jordan not speeding around other vehicles. The late-afternoon traffic had long since disappeared and the Rue de Rivoli was far from being clogged with vehicles. Nonetheless, Jordan did not want to take the chance of being pulled over to the side of the road by an *agent pivot.* French traffic policemen, whether on motorcycles or directing traffic on foot are permitted to ask questions that would not be allowed in the United States.

"It won't be completely dark by the time we get to the Sovey farm," Jordan said. "What do we do, drive right up to the place?"

He gave Camellion another quick glance and felt vaguely irritated when he saw that the Death Merchant's expression remained unfathomable. Damn it! What was really going on?

"Drive right on through Sainte-Villeneuve," Camellion said. "We'll go ten kilometers south of the village. We can then turn around and come back. By then it will be dark."

"Do you want me to go in with you?"

"There's a dirt road, a side road, about a quarter of a mile north of the farm," Camellion said. "We'll take that road and you can pull off among the trees."

Jordan drew back in slight surprise. "You're saying you're going to sneak onto the farm! But why? And isn't it about time that you let me in on what's going on?"

Camellion glanced up into the rearview mirror. As far as he could tell, no one was following them.

"I've got to sneak in because I don't know who else

might be at the farm," Camellion explained. "At the proper time you'll know why I came to Paris and the nature of the mission."

"The tragedy of being a street man," Jordan said mechanically. "We're always the last to know."

"Because you're usually the first to get tagged by the opposition," Camellion reminded the man, who was a large, puffy-faced individual with a talent for dressing meticulously. For example, the clothes he was now wearing: The soft yellow of his shirt, open at the neck, was muted tastefully by his brown slacks and camel blazer. He neither smoked nor drank, but, curiously enough, he had a fear of cockroaches.

Jordan slowed the Citroen as he drove through the village of Creteil, which was only three miles north of Sainte-Villeneuve. Within minutes he and Camellion had driven through the small settlement, and Jordan increased speed. Quickly the Citroen began to close the distance between Creteil and Sainte-Villeneuve.

The Death Merchant took a pair of 9-mm MAB[1] autoloaders and two silencers from a special compartment underneath the seat and started attaching the silencers to the extralong barrels.

"Let's hope you don't need them," Jordan said. He tacked on, "I suppose you know that Madame Sovey's two sons live with her. I don't think they'll take kindly to a stranger busting in and asking their mother a lot of questions, especially since Monsieur Sovey was murdered only a month ago."

"The sons won't have anything to say about it," Camellion said. He pulled a magazine from the butt of one of the MABs and checked to make sure it contained a full fifteen rounds of 9-mm "Sure Kill" cartridges. The cartridges were special in that each thin copper-jacketed bullet was prefragmented. The result was that no energy was wasted

[1]*Manufacture d'Armes de Bayonne.* Bayonne is a port town in the extreme south of France and is famous for more than the MAB. The earliest references to the use of the bayonet are connected with Bayonne. And although the origin of that weapon is obscure, tradition maintains that the bayonet was first designed in the early seventeenth century in Bayonne, where it derived its name.

as with a hollow-point bullet. Being struck by a "Sure Kill" bullet made a wound that always looked as if it had been made by a runaway rip saw, a wound that was a surgeon's nightmare.

"One village of Sainte-Villeneuve coming up," Jordan said.

By now the twilight was very deep, marred only by the headlights of passing cars and the street lights of Sainte-Villeneuve, street lights that grew brighter as the Citroen drew closer to the village. At this early hour of the summer evening, Rue de la Buffa, the main street of Sainte-Villeneuve was alive with people, either strolling on the stone sidewalks or relaxing at the town's two sidewalk cafés . . . drinking the inexpensive peasants' wine, *vins ordinaires*, the common wine most places served in carafes.

Patiently, Jordan guided the Citroen through the two-block area, past other cars, bicycles, and people leisurely crossing the street. Camellion's eyes were everywhere, darting from the rearview mirror to either side of the street. There was a clothing store, a butcher shop on the left and a butcher shop on the right, the latter a *boucherie chevaline* that sold fresh horse meat and its conserved derivatives. Several *épiceries*—French versions of grocery stores that make the American ones look like Mother Hubbard's cupboard. A few cheese shops. Then, once more, the open highway, with pasture land on each side of the road . . . wire fences . . . cattle chewing grass.

"You're armed, aren't you?" Camellion inquired.

"If I had had my way, I'd have brought along an atomic bomb," said Jordan with a laugh. "But I've settled for two Brownings. There's also a Terry carbine with a silencer in the compartment under the back seat."

Forty-two minutes later, Jordan was driving the Citroen slowly along a dirt road, dust flying back over the car whose headlights were dimmed. A small patch of woods—really nothing more than a long, narrow windbreak of beech trees and evergreen shrubs—insured their not being seen by anyone at the Sovey farm, a quarter of a mile to the south.

A slight breeze ruffled the leaves. Crickets and other creatures of the dark sang their night songs.

"Just up ahead, to the right, is a good spot," suggested Jordan. "There's a break in the trees."

"Good enough," Camellion said. "Pull in as far as you can."

A very short time later, Jordan had parked the car, and he and Camellion made the necessary preparations. Jordan took out the 9-mm Wilkinson "Terry" carbine, and the Death Merchant checked a Bio-Inoculator, an electrically fired dart pistol that was totally silent.

Jordan put on a pair of rubber hip boots as protection against chiggers, then proceeded to spray his face and hands with insect repellent. The Death Merchant, having sprayed himself from head to foot with insect repellent before leaving the Champs-Élysées-Étoile hotel, did not have need of such a precaution.

The Bio-Inoculator in his left hand and a silenced MAB in his right, he turned to Bernie Jordan, who had completed all he had to do and was waiting by the left side of the car with the thirty-round carbine.

"Give me an hour and a half," Camellion said in a low voice. "If I'm not back by then, pull out."

"That's a pessimistic attitude," growled Jordan.

"But a realistic one," Camellion corrected him. "If I get the business, you won't prove anything by coming to investigate."

"You're right," Jordan said. "Two dead men only add up to two bad mistakes. By the way, I'll be twenty feet to the left of the car—to your right when you're coming back. Good luck."

He watched the Death Merchant move off through the trees, confident that "Leonard Kidd" would return, sensing by experience that Camellion was the type of pro who could put a Swiss watch together—while blindfolded and wearing boxing gloves!

Moving as swiftly as possible and using Ninja techniques, the Death Merchant skirted the wheat field between the windbreak and the farmhouse and the other buildings. As silent as a shadow, he made the approach from the east, closing in on the farm from its rear. He crept through a grove of maples, on past a long grape arbor, and moved to the side of a tool shed. Seventy-five feet ahead and a hundred feet to his left was a large stone barn and its silo, the back of the barn fenced in. A chicken house. A long shed for goats. A typical French farm.

His concern at the moment was the four hounds that

were on the farm. He wasn't worried that any of the dogs might get to him, but their barking could sound an alarm and bring down the curtain before the first act began.

His eyes probing the darkness, Camellion crept forward, all his senses of survival on full alert, the tune of "I Hear the Sound of Music" skipping lightly through his consciousness.

He studied the farmhouse—two stories of stone topped by a saddle roof, half a dozen dormer windows on each side. Lights burning downstairs, shades pulled over the windows. A porch across the back of the house, a roofed-over veranda along the south side and clear across the front of the house, part of which, on the south side, was glassed in.

Camellion hurried to the north side of a wooden tractor shed. Nothing moved. There was only the sound of crickets and other insects. From far in the distance, an owl hooted.

I don't like the setup. It's too quiet. Well, every man is a fool for at least five minutes of every day. I hope my five are not within the next three hundred seconds.

He stared at the back porch, blinked again, stared again, and was positive that the two dark bundles on the ground were dogs. *From the way they're stretched out, they're not sleeping. Either they have been tranquilized. Or they're dead. Ohhhh boy!*

The house or the barn? *If I take the house, the barn will be behind me.* From where he stood, cloaked in darkness, he couldn't tell whether the barn doors were open or closed.

He chose the house.

A sixty-foot run. Camellion raced straight in, noticing on the way that he had been right about the two dogs. They either were dead or had been rendered unconscious. He got down behind a clump of ornamental mugha-pine bushes by the southwest corner of the porch and waited, his ears straining to pick up any unusual sounds. He got what he wanted. Loud voices came from inside the house, the tones angry, the words muffled. No longer was there any doubt in the Death Merchant's mind. Someone had beaten him to the André Sovey farm. The FLB? Possibly. Yet he couldn't rule out the DST, the French FBI, or the SDECE, the French intelligence service.

Camellion holstered the Bio-Inoculator in its special shoulder holster and pulled out a second MAB. He left the safety of the bushes, stepped up onto the porch and crept to one of the southside windows. The shade was down so he couldn't see who was in the room, but he could hear the conversation.

The terrified voice of an older woman, the words in French—"We don't know about any boxes. He didn't tell me or my sons."

"*Menteur! Cochon!*" The brutal voice of a man, the words snarling with a German accent. "You were his wife! He must have told you where the boxes were hidden—you or those two pig sons of yours!"

There was the distinct sound of a slap, the gasp from the woman, then a man's voice crying out in French, "Leave her alone! He didn't tell her the secret. He didn't tell us. What can we do to convince you?"

"*Zum Verheizen!*" another voice said in German. The man then switched to French. "They know nothing. Let's kill them and leave. The longer we stay the more dangerous it becomes for us."

The Death Merchant's mouth became a tight line of hate. *Zum Verheizen* was Nazi slang for "incineration." It was a term that meant kill, that meant murder!

The men inside with Madame Sovey and her sons are ex-SS! The Death Merchant did some more thinking. The Germans sure as hell hadn't walked or used pogo sticks to get to the farm. Where were their cars? There weren't any vehicles in front of the house. Could they have parked their cars in the trees to the north—*Like Bernie and I did? If so, Jordan could be in trouble. . . .*

Camellion weighed the odds. Lag time was on his side. Kick open the front door and go in shooting, the most direct and logical way. He could kill the SS men before they'd be able to get off a single shot.

Camellion was about to move from his position when twin beams of headlight shot through the open barn doors, an engine started and out came a Porsche Targa. The beams of headlight caught and outlined Camellion as the driver turned the car toward the front of the house.

Behind the Porsche came a larger car—a Mercedes.

During that nick of a second, the Death Merchant saw that two men were in the front seat of the Porsche and that a man who looked German was driving the Mercedes. What really mattered at the moment was that the man on the left side of the Porsche had his arm out the window and was about to open fire with a pistol.

Camellion darted to his left just as the man fired, the loud boom of the Beretta shattering the eerie silence. The 9-mm hollow-point passed within a foot of Camellion, broke a window, poked through the shade and, zipping between Horst Zimmermann and Oscar Ehrlinger, thudded into the wall. The Germans made a dive for the floor, Willy Kurst muttering "*Hurensohn*!" ("son of a bitch") in surprise and fear.

Kurst wasn't any more surprised than the Death Merchant, who fired both MABs as he jumped from the porch to the grass—four audible *bazits* from the special Lee E. Jurass–designed noise suppressors, and it was Doomsday for Fritz Bauer, the man who had fired the Beretta, and for Henri Bidault, the driver of the Porsche. One of the Death Merchant's "Sure Kill" 9-mm bullets ripped into Bauer's right shoulder and shattered the knob at the top of the humerus, the top long bone of the arm. A second 9-mm prefragmented slug tore off the end of his chin bone, zipped upward and buried itself in his hard palate. The third and the fourth bullets from Camellion's MABs, boring in through the windshield, had lost much of their power; yet they still had more than enough momentum to terminate Bidault, hitting him in the chest.

With Bidault unconscious and dying, the Porsche went out of control and began to weave back and forth. It began to slow down as Bidault's foot relaxed on the pedal. Then the dying Bidault fell left, his head and left shoulder falling into Bauer's lap and forcing the Bauer's leg and foot to press down on the accelerator. Like a charging bull, the Porsche headed for the southwest corner of the porch.

Camellion didn't waste time by opening fire on the Mercedes. Knowing he was up against heavyweights, he raced east toward the rear of the house, his years of experience warning him that the ex-Nazis inside would be employing—maybe—the same strategy. The ex-Nazis might be the dregs of the scum barrel, but they weren't novices in the violence and survival department.

He was almost at the rear of the farmhouse when he heard three shots in quick succession from the room in which the conversation he overheard had taken place. No sooner had the shots been fired than the screen door to the back porch was thrown open, and three young goons stepped out, weapons in their hands.

Webber and Kurst, who came out first, turned to their right, Webber swinging up a Heckler and Koch P9S autopistol, Kurst trying to get his Walther P-38 into action. Horst Zimmermann, the last man to come out onto the porch, brought up a Polish P-64 pistol.

Camellion jerked to his right and fired both MABs simultaneously at hip level. Webber cried out from the impact of the MAB's "Sure Kill" bullet striking him in the stomach, the slug then tumbling around inside his visceral region like a razor blade weighed down with an anvil. Dying on his feet, Webber fell sideways against Kurst who was doing a fast backward two-step with a slug in his chest, the front of his blue sport shirt torn and bloody.

What dumbbells! They're not old pros from ODESSA. Camellion jerked to the right just as Zimmermann snapped off a quick shot with the P-64 pistol. The metal-jacketed bullet burned by Camellion, missing him by only a few inches. Before Zimmermann had time to regain that half second of lag time, Camellion placed a "Sure Kill" 9-mm bullet into his chest. At once the German was unconscious from shock and dying, the slug having cut through one of the coronary arteries.

Behind Camellion the Porsche slammed into the southwest corner of the porch, the crashing bringing down several of the square posts supporting the overhang.

The driver of the Mercedes shot his vehicle around to the front of the house, slammed on the brakes, pulled out a 9-mm MKE pistol, hunched down in the seat and waited.

The Death Merchant jumped up on the back porch and leaped over the corpse of Webber. He had iced the three men so fast that he didn't even have to open the screen door, which was prevented from being closed by Zimmermann's corpse that acted as a doorstop.

He rushed into the kitchen, almost stumbled over a dead dog lying by a table, and ducked when he saw several men in the second room ahead turn in his direction and bring up pistols. Two quick shots from the men, but both bullets went to waste.

Crouched by one side of the door to the dining room, Camellion had no way of knowing if the men in the front room of the house might be charging toward him. He didn't think so. He assumed that they would rush out the front door, get into the Mercedes and get the hell away from the farm. Not willing to take any chances, he thrust one of the MABs around the edge of the doorway and triggered off four quick shots, spreading them out so that a four foot square was covered.

No cries of pain. No sounds of falling bodies. He heard the front screen door slam—*Which could be a trap! One man or all of them might still be waiting.*

Camellion sent five more shots toward the front of the house, then jumped up, charged through the door, raced across the dining room and, upon reaching the living room, heard an engine throbbing with increased power and tires screaming in protest. The Germans in the house had piled into the Mercedes and were escaping.

Camellion pulled back the shade slightly from one of the windows and saw the Mercedes pulling away, the driver increasing speed. Still, taking no chances, he raced into the first bedroom and inspected it, including looking under the bed and into the closet. He checked out the two other bedrooms—all empty.

He hurried back to the living room and looked down in disgust at the bodies of Madame Sovey and her two sons, men in their thirties. The three corpses were on the floor, lying on their stomachs, hands tied behind their backs. All three had been shot in the back of the head. *And not by amateurs either!* noted Camellion. The muzzle of the pistol had been placed against the hollow of the back of the head, at the level of the ears, with the weapon pointed slightly downward. The most efficient method of execution. In this manner a bullet will pass through the medulla oblongata, that part of the brain that controls heartbeat and respiration. The woman and her sons had died instantly, as fast as if they had been struck by a bolt of lightning, which delivers its punch in one-tenth of a microsecond (or ten-millionth of a second).

In spite of this phase of the mission being held a total flop, Camellion felt a certain amount of satisfaction. At least he now knew that he was up against the experts of ODESSA, which doesn't have anything to do with the port on the Black Sea. ODESSA (*Organization der ehemaligen SS Angehorigen*) is the Association of ex-SS Members. The men who had murdered the Soveys were probably former *Sicherheitdienst*; the intelligence service of the SS and the Nazi Party. The SD was also part of the *Reichs-*

Sicherheits-Hauptamt, ("the Head Department for the Security of the Reich"). Ex-Gestapo agents would have used the *Genickschuss* ("neck shot").

There wasn't any sense in searching the house. Camellion didn't have the time. Besides, the Germans had already made a search and hadn't found anything, or they wouldn't have been questioning the Soveys.

Camellion reloaded the two MAB autoloaders and hurried toward the rear of the farmhouse. His work here was finished. A few minutes later, he was outside in the darkness and running in an eastern direction.

Bernard Jordan stepped out from behind the tree as Camellion cautiously approached the Citroen.

"I heard the shots from the farmhouse," Jordon said simply. Moving to the car, the Company man didn't press for answers.

It wasn't until Jordan had driven the car onto the brick road that Camellion gave him the details of what had happened at the Sovey farm.

"ODESSA, huh?" Jordan's voice was casual. "So it goes all the way back to World War Two. It might help if you gave me a clue to what we're supposed to accomplish."

"We're after gold," Camellion said, staring at the lights of Sainte-Villeneuve in the distance. "At today's prices, about half a billion dollars in stolen Nazi gold. And that's only a part of it."

"And the other part?"

The Death Merchant didn't answer.

CHAPTER TWO

No one suspected that the tall and distinguished Senhor Alfredo Pinheiro, a coffee salesman from Rio de Janeiro, was actually ex-SS-*Gruppenführer* Ernst Rudolf Müller. Ex-lieutenant general Müller hated being in France. Even worse was having to deal with such *Schweine* as Fauvet, Duchemin and Jaffe. Those *dumm Esel* were so unrealistic that they actually thought they could force the French government to eventually grant self-government to Brittany. Yet Muller realized that ODESSA needed the help of the FLB terrorists. Without *Front de Libération de la Bretagne*, ODESSA would never find the gold that had been stolen by the Americans so many years ago. Once the gold was located, then Fauvet and the others could be dealt with.

Standing by the window, looking out over the peaceful French countryside, the seventy-one-year-old Müller remembered those days of glory, especially that day forty-one years earlier, on June 21, 1940, when he had been a member of the entourage that accompanied Hitler to the forest of Compiègne where the French surrendered. The führer had insisted that the same railroad car be used, the very same dining car, in which the defeated German generals had signed the documents of surrender that had ended World War I.

Ya . . . Müller remembered with pleasure. He had been a captain in the SD, and Reinhard Heydrick himself had assigned him to be a member of the Führer's personal bodyguard. How he recalled that glorious day in 1940. The band of the *SS Leibstandarte Adolf Hitler* had given a resounding performance of "Deutschland über Alles." Hitler and his party had strode under the great oaks and elms, the face of *der Führer* contracted into a mask of angry scorn and brutal contempt for the defeated French. So very long ago. Then, five years later, total defeat, the Reich in total ruins. By then, however, certain far-sighted people in the SD had made preparations to survive the catastrophe. Müller—by then a lieutenant general—had made it safely to Brazil and, well supplied with money and an excellent job of plastic surgery, had established himself as Alfredo Pinheiro. The Israelis had chased Dr. Mengele and other German "war criminals" all over South America, but not once had they even developed a clue as to the real identity of Senhor Alfredo Pinheiro.

But now he was back in France. He had returned because the command of ODESSA had ordered him to go to Paris, because this particular situation called for a highly experienced man, an expert in duplicity and double-dealing. And Müller was one of the best.

Dressed in off-white slacks, blue loafers and a sky-blue shirt, Müller turned and walked slowly back to the table where Karl Scherhorn, Heinz Wallesch and the three Frenchmen were poring over an old map that showed General Patton's rapid advance through Europe during World War II.

"All of this speculation is useless," grunted Karl Scherhorn, standing erect. "This map tells us nothing of any importance. Patton himself didn't help steal the gold. It was a handful of his officers."

"Yes, that's true, but only on the surface," Heinz Wallesch said. "Patton's officers—whoever they were—wouldn't have had the time to journey too far from the main force of the American Third Army." Wallesch glanced at Scherhorn, then at a dour-faced Müller. "For example," he continued, "Patton had pushed his Twelfth Corps to a point ten miles below Linz on the Austrian Danube—this on the day of the German surrender. His Third Corps was at the foot of the Bavarian Alps. On May 2, 1945, his Thirteenth Armored Division crossed the Inn at Braunau. That should tell us all something."

"You're only reinforcing what I just said," countered Scherhorn. "We know that there were three main thrusts by Patton's Third Army But none of that tells us which American officers participated in the theft of the bullion."

"Of course not," Wallesch said. Annoyed, he stood up straight. "We have to make assumptions. Munich is only one hundred and twenty kilometers west of Linz, and the gold was stored in Munich, in the basement of a brewery. It's safe to presume that some of the officers in Patton's Twelfth Corps were involved in the theft."

"*Oui,* that makes sense," Jean Joseph Duchemin said, nodding in agreement.

"Nonsense. The American officers are not important," Charles Fauvet said, sounding annoyed, his voice unusually high. "Why, all of them could be dead by now for all we know."

The thirty-four-year-old Fauvet didn't look like a terrorist either. Muscular, but only 5 feet 3 inches tall, he gave the impression that someone had chopped a foot or so off his legs. His face was round and fleshy, yet his jaw was sharp and firm, his eyes as mean as a barracuda's.

"It's where the gold is hidden that matters," he said, "and we of the FLB don't have a single clue." He grinned maliciously at an expressionless Muller. "And neither do you Boche!"

"We are Brazilians, Monsieur Fauvet," Müller said tolerantly, looking at the terrorist leader who was smiling slightly. "If you feel we are Germans, why then are you dealing with us?"

Heinz Wallesch, whom the French knew as Jimenez Cuença, faked a laugh. Only thirty years old, tall and good looking, he was the son of ex-SS general Jurgen Wallesch.

"It always amazes me how you French always think that anyone from South America is a Nazi in disguise!" he said, laughing again. "Why I wasn't even alive during World War Two."

"*Non, mon ami,* you weren't," Fauvet said slyly, putting his hands on his hips. "But Monsieur Pinheiro and Monsieur del Rosa were very much alive."

André Jaffe extended his arm in a mocking Nazi salute. "*Vive la France! Sieg Heil!*" He walked with quick steps across the thick white rug and dropped into a heavy armchair.

"We were in Brazil all during the war," Müller said sincerely, knowing fully well that not one of the three French terrorists believed him. Not that it actually mattered. The French terrorists needed the ex-Nazis to dispose of the gold on the foreign market. Unless they had proper knowhow and expertise in international banking, the gold was just so much yellow metal. The ex-Nazis needed the FLB to help find the gold. The FLB knew the countryside, and it had contacts in the French underworld.

Müller glanced furtively at José del Rosa, who—his junior by four years—was actually ex-SS *Standartenführer* Karl Victor Scherhorn—or the "Butcher of Brussels" as the police of a dozen nations had called him. Muller realized that Colonel Scherhorn didn't trust the French pigs anymore than he did. *Ya* . . . there was just a little more than the possibility that Fauvet and his gang of cutthroats would cooperate only until the gold was found, then—*Zum Verheizen!* The French terrorists might attempt to dispose of the gold on their own. It was indeeed a dangerous game for both sides. For the FLB had to suspect that the Nazis had the same fatal plans for them, that "Senhor Pinheiro" and his two companions from Brazil had not imported Nazi sympathizers from West Germany merely to help the FLB search for the gold.

As Müller and the other two Nazis sat down on a long couch, Jean Duchemin leaned back and blew cigarette smoke toward the high, baby-pink ceiling. Of medium height, he was built like a boxer, lean and quick. He had a head of heavy black hair and a bushy black mustache under his long beak of a nose.

"*Assez, monsieurs,*" he said pleasantly and smiled at Müller and the other two Germans. "We are talking like petty shopkeepers. It is only that we are not fools and do not like being played for *faire l'idiots.* You three 'Brazilians' rent this fine chateau, only a few kilometers from Versailles, and then know exactly how to contact us. That alone, *mes amis*, proves you are not ordinary businessmen."

Charles Henri Fauvet further surprised the Germans by saying, "My father was a *Louisien,* a Resistance fighter, during the war. We are not interested in refighting the wars of our fathers. It is the future that counts with us, a future in which *Bretagne*[1] will be an independent nation . . . after we help you find the gold. But"—he shrugged —"*on se défend.* It is only natural that you keep your guard up."

Müller carefully brushed the left side, then the right side,

[1]Brittany, a region in northwest France. Many English—British—people moved to this part of France about fifteen hundred years ago, and that is how it got its name.

of his mustache with a forefinger. Fauvet and his crowd, totally unscrupulous, couldn't care less where the power came from—as long as it wasn't used against them personally, and as long as they got what they wanted. Müller, an expert in treachery, knew that one could only retain the allegiance of such men by deception, and even then not indefinitely.

"*Oui*, you are right, Monsieur Fauvet," Müller finally said, smiling slightly. "We must trust each other and work for the good of all. After we have succeeded, we can go our separate ways."

"*Bon!* Let's discuss last night's activities," Fauvet said.

Senhor del Rosa—Colonel Scherhorn—made an angry face. His florid cheeks looked strangely gray and sunken. "What is there to discuss? Last night was a disaster. Four of our people are dead, and—"

"And one of ours," interjected André Jaffe quickly.

"With them went our last clue to the gold—Madame Sovey and her two sons," intoned Fauvet thoughtfully. His gaze went accusingly to Ernst Müller. "Your man Glucks had to kill them. *Oui!* I know he had to do it. After last night, the DST and the SDECE would have returned and pulled answers from the Soveys. Once the Soveys talked, we'd have lost all our opportunities to get the gold."

Heinz Wallesch almost said "*Ya*," but caught himself in time. "*Si*, all that is true. But that leads to the question of, where do we go from here? We don't know of anyone else who helped the American officers hide the gold."

Scherhorn uncrossed his legs and leaned back on the couch. "Glucks and Berger are convinced that André Sovey didn't impart any information to his family. I, too, don't believe that he did. I think he would want to protect them."

"I was against it from the beginning," Heinz Wallesch said sarcastically. "The three Soveys should have been kidnapped. They should have been taken to a safe place where we would have had enough time to torture them into telling the truth. Any person can be made to break under pain. Now they're dead."

"We can be certain that the gold is buried somewhere in northern France," Müller said in a soft tone. "On the assumption that André Sovey was telling the truth in his interview with *Paris Match*."

Charles Fauvet shifted uneasily in his chair. "Suppose

Sovey was telling the truth? That's no guarantee that the gold is still there. After the war, the *officiers américains* could have returned to France and picked up the gold. Why else would they have stolen it?"

"*Non*, the Americans did not come back for the gold," Scherhorn said stubbornly. He stared at Fauvet, who was not moving a muscle. Duchemin was nervously manipulating his long, thin cigar. André Jaffe was toying with a cigarette lighter. "In the first place, consider the weight. Each box weighed 45 kilograms, or a hundred pounds American weight. One hundred boxes would be five tons, or 10,000 pounds."

"Nonsense!" There was a surprising undertone of vehemence in Jean Duchemin's voice. "A large truck could easily carry the boxes of gold. The real trick would be in getting them out of the country."

"You're forgetting other facts which indicate the gold is still in France," snapped Scherhorn. "Sovey was murdered two weeks after *Paris Match* printed his exposé. During the same week that he was murdered, three other Frenchmen were also killed. All three lived in northern France. We would be idiots to ignore that someone wanted to keep them from talking and, no doubt, revealing where the gold is buried."

"It wasn't the FLB that killed them," Fauvet said, frowning. "We wouldn't kill the geese that could lay golden eggs."

"Whoever killed them was working for the American officers who stole the gold," Müller said briskly. "Perhaps the same man—or men—who interrupted last night's operation at the Sovey farm."

"I wonder if he could be working for the American CIA," said Duchemin, staring moodily at the cigar he had lighted. He looked up and locked eyes with Müller. "I don't think so. If he's working for anyone, he's a paid assassin to the officers in the Third Army who stole the gold. They wanted to shut up Sovey and the others, and they succeeded."

André Jaffe fidgeted nervously with the cigarette lighter. "I don't think we'll ever find the hot gold." He kept his eyes on the lighter as he talked. "We're going to have enough trouble just keeping the flics, *the agents de police*, from slitting our throats. And those *fils de putes* ("sons of bitches") of the ARC.[2] The ARC had a lot of ex-legionnaires and ex-marines in its membership, and they're as tough as nails. These terrorists who want to free their beloved Corsica from France! Add to them the *porcs* of the DST[3] and the agents of the SDECE[4] and we have plenty of trouble. *Mon Dieu!* We don't have a single clue as to where the gold is hidden."

SS *Standartenführer* Karl Victor Scherhorn looked sternly at Fauvet. In his best days, Scherhorn had been a mild-looking man who resembled a county clerk. Now he looked like a retired county clerk, still slim—for he was very careful about his weight—but wrinkled, with small bags under his eyes. "We were under the impression that some of your people had infiltrated the Corsican liberation group." His voice was cold and scathing. "Haven't they given you any information of value? After all, the ARC is also after the gold."

"*Rien de valeur* ('Nothing of value')," replied Fauvet. He sat up straight and squared his shoulders. "We have agents only in the rank-and-file membership. We have no one close to Jules Laroche and Antoine Argoud, the leaders. Furthermore, we are certain that the ARC and agents of the DST have infiltrated our own organization at the rank-and-file level."

The French terrorist—he was wanted for seventeen murders—glanced at Senhor Alfredo Pinheiro, but Müller's thoughts were elsewhere. In a sense, this chateau, with its tall, narrow windows reminded him of a miniversion of the Reich Chancellery on the Wilhelmstrasse. Completed in 1939, the new Reich Chancellery had vast columns, slot-like windows and endless corridors of blood-red marble from which tapestries were hung. Came the end of the war, and the Chancellery was but rubble. *Gottverdammte noch-'mal!*

Müller's mind snapped back to the present. "We're ana-

[2]*Action pour la Renaissance de la Corse* is a group of terrorists dedicated to freeing Corsica from French rule.
[3]*Direction de la Surveillance du Territoire*, similar to America's FBI, is responsible for all internal security in France.
[4]*Service de Documentation Extérieure et de Contre-espionnage* is the same as our American CIA. In the old days, the SDECE was the *Deuxième Bureau*, "Intelligence Service."

lyzing in the wrong direction," he said coolly. "We—my associates and I in South America—are almost positive that it was the American Counterintelligence Corps that first learned that the gold was stored in Munich, that the CIC tortured the secret from an SD agent who had the misfortune to fall into their hands."

André Jaffe's eyes widened. "I didn't know the *Américains* went in for such brutality. I thought only the Nazis and the Russians went in for that sort of thing?"

Müller let Jaffe's remark slide by, while memory flashes scenes of the past through his mind. *Nein!* The damned Americans had not tortured the body of a German POW. They were more subtle; they broke his mind. For example, a man might be kept chained—stark naked—to a hot radiator, in a such a manner that he could neither sit nor bend. He was fed only salty food and given only one cup of water a day. By the end of the second day his ankles would be swollen to twice their normal size. All the while, loudspeakers, only twenty inches from his ears, would blare distorted music. Now and then, the music would stop and he would hear the desperate screams and pleas of a German woman from a cell close by. More often than not, one of the Americans tormenting the woman would call out her name, which would just happen to be the name of the POW's wife. Only after he "confessed" would he learn that his wife had been at home all the time and that no one had even bothered to question her. The entire torture scene had been staged. Yet to save his wife, the POW would confess to anything that the CIC wanted him to confess to—*anything!*

Fauvet licked his lips nervously. Jean Duchemin and André Jaffe sat quietly, watching the three Germans, none of whom they trusted.

"Get to the point," Fauvet said sullenly to Müller. "What's the difference how the *Américains* learned about the gold? It is apparent that the *Américain* CIC worked with officers in General Patton's army. Together they shipped the gold, no doubt by truck, to France."

Heinz Wallesch said, "They didn't dare leave the gold in Germany. "At the time, they had no idea of how the Reich might be cut up. Munich and the surrounding area could have ended up in the Russian zone. In France the gold would be safe."

"Let us presume all this is accurate. The *Américains*

would hardly keep a record of such a shipment," commented Jaffe, smiling faintly. "What remains a mystery is why they didn't kill the Frenchman who assisted them. To have let them live—*Stupide!* It makes no sense!"

Smiling, Müller placed his arm on the armrest of the couch and crossed his legs. "I think the Americans didn't kill the Frenchmen because they couldn't, because they didn't dare. I think that Sovey and the other Frenchmen were members of the Marquis, the French Resistance. To have slaughtered them would have brought retaliatory action and have caused a stink all the way to the Allied High Command in London."

Fauvet smiled. "there's only one flaw in your theory, Monsieur Pinheiro. "What was to prevent the members of the Maquis from returning and claiming the gold for themselves—years later if necessary?"

"*Oui.* What assurance would the *Américains* have that the gold would be safe from the very men who had helped them hide it?" pointed out André Jaffee. His shook his head vigorously from side to side. "*Non, mon ami allemand!* It is all nothing more than dangerous speculation."

Heinz Wallesch turned and looked searchingly at Müller. "He's right," he said in Portuguese to keep up the act that he and the two other Germans were native Brazilians. "The Americans would never have trusted the French freedom fighters."

Lieutenant General Müller replied in French for the benefit of the three Frenchmen, "There could be any number of explanations. We can't be absolutely certain that the Frenchmen who helped the Americans knew the boxes contained gold bars." He held up a hand when Fauvet and Duchemin started to speak. "For all we know, it's possible that André Sovey was only guessing at the contents when he gave that interview to *Paris Match*. The man was dying of lung cancer. He wanted money for his family. He would have said anything." He paused, then went on, "Or, even if the French knew the boxes contained gold, there might be another reason why they weren't able to return and claim the boxes."

Fauvet dismissed Müller's words with a wave of his hand. "It's nothing more than sheer speculation that can't help us."

"Oh, but it can," Müller said without rancor. "The maquis kept records of their activities. One, or all, of the

Frenchmen who assisted the Americans just might have made a report to his commander. Such a report would include the name of the town closest to where the gold is hidden. It's not impossible that the actual location of the treasure itself might be in the report."

For the first time, Fauvet's eyes glowed with interest, "Now you're talking sense—for all the good it does us. If there are any written records, they're buried somewhere in the files of the SDECE and beyond our capacity for research."

"Written reports, yes. But there are still a lot of the Maquis alive," Müller went on hastily, striving to conceal his agitation. "Your organization has the manpower and the contacts necessary to help us find not only many section leaders of the Maquis, but also the other Frenchmen who helped the Americans hide the boxes."

"In the *Paris Match* interview, Sovey did say there were twenty of them," Scherhorn said ponderously. "Yet only Sovey and three others were murdered. Either the Americans don't know the names of the other sixteen or can't find them."

Jean Duchemin sighed. "Statistically, at least a fourth of that number would be dead by now. On that basis, we are seeking either eight men—at minimum—or eleven—at maximum."

He glanced somewhat disdainfully around the large room. There were comfortable chairs, thick pile carpets, paintings and sculptures, and he felt out of place amidst all this luxury, in this chateau that the Germans had rented from a French count who was in desperate need of money.

"We should wait," SS colonel Victor Scherhorn said firmly. "We should wait until we find out the result of tomorrow's raid in Paris." His frigid stare stabbed at Charles Fauvet. "The operation is strictly FLB. Should it fail, don't throw any blame in our direction."

"There will not be any failure," Fauvet said in an easy manner. "We've been watching that place in Montmartre for months. We're positive it's a safe house for the Corsican terrorists. Believe me, we're sure."

"We might even succeed in kidnapping the man who killed your German *Kameraden* at the Sovey farm," smirked Jean Duchemin, who could not resist the insult. "Our people are experts."

"We wish you good luck," Müller said evenly. "But suppose we wait and see. Talk is very cheap; it's results that count."

Privately, Müller had one deep fear, one that he had not as yet even conveyed to Colonel Scherhorn and Heinz Wallesch. Based on how the single attacker had acted at the farm, such incredible daring and precision, Müller was very much afraid that ODESSA was fighting its old nemesis—*Der Tod Kaufmann.* The Death Merchant.

CHAPTER THREE

It wasn't the dinginess of the room nor the lack of space that worried the Death Merchant. All apartments in Montmartre had the space of extralarge sardine tins, especially on Liberté, Fraternité and Égalité streets, where there were hundreds of tiny two-story houses the French called *pavillons*. Workers live in *pavillons*, and the bourgeois live in *villas*.

The apartment of Monsieur and Madame Debray was on the first floor of an old three-story building on Rue du Chat-qui-Peche. Only two feet beyond the front door was the curb of the cobbled street. It was this close proximity to "Fishing Cat Street" that troubled the Death Merchant. *Why, damn it! A joker could pedal by on a bicycle and toss a grenade into the living room through one of the two front windows. What a setup! We might as well be in a display window, even if the drapes are drawn!*

From where Camellion sat, in a rocking chair in a corner of the front room, he could see Bernard Jordan, who was cleaning a Beretta M-12 submachine gun, and Roger Silour, who giving an oral history of the guillotine to Ralph Stanley Gerstung, the second Company "street man" in the room. Georges Debray was in the small kitchen, helping Camille, his wife, prepare a lunch of *boeuf à la ficelle*, beef boiled with garden vegetables.

A long-time member of *Action pour la Renaissance de la Corse*, Silour spoke English very well and talked like a record player that never ran down. In his early forties and with an untrimmed mustache, he was wiry, intense and so skinny that it seemed as if he would get a hernia from opening an envelope.

"A lot of people to this day don't realize that the guillotine—or *la louisette*, as it is called—was conceived by a doctor of anatomy, one Joseph Ignace Guillotin, as a humanitarian gesture, to ensure a quick and painless end to the tribulations of those condemned to death. You see, before that, only the nobility had been accorded the privilege of death by decapitation. Ahhh, but Monsieur Guillotine only proposed such a device. The actual design was entrusted to Doctor Antoine Louis, an officer of the Academy of Surgery. But the first working model was built by Tobias Schmidt, a German harpsichord maker. Schmidt tested his chopping machine on corpses at the Hôpital Bicêtre and on live sheep. A robber—I think he was called Pelletier—was chosen as the first human guinea pig." Silour giggled oddly. "The first live human guinea pig. He was executed in April of 1792 at the Place de Grève in front of the Hôtel de Ville."

Bored, Camellion listened to the monotonous oscillations of the two fans in the room. One sat on an end table, the other on top of the piano.

"Ah huh," said Gerstung, a mild-looking, round-faced man in his early thirties. In spite of his harmless appearance, he was rated as one of the Company's best terminators. "So that's where the Revolution lopped off all the heads."

"No. Seventy-three people were executed at Place de la Bastille," responded Silour. "Another couple of thousand were executed at Place de la Nation on the eastern edge of the city. But it was Dr. Guillotin who was the most pitiful victim. He died peaceful in bed in Paris—either 1814 or 1815—his head still attached to his shoulders. Until the very end he complained bitterly because his name had been given to Schmidt's machine."

An amused smile spread across Gerstung's face. "I think you will admit that *guillotine* has a better ring to it than *schmidt*. When you hear the name Schmidt, you think of a German army private or a butcher. It's really a matter of conditioning, of psychology. *Schmidt* would never have worked as a name for the machine. How would it sound if a judge said, "I sentence you to die by the schmidt?"

Both Silour and Gerstung laughed heartily. So did the Death Merchant whose eyes, at the moment, were on a heavy wooden bookcase filled with mostly bric-a-brac . . . a row of gold-plated tankards, a metal cannon, small vases; on top a tall bud vase filled with half a dozen roses fashioned from thin copper. The wire stems were painted green.

"The hell with a guillotine," Jordan said with a half-laugh and shoved a full magazine of 9-mm cartridges into the Beretta sub-gun. "This baby can kill twenty times faster and with more efficiency and less blood. I'm hungry. I wonder how soon we'll eat?"

"Madame Debray said lunch would be at one," Camellion said. He shifted his weight in the rocking chair, slipped his thumbs through his unbuttoned white sport shirt and, hooking the leather straps of the filled holsters nestled underneath his armpits, moved the straps over his shoulders. Each holster contained a fully loaded MAB auto-pistol.

Camellion again thought of his position. The decision to come to the Debray apartment had not been his. Jordan—connected to the CIA "Station" at the American Embassy in Paris—had made all the arrangements. After leaving the area of the Sovey farm, Camellion had Jordan had taken a circuitous route to Paris. According to Jordan and Gerstung, Georges and Camille Debray were trusted members of the ARC. At four o'clock that afternoon the Debrays would take Camellion and the two Company men to meet direct representatives of the Corsican terrorist organization.

What is, is! Camellion told himself. Under a different set of circumstances, he would have enjoyed the district of Montmartre. Of all the villages that Paris had absorbed as it had expanded over the centuries, there were still a few that had managed to maintain a separate identity, a character that was somehow different from the bulk of the city surrounding them. Montmartre—incorporated into Paris in 1860—was such a place.

Situated on a hill—at 423 feet, the high point of Paris—Montmartre remained strikingly provincial, a gem of a little town, whose twisting little streets and alleys are an intricate web of stores, old apartment buildings, and hotels that have hardly changed in three hundred years. Each block was like a self-sufficient unit, with its own butcher, *boulangerie-pâtisserie* (bakery and pastry shop), and of course a bistro or two and a *brasserie*[1]. On every third or fourth block would be a *charcuterie* (a delicatessen and pork specialty shop).

To Camellion, there was always something very special about Montmartre, more so than, say, Belleville, whose highest point was only six-and-a-half-feet less. At Montmartre, early Celtic tribesmen had worshipped their gods, and so had the Romans. The very name of the hill was a religious origin—probably derived from mons Martis or mons Mercurri, the Roman gods Mars and Mercury. Then again, possibly from mons Martyrum because Saint Denis—Paris' first Catholic bishop—was decapitated on this hill in the third century before all the citizens of Paris had become convinced of the benefits of Christianity.

Bernard Jordan put the Beretta machine gun behind the wooden bookcase, then looked over at Camellion and grinned.

"*Snakker De norwagen*? Kidd?"

"*Jo.*" Camellion said, not showing his surprise that Jordan had spoken to him in Norwegian.

Jordan said quickly in Norwegian, "The trouble with these people is that they have no sense of time, no sense of urgency. It's something you have to live with."

"Yes, only the Greeks are more lackadaisical," replied Camellion. "Tell a Greek a joke on Sunday, and he won't get around to laughing until the middle of Monday afternoon."

Hearing Camellion and Jordan speaking a foreign language, Silour looked at both men, his eyes narrowing in slight suspicion.

"We are now having lessons in a language other than French or English?" he asked in French and smiling.

"We like to keep in practice," answered Jordan, who glanced toward Georges Debray, who was coming in from the kitchen. Almost thirty years old, Debray did not resem-

[1]Bistros offer cheap meals in a simple setting. *Brasseries*—literally, "breweries"—are several cuts above bistros and often achieve a high status because of their specialities. *Brasseries* offer less ambitious dishes and cheaper prices than restaurants that serve *haute cuisine.*

ble the average person's conception of a terrorist. With his horn-rimmed glasses, a mustache and a goatee, Debray looked more like a professor at the Sorbonne.

Full of exuberance, Debray rubbed his hands together. "*L'appétit vient en mangeant!* 'Eating awakens the appetite.' It's an old French proverb, *mes amis.* Lunch will be ready in fifteen minutes."

"*Parfait. J'ai faim,*" Ralph Gerstung said pleasantly, with a nod of approval. It was okay with him; he was hungry.

Gerstung's watchful eyes went from Debray to Camellion, who, at the moment, was thinking that Georges Debray himself was another crack in the dam of security, a danger because he was a known radical. A one-time member of the French Socialist party, Debray had been arrested at least a dozen times during protest demonstrations. He had given speeches offering ready Socialistic solutions to such complex problems as unemployment ("Reduce the work week to thirty hours!") and the high cost of gasoline ("Nationalize the oil industry!"). He was also convinced that the way to help the inflation-burdened workers was to give them automatic escalations in pay as prices would rise. To Camellion Georges Debray was an extremely dangerous man—an idealistic dreamer who didn't understand the realities of economics. Worse, Debray was known to the French DST.

Camille Debray—*Just as unrealistic as her fruitcake of a husband. The French FBI also consider her a radical*—was a very shapely young woman, Camille had once been a dancer at the famous Crazy Horse Saloon, the oldest and best striptease establishment in Paris. The high quality of entertainment at the Crazy Horse is due to Alain Bernardin, the owner, whose standards include drivng his dancers hard in rehearsal. All twenty to twenty-five have to be superb dancers; the original routines, taking weeks of practice to perfect, are in the most demanding tradition of modern dance. And when Camille Debray had been a naked hoofer, she had been known by her stage name—Mona Banana.

Camellion was more interested in meeting the representatives of the ARC than in eating lunch. "Listen, Debray. I don't want any slipups with this meeting. If there are any 'ifs' or 'maybes' connected with the meet, now is the time to say so."

"I'm concerned about *agents provocateurs,*" Ralph Gerstung said stoutly, cupping his chin on folded hands.

Debray, who had sat down on the old red couch, took a long and enjoyable pull at his goatee and let out a defensive little laugh. "Oh, you *Américains!* Your national trait must be pessimism!"

"We Americans are too much of a heterogeneous society to have any national traits," Camellion said drily.

"Unless it's violence?" inserted Roger Silour.

"Most of the violence is due to the trash our powderpuff government refuses to deal with!" snapped Jordan. "Foreign trash and so-called native-American trash that should never have been brought to the U.S. in the first place. But that isn't the issue. Can you trust the people we're going to meet?"

Debray was suddenly very serious, his voice low and firm. "I personally know the two men and one woman we are to meet. We'll leave here at four as planned. That will give us plenty of time to drive to the Champs-Élysées. We'll make contact in the Place de la Concorde, close to the Obelisque de Luxor[2]. All will go well. You'll see."

Roger Silour added quickly, "We chose the Place de la Concorde because there is always safety in numbers. At five-thirty in the afternoon la Concorde is always crowded with tourists. No one will take any special notice of us."

"Once Laroche and the others see us, they will return to their car," Georges Debray continued the explanation. "We'll return to ours and drive back here. Laroche and his companions will follow. They will park down the street and then come here."

Camellion wrinkled his nose in distaste. "Why bother to meet them at all?" His voice was slightly sarcastic. "Why couldn't this Laroche and Company just come here and be done with it?"

"Well, six people in the Citroen are going to make it damned crowded," Gerstung said thoughtfully. "I suggest that two or three of us remain here." His gray eyes went to Camellion, as if he were hoping that the man known as Leonard Kidd would agree.

[2]*Obelisque de Luxor* is the oldest monument in Paris. The 75-foot-high monolith is over three thousand years old and was given to Charles X of France by the Viceroy of Egypt in 1829.

Debray said to Camellion. "Going to meet them is a matter of security. The ARC leadership insisted that we make contact in that manner. Camille and I have to go. And my orders are to bring at least one of you. Two of you could remain here."

The stone-faced expression of the Death Merchant didn't change.

Jordan smiled slightly. "A good idea. How about it, Kidd? Who goes and who stays."

The Death Merchant did some thinking. Gerstung, the CIA termination specialist was a DC—*A deep-cover man is more valuable than Jordan.*

"Gerstung and I will stay here," Camellion said. "Hopefully we won't be attacked in this crackerbox. As far as security in this apartment exists, we might as well be sitting on the curb out front.

"We are open to attack, front and back," amplified Jordan. He wiped his face with a white handkerchief and glanced toward the front door. "Ever since we arrived, I've felt like a target living in a storefront window."

"Oh, it's not quite as bad as you think," amended Debray. He got up from the couch, a look of annoyance on his face. "You, Monsieur Kidd, and you, Monsieur Jordan, came in from the garage in the rear. I don't think you have noticed that the front door has a double shunt lock and an extrawide one-way viewer."

"Big deal!" said Jordan. "What about the windows?"

"You haven't seen what lies behind the drapes," Debray said. "Come. I'll show you."

He walked over to the drawn, cream-colored drapes that would permit light to filter into the room, but at the same time made it impossible for anyone on the outside to see into the living room.

Debray pulled one of the cords on the side of the drapes closest to the front door, opening them to maximum. At once, the Death Merchant and the two Company men saw that the windows were covered with cream-colored bars. Horizontal bars crisscrossed vertical bars, so that four-inch squares covered the glass.

"Those bars are not hollow," Debray said. "They're solid steel."

Camellion merely stared at the bars.

"I didn't see them and I came in from the front," Gerstung commented. "I suppose it's because their coloring blends in with the drapes. Personally, though I don't think those bars are worth a damn. A grenade would tear them apart as though they were made of papier-mâché."

Camellion saw the postal delivery van a moment before Debray closed the drapes. The dark brown postal van was on the opposite side of the street and parked a hundred feet to the right of the window.

The other men started to move away, but paused when Camellion pulled back the end side of the left drape a few inches and looked toward the north. A man was getting out of the left side of the van, a large, brown-paper-wrapped package in his hands, a box twenty inches long and almost the same width and depth.

Intuition bubbled within the Death Merchant's compartment of survival. *The hell with Denmark! Something's not right here on Fishing Cat Street!*

"What is it, Kidd?" Ralph Gerstung was by Camellion's side in an instant. He moved in closer, hunched down and looked around the edge of the drape.

"What's wrong with a postal truck and a postman with a package?" he asked. "Hey, a second man has just stepped out of the van. He has the same kind of package as the other guy."

The Death Merchant swung from the window and said darkly to a nervous Debray, "Are you or Madame Debray expecting any packages?"

"I'm not." Debray looked alarmed. "I'll go ask Camille." He hurried toward the kitchen.

"Jordan, you and Silour break out the hardware," Camellion said, then turned back to the window. "I have tacks tapping on my spine, and that means trouble."

Camellion and Gerstung watched the two postmen who, by now, were halfway between the van and the front door of the ground-floor apartment. The two postmen, both in their twenties, wore regulation uniforms and caps. But there was something odd about the way they carried the boxes—with too little effort.

The Death Merchant's eyes became as hard as diamonds. An old trick—of shoplifters and assassins.

Gerstung, old pro that he was, also saw through the ruse. "The boxes are empty," he said scornfully, his voice filled with contempt for the would-be assassins who were walking at an ordinary pace, who were getting closer to the front door.

"Yes, empty," Camellion said, "except for pistols and maybe grenades. "Of course, the side of the box facing each man has a swingin door. And take a look at their shoes. One man is wearing loafers. The other dummy has slip-ons. A little item of dress they overlooked."

"How do you want to scratch them?" Gerstung pulled back from the window. So did the Death Merchant. Both saw that Bernard Jordan had taken the Beretta sub-gun from the back of the bookcase and that Roger Silour had removed the two chatter boxes hanging from the back of the red couch—a 9-mm MAT and a 9-mm Hotchkiss.

"One of you—catch!" called out Silour, and tossed the Hotchkiss toward Gerstung who held out his right hand. Just as Gerstung caught the submachine gun, Camille hurried into the living room, her husband right behind her. She had large brown eyes and full lips under short sand-blond hair, and was wearing a halter and cotton shorts. She was barefooted.

"We have no boxes of that size ordered from any mercantile establishment!" Camille cried, her small breasts rising and falling rapidly from tension.

"All of you get into the kitchen," ordered Camellion, moving to the rocking chair. He gave further orders as he pulled his coat from the back of the chair and put it on. "Jordan, watch the back door. Silour, keep an eye on the kitchen window. Debray, you and your wife get the other weapons out of the pantry—and stay in the pantry. If you two get knocked off, we'll never make contact with the *Action pour la Renaissance de la Corse.*

Debray, not a man to take orders from a stranger, protested.

"Damner! What about the front door and the front windows?"

He placed a protective arm around his wife's slim waist.

"*Tire-toi! Barre-toi!*" ("Beat it! Take off!") Camellion said sharply, his eyes flashing angrily. "Our friends will be ringing the doorbell any moment."

The ever-efficient Jordan, who had slipped into his suit coat, ran into the kitchen and positioned himself to one side of the refrigerator. Silour, with a fearful glance at the Death Merchant, shepherded the Debrays into the kitchen, thinking that if the tall Kidd was the Christ of Death, the rest of them in the apartment were his disciples.

"There could be more than two of them," Gerstung said

in a low voice. He moved with Camellion, who had pulled out the two MABs from their shoulder holsters, to the doorway between the living room and the kitchen. "I know that if I had planned the smear-out, I'd have mechanics come in from the rear as well as the front—and I guess you know we've been set up?"

"So what else is new?" snapped Camellion. "I'm going to the side of the far window. The instant the doorbell rings, stitch the door."

"Right."

The Death Merchant was halfway across the living room when the buzzer sounded. Camellion raced to the northwest corner of the living room and took a position between the wall and the right end of the window to the north.

The buzzer on the door sounded again.

In order to get a straight-in trajectory at the door, Gerstung stepped back into the living room, moved six feet to his left and, as the buzzer sounded a third time, opened fire with the Hotchkiss, the explosions of the 9-mm cartirdges stabbing the silence to bits.

Gerstung first placed a dozen slugs horizontally—at waist level—across the door. He used the remainder of the magazine to "draw" an *X* across the door.

While the first projectiles were tearing through the front door and the first splinters were flying, Camellion gently pulled back—for only a few inches—a portion of the drape at the right side of the north-end window.

What he saw pleased him more than would be a Moslem who had just reached Mecca. One gunman was standing in the front of the door, the second hit man behind him; the right hand of the first man was inside the box in front of him. Gerstung's first projectiles ripped through the door, cut through the cardboard box and stabbed into the first gunman, the solid-point slugs stabbing him high in the stomach. With a loud cry of agony, the man relaxed his hold on the silenced Heckler and Koch VP70 automatic pistol in the box, dropped both box and weapon, and staggered back against the second triggerman, who made a desperate attempt to pull his own Heckler and Koch VP70 from his box while throwing himself to one side of the riddled door. He was too slow. Three of Gerstung's *X*-design slugs cut into his chest and turned him into an instant corpse.

The Death Merchant was surprised to see that, as Gerstung fired, the post-office van had backed up, stopping when it was even with the windows of the Debray apartment—surprised yet double angry because the van's backing up proved there was a third triggerman.

I'll be a jackass on roller skates! Camellion did a double take when not one but three men jumped from the open rightside door of the van, all three carrying Swiss SIG MP-310 submachine guns. Close by, a man and a woman, seeing what was taking place, started to run. *I don't blame them! If I had half the sense of a moronic doodlebug I wouldn't even be here!*

Disgusted with the turn of events, Camellion instantly deduced that vital lag time was on his side. He edged himself between the drape and the window, stepped back to the extent that the inside of the drape was spread over his head and shoulders and cut loose with the two MABs. He was seventy-five percent lucky. His first two 9-mm slugs first shattered the glass of the window, then caught the first two men. One man was knocked off balance by a bullet that chopped into his chest. The second man doubled over with a slug in the top of his stomach, just below the breastbone.

It was a passing car that saved the third gunsel. During that half-blink of a minimoment, the car came between Camellion and the man with a SIG sub. The frantic driver, seeing that he was in the middle of a gun battle, speeded up.

By then it was too late for the Death Merchant. He realized that he had lost the initiative. The instant the car had passed, the third man with a machine gun would be in action. Camellion dropped from the window to the floor and yelled at Gerstung, who had gone back to crouching by the side of the doorway between the kitchen and the living room—"Get down! There's one left with a chopper. He'll be headed this way."

"Balls!" muttered Gerstung. "It can only get worse." He dropped to the floor and started to crawl into the kitchen, dragging the empty Hotchkiss with him.

Behind him, Camellion crawled on his hands and knees across the living-room floor. Camellion was almost to the kitchen when a submachine gun outside began to chatter. Nine-millimeter Parabellum slugs knocked out the rest of the glass of the north-end window, then demolished the glass of the other window. Some of the slugs ricocheted from the solid-steel bars. Others went through the windows and struck the bulky wooden furniture and the eastside wall of the living room.

By then, a cautious gunman would have jumped back into the postal truck and driven off. But Robert Chaffard, the last of the gunmen from the van, had let blind rage and hatred overcome common sense, for one of the men who had carried one of the ruse boxes had been his brother Joseph. Joseph was now a corpse sprawled out on the cobblestones, and Robert Chaffard wanted revenge.

Ignoring shopkeepers, up and down the street, peering from doorways, and a few people screaming, *"Appelez la police! Appelez la police!"* ("Call the police! Call the police!"), Chaffard charged across the street, thrust the muzzle of the SIG machine gun through one of the squares formed by the bars and finished off the magazine, moving the weapon from side to side. Bullets thudded into the wall. Several slugs struck the rocking chair, and it began to move back and forth as though an invisible body were sitting in it. More high-velocity lead demolished the gold-plated tankards and the small glass vases on the first shelf of the wooden bookcase. *Ping!* And the tall bud vase dissolved into a hundred pieces of glass, the copper roses and their green wire stems falling to the floor.

Still ignoring everything around him on Fishing Cat Street, Chaffard jerked the empty magazine from the submachine gun, pulled a full magazine from his belt, thrust it into the weapon, pulled back the cocking bolt, ran to the front door and triggered off a dozen rounds; the blast of such violence that the impact of the slugs, after reducing the lock to junk, kicked the door half open. He grinned when he heard another SIG machine gun chattering from the rear, Chaffard shoved the door wide open and charged into the living room.

When Camellion yelled a warning at Ralph Stanley Gerstung, Bernard Jordan, who was crouching by the side of the refrigerator that faced the door between the kitchen and the living room, moved to one side of the table. He acted just in time. No sooner had he moved to the table than SIG 9-mm Parabellum hollow-points began stabbing through the windows, punching holes in the drapes and making them shake and quiver in the process. While most of the hollow-point projectiles thudded into the living-room wall, three came through the doorway, all three passing a foot over Camellion—still in the living room—and Gerstung, who was crawling toward the gas stove by the wall. Two slugs missed the refrigerator. They zinged all the way across the width of the kitchen and thudded into the opposite wall, a few feet to the left of the back door. With a loud, clanging ring, the third bullet ripped into the side of the refrigerator. If Jordan had been in his original position, the slug would have caught him in the left hip.

"*Mon Dieu!*" exclaimed Roger Silour who, opposite Jordan, was down at the other end of the table. "The damned flics will grab us before we get out of here."

The Death Merchant crawled through the doorway on his hands and knees and quickly took a position to the right of the opening that lacked not only a door but even a curtain.

Jordan swung around and looked at Camellion, who was peering around the edge of the woodwork into the living room.

"Look Kidd, he's right. Let's get to the garage. We still have more than enough time to get to the Place de la Concorde."

"*Oui,*" said Georges Debray. "If we stay here much longer, we're going to have to fight the police." With his wife, he stood in the doorway of the pantry on the north side of the kitchen, a 9-mm Franchi M-LE57 submachine gun in his hands. Camille Debray was armed with a Walther P-38 pistol.

"Watch the kitchen door and the window!" Camellion snarled. "We can't run for it until—"

He was cut short by the roaring of a machine gun outside the front door, the blast tearing away the lock and pushing the door half open. Almost during the same moments, Silour spotted a face outside the narrow kitchen window—also covered with steel bars—, a short bust of slugs shattered the lock of the kitchen door, and Robert Chaffard shoved open the front door and rushed into the living room—straight to his own execution.

The Death Merchant's two MAB pistols exploded together, both 9-mm slugs slamming into Chaffard's chest. He screamed a short scream, did a soft-shoe shuffle and started to fall back at the same time that Roger Silour muttered, "*Fous le camp, espèce de salaud!*" ("Go to hell, dumb bastard.") and opened fire with his MAT music box.

With only a French MAS M-50 pistol and the empty Hotchkiss, Gerstung was almost helpless and crouched in front of the stove while Georges Debray fired from the pantry door and Bernard Jordan triggered the Beretta from the end of the table, both men sending a storm of steel at the kitchen door.

Perfectly at home among all the noise and the cloying odor of burned gunpowder, the Death Merchant shoved one of the MABs into his belt, jumped to his feet, ran into the living room, dashed out the front door and picked up the SIG machine gun lying next to the dead Chaffard. For a moment, he glanced in satisfaction at the corpse, which lay on its back, eyes wide open and staring into infinity. He ran back into the apartment, jammed the other MAB into his waistband and rushed to the side of the refrigerator.

There had been five FLB terrorists in the rear. Jordan and Debray had killed two of the three who had tried to charge in by way of the kitchen door, the blast of Beretta and Franchi projectiles boring through the door and stabbing all over the front of the hit men's bodies. They went down in a cloud in cloth fragments, tiny bits of flesh and splashes of blood, some of the projectiles, coming out of one man's back, narrowly missing Gilles Soustelle, the third man at the door.

Roger Silour had also been lucky. Most of his 9-mm MAT slugs had missed Raoul Girardet, the man he had seen at the window, except for one, which grazed the right side of Girardet's skull, the impact knocking him out. The SIG machine gun slid from his hands and he sank to the ground. Alain Monteil, the second man by the window, cursed and jumped to one side. He turned and looked at Soustelle, who had run over to the window from the doorway.

"Let's get out of here," Monteil said hoarsely. "The others are dead. They've got two machine guns in there; we'll never get them."

"We must," Soustelle responded grimly. "We must. Fauvet will not tolerate failure." He moved around Monteil, got down almost to his knees, crawled over the unconscious Girardet, crept to the other side of the window and stood up.

"We'll fire together on the count of three," he whispered, looking over at Monteil.

Not liking the odds, Alain Monteil was not at all enthused; yet he didn't want Soustelle to report that he had acted like a coward.

"Very well," he finally said, "But I'll do the counting."

In the kitchen the Death Merchant and his people were still waiting, still watching the kitchen window and the kitchen door—all except Ralph Stanley Gerstung, who had crawled to one side of the inside doorway and was keeping an eye on the front door.

Gerstung didn't know it, nor did Camellion and the others, but Monteil and Soustelle had a two-second monopoly on surprise: Only one man, Roger Silour, was watching the window. Camellion and the others were watching the door. Consequently, when both Monteil and Soustelle reared up and fired at once through the window, Silour was at a disadvantage.

Gilles Soustelle's first chain of pointed projectiles came into the kitchen from the opposite side of the window—to the right of the Death Merchant and the others. Four chopped into the door of the refrigerator. Six more would have found their way into Richard Camellion if he had not jerked all the way back to the side of the refrigerator. Soustelle then began directing his fire to the left of the group.

Monteil's first burst of slugs raked the table that Camille Debray had so carefully set with her best china and the silver that had belonged to her grandmother. Plates, glasses, cups and saucers exploded. Knives, forks and spoons jumped from the impact of slugs, along with bits and pieces of the tablecloth ripped by the hot lead. During those six seconds, several of Montiel's slugs also raked Bernard Jordan. One burned through his coat and shirt on his left shoulder, the lead barely cutting the skin. The second projectile cut through the hair on top of his hair, missing his skull by only a fourth of an inch. Those two slugs and three more struck the front of the stove, four of them clanging loudly as they cut through the metal. The fifth struck the side of a coiled-steel burner, glanced off, shot across the room and broke the glass of an electric clock on the northside wall.

Caught off guard, Georges and Camille Debray acted

instinctively. With a gasp they jerked back into the pantry, as Gerstung and a cursing Jordan threw themselves flat on the floor, Jordan reacting with the instincts of a born survivor. He knew he didn't have time to crawl to the other side of the table to rear up and fire, or to rear up between table and stove. He did the only thing possible: He judged where the window was and raised the Beretta. He'd fire through the top of the table. His finger was about to squeeze the trigger when four of Monteil's slugs found Roger Silour, who was standing up and firing. Three of the terrorist's projectiles struck him in the chest. The fourth hit him in the forehead, went all the way through his brain and sent a piece of the back of his skull striking against the stove. The impact of the four projectiles sent him reeling backward, the MAT chattering off its last six rounds into the ceiling as he fell.

But Silour's own projectiles had not murdered empty space between the bars. Even as Monteil was firing at him, Silour was getting off a short seven-round burst, and five of the boat-tailed bullets blew away Monteil's face, turned his brain into scrambled gray matter, and tore off the entire back of his skull. Practically headless, Monteil sagged with blood spurting against the back of the building.

When Jordan finally did pull the trigger, his slugs failed in their mission, all of them striking the bottom of the windowsill. And it was the Death Merchant who saved his life.

From his position by the side of the refrigerator, Camellion—because of the sharp angle of vision—could see only the barrel of Gilles Soustelle's SIG sub-gun and the man's left hand wrapped around the top of the magazine. Soustelle was shoving the barrel through one of the squares between the bars when Camellion triggered a long burst from the SIG he had picked up from the sidewalk in front of the building.

Zing! Zing! Zing! Three of the projectiles ricocheted from the bars across the window. Five more amputated Soustelle's left-hand fingers and knocked the machine gun out of his hands. The terrorist let out a loud scream of pain and horror, fell back and stared at the bloody stumps where his fingers had been. His mind reeling, he looked down and saw his little finger lying at his feet—the bloody digit somehow making him think of the undersized penis of a midget!

* * *

"Gerstung! Catch! It's on safety!" The Death Merchant switched on the safety of the SIG sub-gun, tossed the weapon to Gerstung, pulled the two MABs from his waistband and streaked toward the back door, which had been kicked open by the enemy slugs that had ripped off the lock.

Camellion darted out the door, swung to his left and opened fire on Gilles Soustelle, who, already overcome with shock, was bent over and vomiting. One 9-mm bullet caught Soustelle in the left side, just above the hip, the second in the left rib cage. Dying, Soustelle started to make the final fall of his life.

The unfortunate Raoul Girardet, who had been skull-grazed by one of Roger Silour's slugs, had all the luck of the navigator of the *Titanic*. He opened his eyes, groaned, rolled over on his back and tried to stagger to his feet. It was also the last effort of his life. The Death Merchant put two slugs into the right side of his head and cracked his skull like an egg. Girardet was flopping back to the ground at the same time that Camellion heard Ralph Gerstung's SIG snarling and cries of pain and anger from the front of the apartment.

Well, that's the last cracker in the box of goodies. thought Camellion. The *gendarmes* had arrived. *Gendarmes*, the French national police, are roughly equivalent to American state troopers or Canadian Mounties. *They must have wised up after all these years. They didn't use sirens.*

Camellion rushed to the side of the back door and discreetly looked around the edge into the kitchen, and beyond into the living room. Two blue-uniformed *gendarmes* were sprawled out on the floor, one corpse on its back, the other on its stomach.

Ralph Gerstung, having exhausted the ammo in the SIG sub-gun, was crouched in front of the bullet-riddled stove. Camille Debray was next to him. Gerstung's place by the door had been taken by Georges Debray and by Bernie Jordan, who had reloaded his Beretta machine gun with a magazine that Camille had taken from a box hidden underneath the pantry floor. Two more Beretta magazines were jammed between his belt and his stomach.

"Let's go," Camellion yelled. "It's clear out here, but it won't be for long."

With Camellion, Jordan and Debray covering them, Ralph Gerstung and Camille Debray ran across the kitchen, raced through the back door and took positions behind Camellion. They turned to face the three-car garage, covering the building with their pistols.

Quickly, Georges Debray and Bernie Jordan backed out of the kitchen, firing short bursts at the front door to keep the *gendarmes* from charging in. As soon as Debray and Jordan were outside, they and Camellion, Ralph Gerstung and Camille Debray darted to the side door of the garage. Jordan hesitated only long enough to take out a small metal box, slightly larger than a pack of cigarettes, from one of his coat pockets. He slipped back the metal plate on top, flipped the ON switch, turned the tiny yellow knob to 2-M, and carefully placed the cigarette-pack bomb down, only a foot to the left of the back door of the apartment. He then darted to the garage, where Georges Debray was opening the garage doors and Ralph Gerstung was starting the engine of the Citroen, Camille Debray in the front seat beside him.

"Get in the car," Camellion said to Jordan. "I'll cover you."

Jordan ran to the vehicle, and Camellion took a position by the side of the narrow garage door. He didn't have long to wait. No sooner had Jordan climbed into the back seat than Camellion detected two *gendarmes* in the kitchen by the back door. He saw a third looking around one side of the window.

One of the French cops by the door exposed the left side of his body as he tried to poke an MAT machine gun around the corner. The Death Merchant fired a single round from his left MAB auto-pistol, the policeman cried out in pain as the bullet struck him in the left shoulder. The *gendarme* at the window was poking the barrel of his MAT through the bars at the same time that the ten ounces of TNT in the cigarette-package bomb exploded, the blast shaking the garage and blowing a hole in the kitchen wall large enough for a small car to drive through.

"Come on! Come on!" yelled Jordan, leaning out of the left-rear door of the car."

Camellion ran to the car and got into the back seat next to Jordan. Gerstung was shooting the car out of the garage before Camellion had time to fully close the door. He made a right turn and headed down the alley, calling back to Camellion and Jordan, "Are we still going to the Place de la Concorde?"

"Why not—provided we get out of Montmartre in one piece," Camellion said. He began to reload the MAB auto-pistols with magazines taken from his coat pocket.

"That is madness!" protested Georges Debray. "We can't meet Laroche and the others under these conditions!"

"Monsieur Kidd, the police know who we are—Georges and myself!" Camille said quickly, her voice shaking. "They will be looking for us, and this Citroen. Our neighbors in the two apartments above us must have seen this car."

The Death Merchant's eyes, jumping to the rearview mirror, seemed to become a shade bluer. The Debrays were as nervous as devil worshipers being sprinkled with holy water. Forever suspicious, Camellion wondered if their tenseness had been generated not by the police but by some deeper fear.

"*Oui*, the neighbors have seen this car," Camellion said, and pulled back the slide of one of the MABs. "But Paris is filled with Citroens, and I don't think any of the people in the upstairs apartments bothered to take down the license number. Why should they? The police don't have our license number either."

Jordan had been looking out the rear window. "No one's following us," he said, turning around. "We'll be down the hill and in the thick traffic on Rue Caulaincourt by the time the police get wise."

"The French police are blithering idiots," sneered Gerstung. He slowed at the end of the alley and turned right on Rue de Vanelle. One more block and they would be on Rue Caulaincourt. "I've made fools of them for years."

"Maybe so," Camellion chuckled. "But a little while ago, they were 'blithering' at us with real bullets."

CHAPTER FOUR

At the corner of Rue de Vanelle and Rue Caulaincourt, there was, on the sidewalk, a relic from the past, a tiny bit of a former Paris institution: a *pissoir,* a public urinal for men only, a boxlike affair painted green, with a ten-foot-high "tower" in the center.

"There are only four or five *pissoirs* left in all of Paris," explained Gerstung as he expertly swung onto Rue Caulaincourt, "and none are in use. I'm told that when the first were closed many years ago, the cab drivers almost went out on strike."

Once the car was solidly in traffic, even the Death Merchant relaxed somewhat. Cars of every make and model were on the four-lane route, and many of them were black Citroens.

We are just another piece of hay in the haystack of traffic. . . .

Georges Debray spoke up nervously, as Camellion suspected he would. "I don't think the three representatives of the ARC will come with us, especially after I tell them of the attack."

Camellion, toying with the French terrorist, smiled mischievously. "Why tell them anything?"

Georges Debray and his wife stiffened, their faces fixed in resentment. With some difficulty, Georges managed to turn around in the front seat of the small car, then fixed his eyes bitterly on Camellion.

"Listen, Monsieur Kidd. We must inform them what took place back there. We can't tell them to follow us to our apartment. I—"

Camille Debray thrust in quickly, "They will think it is a trap if we give them another address and don't give them a reason. What you are suggesting is *impossible.* Besides, my husband and I are members of the ARC. Our first duty is to the organization, not to you Americans with your love of luxury, of plastics and chrome and pushbuttons."

"Another thing, where are we going?" demanded Georges Debray in an abrasive tone. "No doubt to one of your 'safe houses.' None of you have said so, but it's obvious you're with the American CIA. When I talk to our people, what should I tell them? What address should I give them?"

"Let's get something straight!" The Death Merchant spoke in French with machine-gun rapidity. "Let's stop this nonsense that the *Action pour la Renaissance de la Corse* is something sacred. The ARC is a terrorist organization pure and simple. You and yours have exploded bombs all over France in your efforts to gain 'independence' for Corsica—not to mention your cute little assassinations and attempts at murder. The ARC has ties with the IRA and the Red Army in Italy. Many of your people have been trained in terror tactics at a PLO base in Lebanon, along with other militant groups such as the American Indian Movement. Only a few months ago, the ARC made off with computer tapes containing material belonging to the French Ministry of Defense and the *Direction de la Surveillance du Territoire* in a raid on a computer center in Toulouse."

"You are well informed, *mon ami,*" Georges Debray said coldly.

"In addition to stealing the tapes, ARC raiders sabotaged computers, erased programs, set fire to the facility and killed four guards."

Growled Jordan, "A few weeks later, you attacked a second Toulouse computer center in a similar fashion, only in that strike you knocked off only two guards. As I recall, the center was owned by C.I.I.-Honeywell-Bull. Shucks, old buddy, we give the ARC a lot of credit for having members who have sophisticated knowledge of computer operations."

"And members who know the threat that computers pose to the world!" Camille Debray said with scorn. "Computers are the favorite instrument of the powerful, of the rich who keep their feet firmly on the throats of the poor. Computers are used to classify, control and repress. We don't intend to become locked up in ghettos of programs and organizational patterns the way you Americans have. We—"

"Knock it off," Camellion said ruthlessly. "We don't care if you blow up half of France. I think it would be an improvement if you did. Just keep in mind that we're very cognizant of why the ARC is helping us. We promised you five million in Swiss francs if the operation is a success. That five million is your reason, plus the fact that the ARC hates the *Front de Libération de la Bretagne*. We're paying the money; we're giving the orders."

Bernie Jordan said softly in Norwegian, "Why not tell the son of a bitch that we're also aware that the ARC will try to double-cross us and grab the gold, once it knows where the boxes are hidden."

"No use to put them on guard any more than they are," Camellion answered in the same Scandinavian language.

"We have every right to hate the FLB." An angry look crossed Georges Debray's scholarly features. "It's a favorite tactic of the FLB to blame us for its murders and other activities. Those fools! Those stupid *porcs*! Why the government will never relinquish control of *Bretagne*—never!"

Ralph Gerstung's laugh was taunting. "*Les gens du pavé, ce sont différents des gens du trottoir!*" ("People of the paving stones aren't the same as sidewalk people," is the French equivalent of our the American expression, "The pot calling the kettle black.") The FLB says the same thing about the ARC trying to gain freedom for Corsica. In case anyone's interested, we're only ten minutes from la Concorde."

"I must explain to the three what has happened," Debray insisted, still looking at the Death Merchant, who sat slumped in the seat and was trying to put pressure on the back of his aching neck. "I must give them an address. And for God's sake, don't try to force them to do anything. There will be—"

"Hit men covering them!" Camellion cut him short. "Just in case—correct?"

"Camille and I must give them an address," persisted Debray. "There isn't any other way." With worried eyes he regarded Bernie Jordan, who had taken a Walther .380 PPK auto-pistol from underneath the back seat and was attaching a silencer to the barrel. "What's that for?" Debray asked. "If you're going to try any nonsense with the people we're meeting, it will be a big mistake. Let Camille and me handle it. That's the only logical way."

"Your wife isn't going to get out of the car," Camellion said candidly. "You and I will make contact with the representatives of the ARC. Just in case you've set us up as targets, Jordan will kill your wife." Camellion make a mock gesture of regret. "Don't argue about it because that's how things are. It's that simple."

Debray regarded Camellion with a look that bordered on hate. Camille Debray stared straight ahead. From her reflection in the windshield, Jordan and Camellion could see that she was more angry than afraid.

Georges Debray did not reply for several moments. Then he said in a toneless voice, "we can't blame you for being suspicious. But suppose the police have learned about the meeting, or more probably the FLB? It was the FLB that attacked the apartment."

"Oh! What makes you think it was the FLB?" asked Camellion in a pleasant manner, testing the French terrorist. Ahead he could see the Place de la Concorde. It was handsome enough, but like so many French national self-glorifications it smacked of the drafting table and mathematical planners. It afforded plenty of spectacular views—the length of the Champs-Élysées, the Tuileries Gardens and, across the Seine, the Eiffel Tower. But the only time it was truly beautiful in itself was when it could least be seen; at night, when the six hundred-odd lamps and spotlights throughout la Concorde were thrown on and would glow like a cloud of giant fireflies.

"Stop this nonsense!" Debray's voice rose in anger. "And stop talking to me as though I might be an idiot. The ruse with boxes the first two assassins tried . . . who else but the FLB? None of the flic departments operate that way. We all know that, just as we know there must be an informer within the ARC. How else could the FLB have known?"

"He's right, Kidd," Jordan said. "Let's get down to hard cases."

Georges Debray went on, "Camille and I can't be responsible for the actions of other ARC members, not if they think they've walked into a trap. Don't be too quick to fire until you know the true facts."

"Don't worry, *mon cher,*" Camille said. "I'll be safe with these American killers. I doubt if the FLB has any knowledge of the meeting. But if there is a shootout . . . we all die. Fortunately the dead know nothing. I sometimes envy them. . . ."

The Death Merchant only smiled. *The dead know nothing? If she only knew the truth. The dead are all around us.*

CHAPTER FIVE

The blood-red setting sun bathed the red-brick *hôtel particulier* (or mansion) in a warm, crimson blush. Not even the imaginative agents of SDECE could suspect that the fine home of Monsieur Jean Gerard deBois was one of five safe houses that the Central Intelligence Agency maintained in Paris. Certainly not. Monsieur deBois, who was a manufacturer of cosmetics and lived in the chic suburb of Boulogne, had a reputation beyond reproach. According to CIA files, he was a man to be admired. The sixty-eight-year-old widower (three children, all married) would not accept one franc in payment for the occasional use of certain rooms of his mansion. He permitted the CIA to use his house for only one reason: He had an intense hatred of communism. Any enemy of the Soviet Union or of Red China was a friend of Monsieur deBois.

At first, there had been some difficulty with Jules Laroche, Antoine Argoud and Marie-Thérèse Morlande, the three representatives of the ARC. After Georges Debray had introduced Camellion to the three, Debray had explained that there had been a shoot-out at his apartment, that the attackers had been the FLB, and that "We were forced to kill some flics in escaping. But we're positive we weren't followed here."

The trouble had been in not revealing to the three ARC representatives where the meeting and layover would take place.

"Even I don't know," Camellion had truthfully told Laroche. "I'm a contract agent. The CIA man in the car didn't tell me. That way if you took me prisoner, you couldn't torture it out of me. All I can tell you is that we're going to a special CIA safehouse and that you'll have to permit yourselves to be blindfolded, if you agree to go."

Jules Laroche had viewed Camellion with eyes smoldering with suspicion. A brawny, deeply tanned man in his late twenties, Laroche looked out of place in his expensive Italian-cut suit. He had tossed away his cigarette and stared at Camellion with cold, ruthless eyes.

"And you expect us to agree to this arrangement?" There had been no humor in his voice.

Camellion had played it straight. "*Non,* I do not. I know you would be safe, but you don't."

"Monsieur Kidd, if our positions were reversed, would you go with us?" Marie Morlande had spoken up. A heavy, plain-faced woman in her forties, with glistening black hair worn in a long swinging Parisian-style page, her smile had been more of a sneer than one of friendliness.

"I'd weigh all the factors," Camellion had promptly replied. "In your case, we need the ARC as much as the ARC wants our help. I'd know that you'd have no reason to harm me. You'd have nothing to gain and everything to lose. *Oui,* I'd go with you."

For several minutes, Laroche conferred with Argoud and Morlande, all three speaking Italian[1], every word of which Camellion understood. The three had done what he would have done under similar circumstances: They discussed all factors and finally had arrived at the conclusion that the CIA would not harm them, based on a priori reasoning that the Americans needed them.

Laroche then turned to the Death Merchant.

"How do you propose to get us to your safe house?"

"What kind of car are you driving?"

"A four-door Audi. What does that have to do with it?"

"We'll drive to the Tuileries Gardens, we in our car, you in yours. After we get there, two CIA men will transfer to your car. One will drive. The other will make sure you keep down in the back seat, and don't try to raise your

[1]About three times the size of the state of Rhode Island, Corsica has only 250,000 inhabitants. While the island has belonged to France for over 150 years, the Corsicans speak mostly Italian.

blindfolds. Madame Morlande will accompany us in our car."

Jules Laroche took off his dark glasses. "And if we raise our blindfolds?"

"Then the deal will be off. Then you can all get back in your Audi and go where you want—to hell for all I care."

Laroche grinned. "Let's get started," he said.

The large attic room would have been an oven without air conditioning. Even so, there were tiny sweat beads on the foreheads of most of the people present. The human body itself gives off heat, especially when one is laboring under uncertainty and nervous strain.

Other than the Death Merchant, the Debrays and the three representatives of the ARC, Jordan, Gerstung and a third Company man were present. The third CIA case officer was Cecil Mintug. He was the contact man between the Company's "street men" in Paris and the Company station at the U.S. Embassy. Street men NEVER go directly to the embassy. A cheerful-faced individual, Mintug was in his thirties and had features that would have fit any number of races or nations. Although he had light blond hair, he shaved his head every morning, so that his totally bald scalp would accommodate hairpieces of various colors and styles. Now and then, he would add a beard or mustache, or both, to his disguise.

Always polite, always the gentleman, Mintug stirred the ice in his glass of Coca-Cola mixed with Volnay burgundy, and looked with cool aplomb from Camellion to Jules Laroche. "Then it is settled. The eight of you will go to Lamballe in Brittany to meet the leaders of the ARC?"

The Death Merchant, relaxed on a Hitchcock chair, nodded and glanced at Laroche. "That's the program as far as I'm concerned. We can spend the night here and leave tomorrow morning."

"Yes, that's agreeable with us," Laroche said pleasantly enough.

"But you will have to use a different car," said Marie Morlande. The *gendarmerie* are looking not only for the Citroen, but for you personally, Monsieur Kidd. They know who you are."

"She's right," Ralph Gerstung said savagely. "According to the news on TV, the *gendarmes* and the DST raided your hotel, looking for you. It's that damned informer. The police couldn't possibly know your name unless they were tipped off." He ground out his cigarette in an ashtray on a stand by the armchair, and shifted his glare to Laroche. "The tip-off couldn't have come from our end of the line. Only I and Jordan knew Kidd's identity. It wasn't until a few hours ago that even Mr. Mintug knew Kidd's identity."

"It boils down to how many people knew of my existence and my name," Camellion said gently. While he had his own suspicions, he went on, "We can eliminate the Debrays. They didn't know about me until Jordan and I went to their apartment on Fishing Cat Street in Montmartre. That means there could be a difference between the informer, who no doubt tipped off the FLB to the apartment and how the police found out my name. The two could have come from the same source, but not necessarily."

Laroche placed his fingertips together. "I suggest we decide how many people knew that you and Monsieur Jordan would be at the Debray apartment."

"That makes sense," Jordan said, twisting his mouth.

"We Corsicans can do more than grow olives and make wine," Laroche said drily. "Now and then we even say something intelligent."

"And not all of us deal in drugs, as most of the world seems to think," Antoine Argoud tacked on bitterly. Like Laroche, he had been born in Corsica and felt more nationalistic than those Corsicans who had gone to live in France. Argoud was plump, half bald and had a huge mustache. *Like a gay history teacher*, thought Camellion, who wasn't impressed with the man. Nor did Argoud's habit of picking his teeth endear him to the Death Merchant.

"Please continue, Laroche; you have the floor," Camellion said. "Let's have your analysis."

The Corsican nodded. "The three of us—Antoine, Marie, and myself—knew only that we would meet the Debrays and then drive to their apartment in Montmartre. We didn't even know the number and the name of the street. Neither did the leadership of the ARC. I feel that in the final analysis of who the traitor might be, we can exclude the ARC."

"Monsieur Kidd, how many people knew your identity before you and Monsieur Jordan arrived at the Debray apartment?" asked Marie Morlande in businesslike tones.

"No one, except Jordan!" Caemllion answered

promptly—*And Grojean, but he's so paranoid about security, he's more close-mouthed than a clam with lockjaw.* "And I've been with him every second, ever since he knew my name."

"I didn't meet Kidd until after I arrived at the Debrays," Ralph Gerstung said slyly.

The Death Merchant made an impatient motion. "We'll never find out sitting here. Our immediate problem is getting to Laballe without any difficulty."

"Maybe so, but if the FLB hits us again, then what?" asked Gerstung. "Hell, learning the hard way is not going to help us. Everybody has twenty/twenty hindsight."

Jordan dropped the cigarette lighter into his shirt pocket and blew out a cloud of smoke. "What do you suggest we do, Ralph? Give everyone a lie-detector test?"

"What about us?" Georges Debray reminded Camellion. "The flics know us, too. By tomorrow, our photographs will be distributed all over France. . . ."

"And in the newspapers," Camille Debray said glumly.

The Death Merchant turned to the immaculate Cecil Mintug.

"Did you bring the two cases?"

"They're in the other room." Mintug finished his drink and put the empty glass on a card table. "The seals have not been broken."

Camellion's smile and deep gaze somehow told the Debrays that their safety depended on the contents of the two mysterious cases. Camellion proved their deduction by saying, "I'll change how you look. I'll change your faces the way a make-up artist at a motion-picture studio does."

Camille Debray gave a nod that might have denoted agreement.

Georges was not so certan. "Are you sure you can do it?"

"I'm positive. By the time I'm finished, your own mother won't recognize you, and neither will the police."

"The two of you will also need new *cartes d'identité,* Cecil Mintug said, loosening his tie and unbuttoning his white shirt, well aware that in France, each citizen must carry a *carte d'identité,* an identity card that lists his name, address, age, and place of birth. "And you, Mr. Kidd, either a passport or an identity card. We can supply either. It's your decision."

"By ten tomorrow morning?" Camellion said.

"I'll be here by nine. All we have to decide on are the names and whether you want to be a native Frenchman or a foreigner."

"I'll take a passport. 'Gunther Ludwig Kramer.' That's who I'll be. Make me fifty years old. I'm an engineer, married, and work and live in Munich. I flew in. Make sure the passport is stamped with the French customs' stamps used at Orly Airport. Date it for today."

"What about the Debrays?"

"You mean 'Marguerite and Pierre Laffont.' Put them both in their sixties. Make Pierre five years older than Marguerite. You've heard enough of the situation. Use your own judgment."

Curious expressions dropped over the faces of Georges and Camille Debray.

"Why those names?" Georges's voice was thick with suspicion.

Camille looked at Mintug. "Aren't you going to write anything down?"

"I have a memory for details," Mintug said in a precise tone.

"No particular reason," Camellion said indifferently. "I grabbed them out of thin air. Anyhow, those names fit how you both will look."

"Speaking of Germans," said Jules Laroche. "How can we be sure that the gunmen who attacked the apartment weren't working for ODESSA? You intelligence people know more about those Nazi swine than we do. Would ODESSA have such capabilities?"

The fingers of Camellion's left hand started to drum on his left knee, and his lofty brow furrowed. "ODESSA is not merely a bunch of old-time Hitler lovers sitting quietly at home by the fire in hobnail slippers. ODESSA has more power than the Mafia, operates worldwide, and has a treasury of billions. Yes, the attack very easily could have been the work of ODESSA. Who knows? ODESSA might very well have used Paris hooligans, *apaches* for the attack."

With a deep, loud sigh, Laroche got up and walked toward an old brass-bound trunk, speaking harshly as he moved, "It's bad enough that we Corsicans are considered France's 'white niggers' and have to fight not only the *gendarmerie*, the DST, the agents of the SDECE and those murderous bastards of the FLB. But now we have ODESSA to contend with. *Enfer!* We go from bad to worse!"

"Will we and the world ever be free of the Boche?" Argoud said belligerently, slapping a hand on top of his leg.

"We had better concentrate on the FLB," Marie Morlande said half angrily. "Laballe is in the heart of Bretagne, the heart of FLB territory." She shifted her chair around and glared at Laroche, who had sat down on the trunk and was staring reflectively at the floor. "And I don't mind saying that I think it was a bad mistake for Gelee and the others to come to France. And to hole up in Laballe—sheer madness!"

"It was their decision." Laroche spoke sharply and swung his head up to stab cold eyes at Marie Morlande. "We only follow orders for the cause. Remember that."

Ignoring his angry tone, the woman did not reply, although her eyes showed that she was infuriated.

"What safer place for our leaders than in Bretagne?" Antoine Argoud said with a hint of wryness. "Laballe is the last place the FLB and the DST would look for them, and should I add"—he made a sweeping motion with both hands—"for us?"

Georges Debray chimed in, "We labored under the same delusion back in *La Butte*," using the Parisian's name for Montmartre. He wiped his glasses with a handkerchief. "Yet we were attacked and were almost killed. Poor Silour was. It was only by sheer luck that we managed to outdistance the flics."

"They have a point there," Bernard Jordan said to Camellion, surveying the Death Merchant with calculating eyes. "Considering there's a leak, what assurance do we have that we won't be attacked here?"

Forever the cynic, Gerstung sniggered. "What assurance do we have that one of us won't have a heart attack by morning?"

"Knock it off!" Jordan's voice was furious. "This is not the time for philosophical bullshit. You know damn good and well what I mean."

"Sure I do." Gerstung's expression became serious; so did his voice. "But the setup here is different than in Montmartre. We're not sitting smack on the street in this place. How about it, Mintug? What kind of security do we have?"

* * *

As the others talked, the Death Merchant did some thinking. Laroche only knew half of what they were really up against. *That thug should have my problems.* Camellion was acutely aware that he was threatened by more than the French FLB, the SDECE, the DST and the sinister German ODESSA. The ARC was also an enemy. No doubt its leaders had already formulated plans to bury him and the other Company men once the gold was located—$250 million in gold bars. *Now worth more than half a billion at today's rate.*

There was only one slight difficulty: The only lead that he and the Company had was that the gold was hidden somewhere in northern France and that the FLB was also searching for it, and so was ODESSA. CIA Stations in Bonn and Paris had developed some evidence that ODESSA and the FLB were working together. At least ODESSA has the same survival problem with the FLB that the CIA has with the ARC.

The CIA couldn't possibly "field" as many men as the FLB. To offset the danger of that terrorist group, the Company had decided to acquire the help of another French terrorist group, the ARC, which was every bit as ruthless as the FLB.

But why should the ARC settle for a paltry five-million-dollar payment from the CIA when it might be able to grab more than half a billion?

Ironic. No one would blame the ARC if it did grab all the gold, since the Company had no intention of paying the ARC as much as one thin dime. . . . *Only if the ARC ends up with the gold, I'll be dead!*

No one knew about *Scorpion II,* the sleek nuclear submarine lying submerged 61.27 kilometers west of Brittany. According to Courtland Grojean, the head of the CIA's Clandestine Section, the Death Merchant's job would be "simple" enough. Once the gold was located, Camellion would flash word to *Scorpion II* by special radio.Then U.S. commandos would come ashore at the beach west of the village of Paimpol.

There were, however, a few "minor" problems. The Death Merchant and the Company men had to transport the gold to the beach—all one hundred boxes—after it was found and after he and the others had outwitted the FLB, the ARC, ODESSA and—*Every damned police agency in France! Poor fool I for taking on this crazy job!*

He almost hadn't. After completing the mission in Northern Ireland[2], he had flown to London and conferred with Grojean, using a special code that only he and Grojean knew. The code had been triple scrambled, then decoded by v-16W computer, so that the radio "conversation" had been instant. After getting all the facts about Pink Slipper 5, the code name for the French operation, Camellion had calmly told Grojean to stick the whole works in his nose. Finding the gold and getting it to the beach bordered on the impossible. Getting the facts on who had murdered General George S. Patton was equally as ridiculous.

Grojean had instantly responded with, I'M PREPARED TO OFFER YOU DOUBLE YOUR PRESENT FEE.

Camellion had instantly agreed, then immediately felt rather foolish. He tapped out on the key connected to the scrambler that fed into the computer before transmission: WHAT MAKES YOU THINK THAT TWO HUNDRED GRAND WILL MAKE THE JOB ANY EASIER?

Grojean's response had been characteristic of the man—blunt and to the point: FOR THAT KIND OF TAX-FREE LOOT YOU'D FIND A WAY TO STEAL THE GATES OF HELL AND COOL THEM OFF IN THE ICY WATERS OF THE SOUTH POLE.

Grojean had them told him that a Company "street man" would meet him at Orly Airport and . . . WILL GIVE YOU MORE DETAILS IN REGARD TO PATTON AND THE GOLD. WHAT NAME WILL YOU BE USING AND HOW WILL YOU BE DRESSED SO THAT HE WILL KNOW YOU? Cynically, Grojean had added, DON'T SHOW UP DISGUISED AS A PRIEST. THE MAN WHO WILL MEET YOU IS AN ATHEIST.

Jordan had met "Mr. Kidd" and had promptly given the correct I.D. signal in Latin—*"Abiit hodie monstrum"* ("The Monster left today").

The Death Merchant had responded in perfect French, *"Les amoureux qui s'embrassent sur les bancs publics"* ("Lovers who kiss on park benches").

The details that Jordan had given Camellion had convinced the Death Merchant that the best time to look for any kill operation was after you had the job!

For years the Central Intelligence Agency had been

[2]See *Death Merchant #41: The Shamrock Smash.*

hearing the strange rumor that General George S. Patton had been murdered, had been poisoned in a Heidelberg hospital where he was taken after an auto accident on December 9, 1945.

En route to Camellion's hotel, Jordan had explained, "The rumor was that Patton was terminated because he was considered highly dangerous to certain powerful people in the States. They considered him dangerous because he viewed the world as a pragmatic, military man and could foresee the rise of the Soviet Union. He had to be gotten out of the way. So they killed him."

Furthermore, *Washington Post* columnist Joy Billington had alleged, in a piece entitled "Spies of the Past Gather to Honor One of Their Own," that (among other things) one of the men present at the veterans of the OSS dinner was Douglas Bazata:

> *Sitting near Colby, former O.S.S. agent Douglas Bazata spoke of his still controversial claim that in 1944 he was assigned to kill Gen. George Patton. "Apparently quite a number of top-level people were jealous of Patton," Bazata said. "I know the guy who killed him. But I was the one who got paid for it—$10,000." OSS Director "Wild Bill" Donovan himself, Bazata added, was the man who gave him the order for the famous American general to be done in. "And if you get me killed, get someone to say a prayer over my grave. . . ." Bazata told the reporter.*

Later, Washington's *The Spotlight,* the nation's leading right-wing weekly newspaper, had printed a long article on Bazata's supposedly being paid $10,000 to "hit" Patton.

Whether Patton had been poisoned was a moot question. The Company could hardly dig up the corpse and have an autopsy performed, without creating a stink in the world press. And after thirty years, how much of the body would be left? Even in an airtight casket, the body would turn to dust when exposed to the atmosphere.

Jordan had explained further, "However Old Blood and Guts was knocked off, the Company has dug up evidence that there's some indication he could have been murdered. But it wasn't any power group in the States that was responsible. Patton was sent into the next world—which by the way I don't believe exists—because he learned that some of his own officers and a group of OSS agents had stolen two hundred and fifty-million-bucks worth of gold bars from a brewery in Munich that the SS was using as a headquarters. What happened is that Patton found out about the big steal after the gold had been transported to and hidden in northern France. Well, you can guess the rest. Patton was going to court-martial his officers and blow the whistle on the OSS officers. There was only one solution—kill him."

"I guess it would be pointless to ask how the Company acquired such tidbits of information?"

"And stupid. You know that the Center back home doesn't give us anything but the minimum facts. Stations are highly structured. We street guys are always in a gray area. You know what the Yale and Harvard idiots at the high levels think of us in the field. We're supposed to be kill experts who can't think. You and I know better, Kidd—or Smith or Jones or Doodlewinkle, or whatever your real name might be. I couldn't care less. And don't tell me. I don't want to know."

There were a few cracks of light in the darkness. British, French, Dutch or Belgium vessels wouldn't be able to detect *Scorpion II*. The best sub-detecting equipment in the world wouldn't be able to detect *Scorpion II,* even if she lay in only a few hundred feet of water. The submarine was equipped with the ultrasecret Gf-Mechanism, a device that, by the use of magnetic lines of force, made the sub "invisible" to sonar and other detection instruments.[3]

The Death Merchant turned his attention to Cecil Mintug, who was explaining to Ralph Gerstung about the security of the safe house. Conscious of the five ARC terrorists present, the contact man was careful not to mention the location of the house, its owner, or how the grounds were arranged on the outside. To Camellion the large structure was a typical *hôtel particulier*—the basic French design for a city mansion, with beautiful stone work, staircases, high windows and a high wrought-iron fence.

"There are hidden infrared alarms all around the grounds," Mintug was saying, "and there are only three servants. That's because half of the house is closed up. It's

[3]See *Death Merchant #37: The Bermuda Triangle Action* and *Death Merchant #40: Blueprint: Invisibility.*

been that way ever since . . . ever since a certain person died. The three servants—cook, butler and chauffeur—can be trusted. You don't have to worry about them. As far as this place being attacked, there are more than enough arms up here, and there are four of our own people in two of the rooms downstairs. You're safe enough up here."

Camellion's eyes roamed around the "up here." The large attic was divided into three rooms, the large central area in which the group was now assembled, a smaller area filled with arms and special supplies such as grenades and plastic explosives, and a third area filled with aluminum-framed camp cots. This sleeping area was partitioned off to accommodate male and female agents. As for the furniture, none of it matched; all of it was cast-offs from downstairs, plus odds and ends that had accumulated over the years and had been stored in the attic.

"Spare rooms below, and we're stuck up here in the attic," Laroche groused to Mintug, a challenge in his harsh voice.

"If we attempted to leave, what would happen?" Antoine Argoud voiced the second mistake.

"Nothing much." Mintug sighed. "The men downstairs would kill you, that's all. Your bodies would never be found."

Jules Laroche smiled evenly. The other four terrorists looked grim.

The Death Merchant caught Mintug's attention with his piercing stare. "We'll need a special van, one with a large compartment in the floor and other secret compartments," he said. "And another car. Nothing expensive that will attract attention. Can you supply both by nine tomorrow morning."

Mintug carefully adjusted his aviator-style glasses. "We anticipated that you would want a certain kind of van. Will you be driving it?"

"Yes," Camellion said. "You'd better bring a forged international driver's license. How about the plates?"

"Both legitimate French plates. The Simca van is in the garage downstairs. There's also a Renault sedan. Keys in both. The Renault also has two secret compartments, front and rear seats, the usual arrangement." Seeing the anxious expression on Camille Debray's face, Mintug turned to her with a slight smile. "I know, *mon chère*. Your husband and you have only the clothes on your backs, and to return to your apartment is quite out of the question. There will be suitable clothes for both of you in the morning. You can buy more on the way. There will be plenty of money."

Jordan laughed good-naturedly. "What do you do, practice mind reading on the side?"

"Part of my job is to anticipate," Mintug replied very seriously. "And by using various research strategies, I'm very good at my job. It all revolves around cognitive-dissonance research coupled with frameworks for implementation."

"Oh sure, we understand!" Gerstung said mockingly.

The Death Merchant did understand and was amused at Mintug's naiveté. The logical-positivist or strict empirical approach made sense, but only up to a certain point. But there were other times when one had to rely on sheer intuition, on a priori reasoning. There was a flaw in this method, too. *One wrong guess and you're dead!*

The real hole in the machine was how much the CIA was covering up—not Jordan nor Gerstung nor the other counterintelligence people at the various embassy stations in Europe, but Grojean and the other high-level spooks back in the States. Suppose the old OSS had murdered Patton? If so, the CIA would be trying for a complete cover-up.

General Patton was correct in his predictions, and there is an international group of power brokers working toward a one-world government.

The evidence was all there, particularly in the new patterns in political corruption and subversion affecting the United States and its Western allies. Bribery of elected and appointed government officials with money, gifts and sex had long been a staple of American political life. A sizable minority had been for sale to the highest bidder, as proved by the FBI's ABSCAM operation. In the past that bidder had been American-based corporations, labor unions, wealthy families and other well-heeled groups with interests to serve and money to spend.

Camellion's face became hard, ruthless. But now, the rise of international corporations has led to a situation where American politicians are now being bought to protect interests that are outside the U.S. and are seldom compatible with the voters. Analyses of political trends show that multinational corporations operating at the level of the Trilateral commission believe national governments are obsolete and cannot be trusted to create a stable world order. This loose international group, based in the USA, Europe and Japan, will attempt to handpick all party candidates for president, prime minister, etc.—*Dummies who can be manipulated toward international ends.* While the taxpayer is still saddled with the enormous expense of a feeble bureaucracy, every attempt will be made to condition the voter that the government is powerless to act decisively. This will preserve cushy political jobs and ensure support from those in office. *What a setup! The present coalition of blacks, women, homosexuals, and all the rest of the minority crap is over fifty percent, and will keep this disaster going for years. Only at the ballot box can this trend be reversed. But it won't. The average voter is too damned stupid to realize that all current officeholders should be voted out, regardless of party.*

Personally, the Death Merchant didn't give a damn. In his opinion, the whole human race was just one big pack of savages—*Too bad a cosmic Hitler can't wipe out all three billion of them.*

The gold? The group of American commandos murdered near Saint-Brieuc in Brittany was the only clue—and a very slim one at that.

The big flaw was that in order to investigate the probable conclusions deduced from the murders of the twenty-three commandos, the CIA needed the help of the ARC.

And the ARC will try to terminate us the instant we find the gold—

If there is any gold!

CHAPTER SIX

The drive from Paris to Lamballe could have been made in one day, since the distance was only 407.152 kilometers (or 253 miles). But why push? Why appear to be in a hurry? Speed and the appearance of urgency could trigger the attention of the motorized *gendarmerie*. Besides, a straight drive would place arrival in Lamballe during the early hours of the next day. Such an early hour, on deserted streets, would be another risk involving the French police.

As it turned out, the actual start of the journey didn't begin until almost noon; the delay due to once more blindfolding ARC members Laroche, Argoud, Morlande and the Debrays, and Gerstung's transporting them in the Simca van to the Luxembourg Gardens. Once in the park, the transfer had been made, slowly and at the proper time, in order not to arouse suspicions among the students of the Sorbonne, who used the benches for the pursuit of reading and of each other; and mothers and children. There was a place for everything in the park. There were miles of intriguingly curved and landscaped paths for promenading, an old stone-and-wrought-iron bandstand for concerts, a few tennis courts, a marionette theater, terraces crowded with statues of French queens and famous women, and a playground full of swings.

At 11:48 A.M., three cars left the park: Laroche and his two companions driving their Audi; the Debrays—"Pierre and Marguerite Laffont"—in the green Renault; and Richard Camellion, Ralph Gerstung and Bernie Jordan in the van—Jordan, who was driving, cursing the French custom of *priorité à droite* (The person coming from your right always has the right of way, unless the intersection is controlled by traffic lights or signs. And you have the *priorité* if you are coming from his right).

"Look at those idiots!" snarled Jordan in a rage. "None of them should be permitted to drive!"

"What can you expect from people addicted to hippophagy?" sneered Ralph Gerstung. "These French are so backward that if they acquired the Rock of Gibraltar, they'd rename it 'de Gaulle stone.' "

Sitting on a metal bench behind Jordan, Gerstung was not attempting to be funny. No, not the cynical Gerstung, who hated not only the French, but all nationalities and races. He especially disliked Germans, blacks, Arabs, and Orientals.

Hippophagy! The eating of horseflesh. Camellion thought of why the Parisians devoured horse meat with so much gusto—not only for budget reasons but because they firmly believed that horse meat was a tonic and "good for the blood." The Monday horse steak and French fries were a typical part of the city's ritual, just as is the Sunday lunch. Why Monday? Because many regular butchers close up shop, having worked hard Sunday morning, the busiest time of the week. Although refrigerators were now in general use, the Parisians had maintained their prefridge habits and continued to do their shopping daily, insisting on absolute freshness and scorning such hideous aberrations as packaged foods, mixes or what they considered to be that American crime against nature—the TV dinner. On Mondays, when regular butchers were closed, Parisians turned to *boucheries chevalines*—the sellers of horse meat—for fresh meat.

Camellion, sitting in the van's swivelseat next to Jordan, swung around to Gerstung, who had stood up and was closing the large plastic bubble in the roof.

"Chacun à son mauvais goût," Camellion said, the trace of a smile on his thin lips.

"Bernie, turn on the air conditioner," Gerstung said crankily. Unbuttoning his brown sport shirt, he glanced at Camellion, as if the Death Merchant's comment had just sunk in. "Yeah, 'each to his own bad taste!' That's one way to look at it. Just the same, I still think the French are a bunch of lice. Hell, they couldn't hang on to Vietnam and they let themselves get kicked out of Algeria; and we can't trust them to do their share in NATO."

"We didn't do so well in Vietnam ourselves," Camellion

said evenly. Feeling in a jocular mood, he laughed. "The Vietnam War began to Hanoi us, but eventually, however, we left and decided to let Saigons be Saigons."

Jordan glanced at the Death Merchant and grinned. The dour Gerstung was not amused. "Remind me to laugh in the year 2000," he growled. "We lost in 'Nam for the same reason we're losing everywhere else in the world. Because of the greedy politicians, the moronic do-gooders and the half-witted unrealists who refuse to see the handwriting on the wall. Screw the American government. It's composed of idiots, traitors, gun-grabbing hypocrites and first-class swine. Fuck the American government ten times over. If I had my way . . . we should keep the gold if we find it." Gerstung got up, moved the short distance across the van, opened the small refrigerator and took out a chilled bottle of red wine.

Jordan pushed at the center of his sunglasses with a finger and then turned onto Boulevard de Grenelle. "Ralph has a point, Kidd. And I don't mean about the gold. I'm talking about the dumb asses in D.C. Did you know that there are more than fifty Soviet-backed 'front' committees operating in Washington? And the majority are located in the one hundred block of Maryland Avenue on Capitol Hill. Most are funded from U.S. taxpayers' dollars through 'study grants' procured by witting and unwitting dupes in Congress. Systematically, their propaganda and lobby efforts—and many of these organizations are allied with the anti-gun groups and would dearly love to see all of America totally disarmed—attack the FBI and the Company for 'civil-rights violations and invasions.' "

Gerstung, who had just taken a slug of wine, belched loudly. "I'll tell you something, Kidd. If you think we in the Company have it rough, you should see what those poor bastards in the FBI have to contend with. The commie front people scream like hell about 'civil-rights violations' every time a poor fed questions one of the slime balls about a federal crime; then the media picks it up and the feds get another black eye."

"You'd better believe it," Jordan said. "Those same anti-democracy groups have no respect for the civil rights of terrorist violence. Yet the FBI, charged with the responsibility to protect the U.S. and the American citizens' rights, is expected to behave like virgin Boy Scouts. Those poor bastards have an impossible job."

The realistic Death Merchant, who couldn't have cared less about American sheep and their Judas shepherds in D.C., changed the subject as he opened a small compartment under the dash on the right-hand side and took out a small transceiver.

"Bernie, you're sure you're on the right route?" he asked.

Jordan heaved a sigh. "Of course I'm sure. I could drive backward to Lamballe. We'll cross the Seine up ahead, make a right on Rue Franklin and turn off onto Avenue Poincare to miss the heavy traffic at the Arch of Triumph. Avenue de Neuilly will take us west right out of Paris." He gave Camellion a speculative glance. The Death Merchant was turning on a walkie-talkie that, having a special transducer and transistor, operated on a totally closed band.

"The Audi should be about a mile in front of us," Jordan said, "and the Debrays about a mile behind us. Frankly, I don't trust any of them."

"What makes you think I do?" The Death Merchant switched on the walkie-talkie, and he and Jordan and Gerstung soon learned that the three ARC representatives in the Audi were only half a mile ahead and that the Debrays were practically behind the rear bumper of the van.

Camellion returned the transceiver to the compartment, and reminded himself that contact arrangement on the highway was as practical as logic would permit. He would contact the Audi and the Renault every half-hour and check their positions electronically every forty-five minutes—just in case "Pierre and Marguerite Laffont" or Laroche, Argoud and the bitchy-faced Marie Morlande should decide to go in the wrong direction, in which case Camellion and the two Company men with him would know that something was very very wrong.

During the early morning, CIA technicians at Monsieur deBois's mansion had attached "drop transmitters" underneath the Audi and the Renault. Battery powered, each transmitter operated in the 137 to 175 MHz frequency spectrum and produced 5 watts of power; its range, 6.34 miles.

By eight o'clock that night, the van, the Audi and the Renault were parked in a campground outside of Argentan, a picturesque village noted for the numerous battles that had taken place around it, the most celebrated being the hard-won victory of the French over the Spanish in 1557.

The Death Merchant and his people had covered a distance of 177 kilometers (or 110 miles), not that they couldn't have made better time. However, they hadn't been in any particular hurry, and there had been numerous stops, particularly with Georges and Camille Debray—so many that Jordan had remarked, "those two must have weak kidneys."

"Maybe they brought along wine from the vineyards of Clos de Montmartre," Gerstung had said. "You know what they say about Montmartre wine, 'He who drinks a pint of Montmartre pisses out four.' "

Each time the Debrays prepared to stop, they would use a walkie-talkie and notify the others in the van and the Audi. The van and the Audi would then pull off the road and wait, starting up again only when the Debrays were under way.

At 4:30 P.M. they had stopped for an hour and a half for a very early dinner at a roadside inn, the occupants of each vehicle sitting at separate tables and pretending to be strangers to the other members of the three-car party.

The same "stranger" arrangement continued at the campground north of Argentan. The campground had a combination bar and *brasserie*—the Brasserie Oignon, so named because, in the local area, it was famed for its onion soup at modest prices.

For those who wanted them, there were cabins. The Debrays, Marie Morlande, and Jules Laroche and Antoine Argoud rented cabins. Camellion, Jordan and Gerstung remained in the air-conditioned van, which had two bench seats that could be converted into bunks. The efficient Cecil Mintug had also provided a sleeping bag.

At 11:30 Jordan reported to the Company station in Paris. His report, once it left the radio, was on the air lanes only .009th of a second. A marvel of modern technology, the radio—or my "*Geheimschrieber,*" as Jordan called the device. The *Geheimschreiber* ("private secretary") was the code name for a cipher machine that the Germans used during World War II. However, the *Geheimschreiber* was not a transmitter, not in itself. The operator would have to sit in front of a keyboard and type out a message, and the *Geheimschreiber* would encipher the message automatically, before pumping the message out by radio at the rate of 62 words a minute. But Jordan's radio was more than a high performance transmitter and receiver. Built into the machine was also a scrambler-timer and a "con box," the latter of which could compress as much as 60 seconds of transmission time into .009th of a second. The scrambler-timer would pick up incoming transmissions, unscramble them, and "stretch out" the message to normal time sequence on the tape recorder. Transmitter, scrambler-timer and "squirt" box were only slightly larger than a portable typewriter.

As usual, the ultracautious Gerstung made no secret of his dislike of their spending the night in the van.

"Sitting ducks, that's what we are," he said, checking the left bay window to make sure it was locked. "Who's to prevent someone from rolling several grenades under this jalopy?"

"It's possible but not likely," Camellion said. "Anyhow, all the glass is bulletproof, and if anyone even touches the door handle, the alarm will go off. We have too much valuable equipment in this vehicle to leave it unprotected. Why do you think the three of us ate in shifts or never went to the john together?"

"Come off it, Ralph," Jordan said. "He's right, and you know it." Sitting on one of the narrow bunks, he started to slip off his pants. "This is vacation time all over France, and the derelicts and thieves are thick all over the highways. Why knock off some wine-sodden down-and-outer if we don't have to?"

"Uh huh. So tell me how we're going to keep this van and its contents out of the hands of the ARC should they decide to appropriate it?" demanded Gerstung, rubbing the chin of his round face.

"We'll work out that problem when we come to it," Camellion said, slightly annoyed, slipping off his leather sandals.

"We had better work something out damn soon because we'll be right in the middle of those terrorist bastards before midnight tomorrow." Gerstung pulled a French coin from his pocket. "Kidd, I'll flip you for the other bunk. Heads I win, tails you lose."

The floor of the van was hot to Camellion's feet. "Take the bunk. I intend to sleep in the lounge chair by the door."

* * *

The next morning. After an 8:00 A.M. breakfast in the Brasserie Oignon, by 9:15 the three vehicles left the campground within five minutes of each other. Camellion got on the walkie-talkie, telling the Debrays and the other three members of the ARC that this day the driving must be precise and timed so that they would arrive in Lamballe on schedule and make contact with the man who would then take them directly to the three council leaders of the *Action pour la Renaissance de la Corse*.

Jules Laroche's voice, coming in over the walkie-talkie, was cutting. "Don't snap orders at us, Monsieur Kramer. You are not the leader of this party. In case you have forgotten, we are taking you. Not you're taking us. Remember that."

Jordan, listening in, glanced at the Death Merchant and winked.

"Que Corsican bâtard," mumbled Gerstung.

Camellion smiled a smile that indicated he considered Laroche a few degrees lower than a diseased cockroach.

"*Mon ami*," he said in a very pleasant voice, "it was your order that we arrive in Lamballe no later than two o'clock in the afternoon. I suggest you put your own memory in first gear."

The transceiver went dead, and there was only background noise. Laroche had shut off his set.

"We're going to have a lot of trouble with that damned piece of trash," Jordan said acidly, "not to mention a hundred or so other members of the Corsican group."

"I doubt if there'll be that many of them in and around Lamballe," offered Gerstung. "I figure we'll be safe enough until we find the gold. Christ! Even if we find it and manage to stay alive, how can we possibly get it to the coast? It can't be done!"

"Is that why you brought those Manville shotgun machine guns?" Jordan asked. "I mean because you're expecting that much trouble from the ARC? For my money, nothing will beat the nine-millimeter M-10 Ingram. With only a little experience you can fire the Ingram with one hand, like a pistol."

Nodding, the Death Merchant pulled the cord of the electric shaver into its full length and plugged the end into the cigarette-lighter opening on the dashboard.

"Shotguns are more effective at close range in that when you blast a man, say with a twelve-guage, you can be certain that he won't have that split-second lag time in which to put a slug into you while he's going down."

The sky was heavy with clouds, although now and then the sun would put in a brief appearance. Still the temperature was in the low nineties, the heat made worse by the high humidity due to the proximity of the English Channel.

Driving demanded caution, for the road was not a *route à grande circulation,* a four-lane highway with the four flows of traffic separated by barrier strips; instead, it was a *route principale,* a main road of only two lanes. Going in a direction opposite to the van, and to the rear of the van were all makes and models of cars and trucks, as well as large and small motor homes—Renaults, Citroens, Peugeots, Volksies; German-, British- and Japanese-manufactured cars; and now and then an American auto. And motorcycles—mostly Japanese-made—complete with high baggage carriers and the inevitable female passenger sitting behind the driver. Many of the vehicles pulled open or folded campers; others dragged small trailers, motorboats or small cabin cruisers—every driver moving as if his life depended on his getting to his destination within the next five minutes.

Gradually, as Camellion and his people drove onto the peninsula of Brittany, the countryside began to take on an old-world flavor. Even the architecture of the tiny hamlets through which they passed was different. For good reason: The Bretons, unlike the rest of the French, were Celts, linguistically and ethnically related to the Irish, Welsh and Cornish; and like all true Celts, they were a contradictory, independent and mystical-minded people. Most Bretons lived the timeless lives of fishermen along the coast. In the interior, though, there was still the haunting atmosphere of the brooding, druidic past—the world of Tristan and Isolde, and spirits in trees—in the rolling hills, flat farmlands, stark architecture and deserted castles.

The Death Merchant found himself feeling the same emotions that had been with him in Northern Ireland[1]. The past lived constantly with the people in Northern Ireland, and he knew that the past had an especially tenacious hold on Brittany, on its markets and shops and parish churches. Women with traditional costume and hair styles

[1]See *Death Merchant #41: The Shamrock Smash.*

were a frequent sight on the cobbled streets as the van passed through tiny villages too small to even be on maps. The language, Breton, was still spoken by members of the older generation and was growing more popular among younger people with the rise of Breton nationalism. Due to the terrorism of the *Front de Libération de la Bretagne*—the bombings, the murders, the kidnappings—the French government had appeased the FLB separatists by permitting the revival of Breton in the Brittany schools.

"From what I've seen of Brittany so far, they can keep it," said Ralph Gerstung, who had taken over the driving. "The government in Paris would be well rid of these backward peasants."

Camellion laughed lightly. "It could be that Paris wants to hang onto Brittany because it has the best seafood in France. The best crab, *crevettes, huîtres* and *saumon fumé* in all France. The Bretons also have a good wine—*muscadet*. It's a superb, dry white wine."

"You've been here before?" Jordan, sitting behind Camellion on the end of the rightside bench-bed, seemed surprised. "You couldn't have been here during World War Two. You're too young."

"I was here some years ago . . ." Camellion said. He finished with a lie, ". . . on a vacation."

Gerstung slowed the van when he saw the sign ahead, TOURNANT DANGEREUX. "That's another thing about this part of France. Either it's a straight stretch of road or *bam!* you come to a dangerous curve. Look at those idiots ahead of us. It's a wonder they don't all pile into each other."

"Those dishes you mentioned," commented Jordan. "*Crevettes*—is that the right word?—and all the rest. What are they exactly?"

"You know what crab is," Camellion said, glancing at his watch. "The rest is shrimp, oyster and smoked salmon. The Bretons also make delicious *crêpes*. It's filled with your choice of cheese, ham, fruit preserves or assorted liquors. Another thing, here in Brittany, they often drink hard cider instead of beer or wine."

Gerstung said, "The krauts are the biggest beer drinkers I've ever seen. I was stationed in West Berlin for several years, and if those krauts weren't guzzling beer, they were eating pastries. They're worse than the Danes in the sweets department."

"I'm not concerned about eating," Jordan said huskily. "Just staying alive will be good enough for me." He bent down and checked the two .25 Mauser automatics, each of which was secure in an ankle holster. He carried another pistol in a Bianchi pancake holster jammed down between his body and belt on the left side—a .38 Smith and Wesson "Bodyguard" revolver with a concealed hammer.

"I don't think much of the Saint-Brieuc theory," he went on, making sure the straps of the ankle holster were secure around his ankles. "Twenty-three murdered commandos don't add up to half a billion in gold. To me, it's only a half-crocked idea, even if the commandos didn't have any reason for being outside Saint-Brieuc."

The Death Merchant continued to watch the cars ahead. "We have to place all the factors in proper perspective. First of all, the commandos were gunned down—machine gunned. If the old World War Two reports are accurate, the bodies lay in such a position that indicated that the men were shot unexpectedly. We might interpret this by saying that they were killed by someone they knew and trusted. Most of them were shot in the back—more evidence that they didn't expect to be killed."

"Well, they did belong to Patton's Third Army," Offered Gerstung. "To be exact, they were in Patton's Twelfth Corps.

"Which still doesn't prove anything," Jordan said.

"Very often from theory comes truth," Camellion said. "In the first place, there isn't a single record of why those commandos were in Brittany. What was their mission? The Allies had driven the Germans from France months before the commandos were murdered. The corpses were fresh, only a few days old when they were found. It was evident that the Germans hadn't killed them. There weren't any Germans in Brittany when the commandos were killed."

"Uhhhh . . ." Jordan frowned. "You're intimating that the commandos helped Patton's officers and OSS agents steal the gold, then were terminated to keep them quiet?"

"I'm not suggesting that. I think the commandos transported the gold to Brittany. It's possible they didn't even know what they were transporting. Or if they did, they were told it was part of some kind of special mission."

Jordon pondered for a moment. "Let's assume, at least for the moment, that you're right. How then did Sovey and the other Frenchies fit into the picture? What I am saying is that twenty-three commandos would have been more than enough manpower to handle the boxes. Why bring in the Frenchmen at all? And it's damned unlikely that Sovey was the only Frenchman involved. He sure as hell wasn't according to the story he gave to *Paris Match.* Six times he said 'we.' Twice he used the phrase 'our group.' So! Why didn't the officers and the OSS agents who originally stole the gold kill Sovey and the other Frenchmen? It doesn't add up!"

"I don't know," Camellion said. "That's why we're here, to try to figure it all out."

Gerstung, having rounded the curve, speeded up the van.

"If we assume that Sovey and the other Frenchies helped the commandos stash the gold, what guarantee did Patton's officers and the OSS have that the French wouldn't come back and grab the gold for themselves?"

"The answers elude me." The Death Merchant shrugged. "There are any number of variables. It's possible that Patton's officers and the OSS agents had to use Sovey and the other Frenchmen. Just because we don't know the reason doesn't mean that one doesn't exist. If our theory is correct, there has to be a valid reason why the Frenchmen didn't return for the gold."

"Your theory, not ours," Jordan said. "As far as I'm concerned, there's a credibility gap wider than the Grand Canyon. If Sovey hadn't been murdered, and if he hadn't run into all that mess at the Sovey farm, I'd say the gold story was a pipe dream."

Gerstung gave a low whistle. "By George, look at that!" he exclaimed in surprise. "A coal-mine tipple—and a slag pile."

"There's also some coal mining in Brittany, or was," Camellion said and glanced at his watch. "As I understand it, most of the mines have been worked out."

"Hmmmmm, a good place to stash gold," murmured Jordan. "In an abandoned mine shaft."

"It's a possibility," Camellion admitted. Time for a signal check. He opened the glove compartment, removed the CL-receiver and flipped the switch. *Beep-beep-beep!* Loud and clear. He looked at the signal-strength meter. The Debrays were less than a mile behind the van. He turned off the switch and flipped a second switch. There were another series of strong beeps. He was glancing at the signal-strength meter when the walkie-talkie in the compartment beneath the dash began to buzz. Camellion turned off the signal station, pulled out the AN/PRC-6T and switched it on, then held the speaking end to his mouth.

"Kramer here."

"We're making good time," Jules Laroche said, his voice friendly enough. "A few kilometers ahead there's a large *brasserie*. We stopped there on our way to Paris. I suggest we stop."

"Sure, that's fine with me." Camellion spoke into the radio. "Pierre? Marguerite? Did you get that?"

Georges Debray's voice came from the set. "*Oui.* What's the name of the place?"

Camellion: "Laroche?"

"It's the Brasserie Lapin," Laroche said. "You can't miss it. It's to the left of the road, and out front is a large sign with a red rabbit painted on it. They specialize in *fricassées* of wild hare."

"Merci. We'll find it," Georges Debray replied.

"Remember, don't take more than an hour," Camellion warned. "And the same security measures will prevail."

"*Oui, nous comprenons,*" Laroche and George Debray said together.

Chuckling loudly, Camellion returned the AN/PRC-6T to the secret compartment.

"We're going to stop to put on the feedbag," said Jordan. "That's funny?"

"I suppose you men know that Paris rests on uncounted miles of stone quarries that have lain under the city since Roman times?"

Jordan was puzzled. "Of course. The catacombs of Paris are well known and very extensive. But what does that have to do with fried rabbit?"

Camellion explained that the limestone and gypsum—used for making plaster of Paris—was so rich in quality and quantity that the city was built by simply digging straight down to obtain construction materials. The first open-pit quarries soon gave way to high-domed mines. "When these were exhausted, they were abandoned. But no one bothered to map the hidden chasms. As the city expanded over the centuries, the mines were forgotten and whole quarters were built over them."

"So why didn't the city fall into the pits?" Jordan wanted to know.

"It started to, in the middle of the eighteenth century. It was then that the city authorities began mapping the underground, filling water-dissolved pits with earth and rubble and sealing off mine entrances. Nonetheless, the vast network of tunnels and caves continued to have their use, as hideouts for *apaches* and other cutthroats, and for 'mushroom-growers.' "

Ralph Gerstung growled, "Get to the point, Kidd. What the hell has all that to do with the baked, boiled, or fried rabbit.

"As I recall, it was early in the twentieth century that workers passing through a quarry beneath the Odeon area came upon a cat cemetery. There were hundreds and hundreds of feline skeletons lying all over the place. The workers began wondering if alley cats had some death instinct like elephants, which impelled them to totter down to this boneyard to die. The explanation was much simpler. Above the workers was a sealed-up, obsolete well that years before had stood in the courtyard of a restaurant famous for its *fricassées* of 'wild hare.' "

Gerstung chuckled, "Well, the French eat horses, why not cats."

An expression of distaste flickered over Jordan's face. "Remind me not to order any wild hare when we get to the Brasserie Lapin."

In a very short time they saw that the Brasserie Lapin was much larger than they had expected and that on the east side and in front, on the south, there were scores of tables covered with red tablecloths, both areas shielded from the sun by a red-and-yellow-striped polyester canopy that flapped in the breeze and was held secure by aluminum poles. From the number of vehicles parked at the east of the building, the Brasserie Lapin was a very popular establishment.

Gerstung turned in and found a parking place in the center of a line of vehicles stretched out by a short, two-foot-high wall that ran from north to south. The second line of cars was parked at the north, in a line that was in an east-west direction.

"You two go ahead," Jordan said slowly. "Frankly, I'm not hungry." He grinned good-naturedly at the Death Merchant. "You and your damned cats."

"Keep the van locked after we leave," Camellion said and reached for the handle of the door.

Halfway to the east side of the restaurant, Camellion and Gerstung noticed that the Audi was parked at the front of the north-south line of cars. As they walked under the east canopy, they spotted the Debrays coming down the highway in the Renault.

Heavily armed, Camellion and Gerstung made their way through the babble of voices, cooking odors and people and found an empty table in the northwest corner under the front canopy. On his left and right sides, Camellion packed Walther PPK/S autos in hugger holsters inside his belt, the weapons hidden by his short-sleeved white shirt jacket. In the left pocket of the jacket was an NAM minirevolver, a weapon that had an overall length of only three and three-sevenths inches, yet could fire five high-speed Long Rifle cartridges. On each ankle was a COP, a unique four-barrel .357 Magnum that was only 5.5 inches by 4.1 inches by 1 inch.

Gerstung, a natural-born terminator, carried the TP-70 .25 autos in ankle holsters and two 9-mm Parabellum Star BKM pistols in under-the-belt holsters, the bulges concealed by his bright yellow chino pullover shirt.

Taking off his dark glasses, Gerstung scooted his chair closer to the table and picked up a menu. "I see Laroche and his two lovelies," he said in a very low voice. "They're front center."

"I know. They had to see us when we came in," Camellion said. He settled back and picked up a menu, a feeling of uneasiness dancing up and down his spine. While pretending to study the menu, he studied the people around him through his dark glasses. They *looked* all right. They *looked* harmless enough. They *looked* like tourists and people on a vacation—*But only fools go on looks, and fools don't live long in this business.*

"I see that rabbit is the *spécialité* of this dump," Gerstung said drily. "They can keep it. I'm going to have four *entrecôtes,* a salad and— I wonder what crêpes Breton is?"

Camellion scanned the menu. "No minute steaks for me. I'm having the Châteaubriand, the sirloin. Crêpes Breton? It's like a pancake. Chopped peppers, chopped onions, some other vegetables. It's not too bad. . . ."

* * *

Fifty minutes later, Camellion and Gerstung prepared to leave. Having paid the check, they got up and moved toward the east canopy, Laroche, Argoud and Marie Morlande only fifteen feet ahead of them. Once outside, Laroche and his two companions walked toward their Audi parked sixty feet to their right. The Death Merchant and Gerstung headed toward the van, eighty feet away and slightly to their left.

It was then that trouble of the worst sort arrived. Camellion and Gerstung were a fourth of the way to the van. Laroche and the two ARC members with him were halfway to their Audi.

It was the sun glinting off a shiny object that grabbed Camellion's attention and made him jerk his attention to the left, just in time to see four or five men—he couldn't be sure—on either side of a car parked in the center of the east-west line. The mirror-like glint had been caused by the sun's rays striking the barrel of a stainless-steel Belgium .38 FN revolver. In that sliver of a second, Camellion could see that the other men were putting weapons into firing positions, one had a submachine gun of some kind.

"Ambush—to the left!" Camellion yelled, his hands streaking inside his jacket as he dove to the cobblestone ground.

"Balls!" muttered Gerstung. He, too, started toward the ground, just as the terrorist with the Israeli UZI machine gun got off the first stream of projectiles. All the hollow-nosed slugs passed over Camellion and Gerstung, both of whom were pulling out auto-pistols. Jules Laroche and Marie Morlande were also lucky. A slug tore through Morlande's hair, but didn't touch her scalp. A bullet ripped through the short sleeve of Laroche's right arm and left a burn line on the flesh. But Antoine Argoud's luck could not have been worse. Two slugs bored into his left hip. A third struck him in the left rib cage. A fourth and a fifth ripped across his back, one cutting a deep, bloody ditch in the flesh, the other cutting through his back and severing the spinal cord. One moment Argoud was alive and in the prime of life; the next instant he was a corpse, a nothing even before his body crashed to the hard stones.

In another few seconds, while the man with the UZI prepared to get off another line of slugs, the other four terrorists got off shots. Camellion and Gerstung—lying on their stomachs—fired, and Jules Laroche and Marie Morlande—also prone—drew their weapons.

The slugs of the terrorists came very close to the Death Merchant and his three companions. A bullet glanced from a large, flat stone only several inches to Camellion's right. A projectile whizzed by Gerstung's left cheek, almost striking his ear lobe. Another slug knifed through the air close to Jules Laroche; and while Marie Morlande would never know it, she had missed death by only a few inches, from a 9-mm projectile that almost kissed the right side of her forehead.

Camellion, who had calculated distance and windage while throwing himself to the ground, didn't miss. Two of his .380 PPK/S slugs slammed into the man with the UZI, hitting him high in the chest. The astonished terrorist fell against another man, throwing off the other's aim. The Death Merchant continued to pull the trigger.

Two of Gerstung's 9-mm BKM bullets banged out a second and a third gunmen, one muttering *"Mein Gott! Ich —"* as he went down. The man who had stumbled when the dead machine gunner had fallen against him tried to duck and pick up the UZI submachine gun. André Mariot, the fifth terrorist on the other side of the car, had more sense. Dropping flat to the ground, he began to back away on his hands and knees.

Fritz Kroen grabbed the machine gun and started to swing the stubby barrel toward the south, toward the three men and the woman on the ground. A moment later he started to die from two of the Death Merchant's .380 Walther slugs and one of Laroche's 9-mm by 19-Parabellum Heckler and Koch projectiles, the three missiles catching him in the high part of his left arm, his stomach and his chest.

The roaring of the shots had an instantaneous effect on the people in the Brasserie Lapin. Instantly, the popular roadside restaurant was turned into a madhouse. Conversation turned to screams and yells of fear. Panic took over, and people began to act like turkeys caught out in the open during a thunderstorm. People were running in every direction, bumping into each other, pushing and shoving. Many rushed out from under the front canopy, some running to the south, others to the west. Those people who had been getting into their cars when the gunfire started now tried to back out and escape, now that the firing seemed to be over with. Including Georges and Camille Debray. The Debrays had sat under the eastside canopy and had eaten only sandwiches. They had just gotten into the Renault when Camellion and the others left the restaurant, and had been getting ready to pull out when Constantine Mauriac had triggered the first blast from the UZI machine gun.

Engine roaring, a blue Jaguar started to back out of the east-west line of vehicles. To the right of the Jaguar, in the north-south area, Georges Debray also decided it was time to leave—a big mistake on his part, but a blessing for André Mariot who jumped over the short wall and ran in fear toward the two cars the gunmen had parked under some trees 150 feet to the northwest.

In the meanwhile, Camellion and Gerstung jumped up and—afraid that if they went directly to the van, someone might see them and report them to the police—ran between two cars a short distance south of the van. They were running along the short wall toward the front of the van when they heard a loud crash to the north.

Jules Laroche and Marie Morlande didn't take such precautions. Knowing that Antoine Argoud was stone dead, they ran straight to the Audi, got in, got down and waited, realizing that if they tried to back out into the mad scramble of cars, they stood a good chance of becoming involved in a smashup.

And that's exactly what happened to the Jaguar and the Renault. The Jag backed out in a rush at the same time that Georges Debray put the Renault in reverse. The result was that the rear end of the Jaguar crashed into the left-rear side of the Renault, smashing in the left-rear door and crumbling the left fender over the left-rear wheel.

Georges and Camille Debray were stunned but otherwise unhurt. The man and the woman in the Jaguar had been less fortunate. The woman's body had jerked forward, and she had hit her head against the windshield and was unconscious. The driver, her husband, was dead. The crash had caught him just right, and his neck had snapped.

The shock and the feeling of unreality passed and Georges whispered, his voice shaking, "Let's g-get out of here. We'll go to either the van or the Audi. Move! Move! Get out!"

Grabbing her small handbag from the seat, Camille

shoved open the door on the passenger's side and slid out. All around them cars were either backing out or racing for the highway in front of the Brasserie Lapin.

Georges pushed Camille toward the short wall. "We'll go on the other side of the wall. Out front, we'd get run over."

"Suppose the van and the Audi have already left?"

"They haven't." Georges's voice was just as fearful. "Kidd and Jules are too cautious. They'll wait."

They crawled over the rock wall and were starting to run south when they saw Leonard Kidd, hunched down, a Walther auto in his right hand, racing toward them. In a few more minutes, the three of them were climbing through the door of the Simca van, whose motor Jordan had started. Almost as icy as the Death Merchant, Gerstung had opened the long rear window, stuck out his head and was watching the wild exodus of vehicles, an Explorer II target pistol[2], with silencer attached, in his right hand. The Debrays sagged to one of the benches. Camellion hurried to join Gerstung.

Jordan, his eyes on the truck-sized rearview mirror outside the van, to his left, called out, "How does it look out there? God damn it! Are we going to sit here the rest of the afternoon?"

"The cars are thinning out, but—Oh no!" mumbled Gerstung.

"What is it?" Jordan asked.

The Debrays looked startled.

The Death Merchant answered Jordan. "There's a traffic cop across the way. He's standing by the southeast corner of the canopy and giving us the once-over."

"An *agent pivot!* Where did he come from?" Jordan was suddenly angry. "Kill him, and let's pull out."

"Laroche and Morlande have just backed out," Gerstung said evenly. "What do we do about the cop— As if I didn't know!"

[2]A brand new .22 Long Rifle target pistol manufactured by Charter Arms Corporation. The weapon is unique in that it is built on the principle of the old broomhandle Mauser, with the eight-round magazine in front of the trigger guard. At the same time, there is another eight-round magazine in the simulated walnut grip to give shooters the option of firing a total of sixteen rounds without having to reload the front clip.

The Death Merchant watched the traffic cop who wore a white hard hat, boots, blue pants, light blue shirt and a white Sam Browne belt. An MAB was in a flapped holster on his right side. The moment of truth arrived. The cop took a pen and a notebook from his shirt pocket. He was going to write down the license number of the van.

"Terminate him," Camellion said quietly.

The *agent pivot* had not printed the first number when Gerstung raised the Explorer II and pulled the trigger four times—*bazit-bazit-bazit-bazit!* The traffic cop cried out, jumped, dropped the pen and the pad, and died almost instantly from the four .22 hollow-points in his chest. He was falling as a red Renault–Le Car, its driver attempting to reach the road, cut too sharply to the right. Its right fender crashed into one of the aluminum poles supporting the canopy. The Le Car kept on going, but down came the canopy on the tables and chairs and on the dozen or so people who had taken refuge under the tables.

"Back out slowly," Camellion ordered Jordan. "We'll let you know when it's all clear."

Jordan began backing out, growling, "Hell, giving an enema to a hippopotamus would be easier than this!"

The Death Merchant thrust his head farther out the window. To the west there were only two cars racing toward the road. The north end was clear.

"Now!" Camellion said. "All the way. Fast!"

Six minutes later, the van was on the highway, moving west.

CHAPTER SEVEN

1:45 in the afternoon.

The van was 64.360 kilometers (or 40 miles) east of Laballe. The Audi was a kilometer closer. The inhabitants of Laballe, who years before had been coal miners, made their living from tourists and from a winery north of the town.

"We won't arrive on time," Jordan commented to Camellion. "But Laroche didn't seem worried when you talked to him on the radio. That clever lad has contingency plans. And he probably has half a dozen for us."

The Death Merchant swung around in the swivel lounge chair next to Jordan and looked at Gerstung, who was in the rear of the van and watching the road through the back window.

"See anything suspicious?" Camellion inquired, his eyes raking the Debrays. He was more than a little proud of the make-up job he had done on them. Only God in his Heaven would have sworn that "Pierre Laffont" and "Marguerite Laffont" weren't in the icy years of life, in their early sixties. Their wrinkled skin and gray hair proved it. Not a single facial feature remained of Georges Debray and Camille Debray.

"Not that I can see," Gerstung answered Camellion. At that moment a Honda motorcycle, weighed down with a young man, a young woman, and luggage boxes on both sides and on the rear, roared past the van and began eating up the road ahead. The closest vehicle behind the van was a motor home, a quarter of a mile away. It was not very likely that the FLB or the French police would be trailing the van in a motor home.

While continuing to stare meditatively out the rear window, Gerstung commented, "I'm bothered by all the unexpected assassination attempts. First in Paris and now back there. They had to be following us. They had to see us turn in. At minimum, they had to be positive we were there."

"Could they have tapped into our walkie-talkie band?" Jordan called out. He answered his own question, "No. They couldn't. They'd have to have a preset receiver tuned to our band."

Clutching her handbag, Camille Debray leaned back and smiled weakly at Camellion. "We were lucky that you spotted them in time, Monsieur Kidd, or we might all be dead. Georges and I were only five minutes ahead of you."

"*Oui,*" Georges agreed. "It's terrible enough that poor Antoine is dead. Thank God he carried nothing with him to connect him with us."

Gerstung suddenly swung from the rear window and laughed. In response to questioning looks, he explained that it was "amusing how young voices can come from old bodies"—referring to the Debrays. He then said in a more serious tone, "I find it odd, though, that the gunmen didn't fire at the two of you. Your car was much closer to them than was the van or the Audi, and like you've already said, you were only five minutes ahead of us and Laroche, Argoud and Morlande." Gerstung's gaze moved to the Death Merchant. "How about it, Kidd? Haven't you wondered why the gunmen didn't fire at Georges and Camille?"

"The world is full of mysteries," Camellion said softly.

Camille looked startled. Apprehension crept into Georges's eyes.

"How should we know?" Angrily Georges looked from Camellion to a hard-eyed Gerstung. "Maybe they didn't recognize us because of how our faces have been changed? For all we know, they got into position after Camille and I were already in the car. But I don't like what you are implying!"

"What makes you think I'm implying anything?" Gerstung said with a slight chuckle that was faintly mocking.

Camille said quickly, "We assumed that as close as we were to the FLB killers, the only thing we could do was stay down and hope. By the time we opened the door and started firing, they could have riddled us."

"You'd have done the same thing, if you had been in our place," Georges lashed out. "Don't say that you wouldn't."

Jordan lighted a cigarette. Camellion shrugged.

"I think we should all be grateful," Camille said nervously. "I thank God that they didn't use silencers the way they did at our apartment."

"It wouldn't have made any difference," Gerstung said. "It was the sun glinting on a weapon that tipped off Kidd."

A red light began flashing in Camellion's mind, and he remembered the Heckler and Koch VP70 auto-pistol that had been lying next to one of the men who had tried to gain entrance to the Debray apartment with the hollow-box delivery ruse. The VP70 had had a silencer attached to the barrel. Camellion recalled seeing the weapon and silencer when he had rushed out the front door to pick up the SIG submachine gun.

"Camille, how did you know that the two men with the fake packages had pistols with silencers?" Camellion's voice was slyly inquisitive, yet devoid of bitterness.

Camille stared at him, dumbfounded. Georges stiffened

and drew back slightly. Gerstung became alert, his eyes narrowing suspiciously.

"W-Why . . . I guess someone told me," Camille responded, each word a shiver. "One of you must have."

"No one did," Camellion said. "I was the only one who saw a pistol with a silencer, and I had to go through the front door to see it. You and the others were in the kitchen."

"Then you must have mentioned it." Camille swallowed hard, her face twisting with conflicting emotions. "Somebody had to tell me, or I heard some of you talking."

"I have an excellent memory," the Death Merchant said, "and I didn't mention the pistol with the silencer. I considered it irrelevant. I'll ask again, How did you know about the silencer?"

"She said *silencers*," Gerstung said, his hand with the Explorer II pistol coming up. "The second crumb with the phony box must have also had a pistol with a noise suppressor." His accusing stare fastened on Camille, who was becoming more agitated. "Kidd didn't say a word to me about it. So answer the man. How could you know about the silencers—?"

"Unless she knew in advance," finished Camellion. "Unless she and Georges were a part of the setup. Both of you"—his voice became very sharp—"sit still and keep your hands in sight."

"Or you'll get a .22 hollow-point where the sun doesn't shine," warned Gerstung. "Georges, get rid of those MABs you have underneath your jacket. Thumb and forefinger only. Put 'em on the floor."

A trapped, sick look on his face, Georges reached under the left side of his green shirt jacket with the thumb and forefinger of his right hand and started to tug the 9-mm auto from its holster."

"This is ridiculous!" Camille managed to say. "We're not part of the FLB. You're both crazy!"

Without warning, the Death Merchant got up, crossed the very short distance to Camille and snatched the handbag from her hands that due to make-up, appeared brown and wrinkled and marked with liver spots.

"Let's have a look," he said. "There are always a lot of goodies in a woman's purse."

Jordan called out, "Do you think they're the informers?"

"I'm almost positive they are," Camellion said. Glancing

at Camille, who was watching his every movement with trapped eyes, he unzipped the imitation-leather handbag and began rummaging around in the various compartments. The usual junk and a .25 Linmoges automatic. Camellion pulled out another object, a small metal box shaped on the order of a pack of king-size cigarettes, only slightly wider.

"Well, well! What have we here? Look at this, Ralph?"

"Yeah, a fuckin' transmitter!" growled Gerstung. He glared at the Debrays. "I'd like to terminate them both right now. Only dead people can't talk."

"Not an ordinary transmitter either," Camellion said studiously, opening the hinged panel on one side of the small device. "It's a German *Beschaffenheit* and initiates the scanning procedure at 2 MHz and covers the spectrum up to 1,000 MHz." With the panel open, Camellion looked at the tiny green light, not larger than the head of a pin, and at the two tiny activating buttons and the ON/OFF switch. "Not only that, but this baby generates a second or lower sub-carrier frequency. This is an expensive job, at least ten to fifteen thousand dollars on today's market. I'd say it has a range of at least twenty miles."

"I didn't think you damned FLBs used such sophisticated equipment," Gerstung said, his manner foreboding.

"We are not with the *Front de Libération de la Bretagne*," Georges Debray insisted loudly. Putting the second MAB on the floor of the van, he straightened up and stared truculently at the Death Merchant, who noticed that, in spite of the air conditioning, the Frenchman had begun to sweat. "We've never seen that transmitter—if that's what it is. Somehow, the enemy must have planted it in her handbag.

Gerstung's eyes never wavered from the Debrays, nor did Camellion's.

"Let's give him a lousy 'E' for effort, and then I can shoot off his kneecaps to get some answers," Gerstung said. "What about the transmitter? Are you going to switch it off?"

"Not yet," Camellion said, his own stare stabbing at Georges and Camille Debray, neither of whom could disguise their sense of fear and expectancy. He dropped the transmitter into one pocket of his white shirt jacket and took out the NAM minirevolver from the other pocket.

"*Mes amis*," he said cordially, "you've been caught with

your hands in the cookie jar. The only choice you have now is how you're going to confess, the easy way or the hard way. But you will tell us what we want to know." When he saw that Georges Debray was about to speak, he held up a hand. "Wait!" The word came out like a pistol shot. "Time is too short for lies. Lie or protest just one more time and Gerstung will blow away your kneecaps. Then, *ma chère*"—he glowered at Camille—"he'll start on your legs."

Camille Debray sighed deeply, and a shudder rippled through her body. "He is right, Georges. They have the transmitter. To deny the obvious would only be a waste of time. May I smoke?" She looked at the Death Merchant, who had her cigarettes in her handbag.

"Keep talking," Camellion said.

"You're either infiltrators from the FLB," said Gerstung, "or else ARC members who sold out to the FLB for a price. Which is it?"

"Neither one," said Georges. He wiped sweat from his upper lip with the sleeve of his right arm. "We're agents of the *Direction de la Surveillance du Territoire*. We are the police."

"I'll be damned!" exclaimed Gerstung. "The French FBI!"

"We can come to some sort of agreement, some kind of arrangement," Camille said swiftly. She seemed to relax, and hope crossed her face. "We're both on the side of law and justice. We're working for our country; you gentlemen are working for yours. Why not work together to achieve the same goal?"

Georges Debray was also quick with the hard sell. "Our goals are the same, Monsieur Kidd. The ARC and the FLB are terrorists, murderers disrupting public order. They are the same as the terrorists in your own United States. The only difference is that the ARC and the FLB are very powerful and well organized."

"Right now you had better start at the beginning," Camellion said. "We won't even consider any kind of deal until we have the full facts, until we have the truth. There is no other way."

Georges Debray explained that, as special agents of the DST, he and Camille had infiltrated the ARC four and a half years earlier, their main assignment being to find out when and where the police might trap the three-man leadership council. All three, Yves Gelee, Marc Lavest and Michel La Bigne, had to be taken—or killed—together.

"Then we came along and offered the answer by wanting to meet with the three," Camellion said.

"*Oui,* that's right," Georges admitted. "The only thing—"

"One moment," Gerstung interrupted. "Since you were using us to get to Gelee and the other two leaders, why set us up to be terminated in your apartment? With us dead, Laroche and the other two wouldn't have had any reason to take just the two of you to meet with Gelee, La Bigne and Lavest."

"But that is just it! We didn't have anything to do with what happened at our apartment," Camille said passionately. "We were as surprised as you were. We're not responsible either for the ambush back at Brasserie Lapin. It's not we who informed the FLB We haven't had any more contact with the FLB than you have. We're not the informer."

Jordan called back from the driver's seat. "We can't make any deals, Kidd. Not without permission from you-know-where."

"You forget, I've got full authority in the field to make decisions," Camellion said roughly. "I'll handle this matter." He tossed Camille her cigarettes and a book of matches. "All those other stops yesterday. That's when another DST slipped you the transmitter. Or did you have it on you when we fled from the apartment?"

"In one of the rest rooms," Camille admitted, smiling slightly. "It was only by sheer luck that headquarters managed to get the transmitter to me—and very good deduction on the part of the DST. After all of us fled the apartment, headquarters in Paris didn't know what had happened to us. They did know, however, that we would eventually meet with the leaders of the ARC in Bretagne, because the day before Jordan and the two of you arrived at our apartment, we had gotten word to headquarters that we and other members of the ARC and agents of the American CIA would be making contact with the leaders. Two days previously Georges had met with Laroche, and Laroche had told him that the leaders were in Bretagne, but he didn't name the town."

"How did the DST recognize you?" Camellion asked curiously. "It was impossible for you to have gotten out any word after we fled the apartment in Montmartre."

There was an ironic quality to Camille's voice. "They didn't recognize me and Georges. Headquarters had no way of knowing that we would be wearing such clever disguises. Their main worry, I assume, was that the *gendarmes* might recognize Georges and me. What happened is that headquarters deduced that we'd all be taking the main route to Bretagne. Headquarters also assumed that Georges and I would stop as often as possible in the hope of making contact. Agents were stationed all along the route, at filling stations, roadside inns, et cetera, each one with a transmitter. God only know how many agents saw us but didn't recognize us. It was Georges who recognized one of them. A woman agent who had once been our contact. He whispered to her and she made contact with me in the ladies' room at the campground in Argentan."

"The DST know what our van looks like and they're trailing us, keeping far behind," mused Camellion. He blinked at Camille. "Of course, you told the contact who gave you the transmitter that our destination was Lamballe?"

"You know I did."

Gerstung grimaced and cleared his throat, sounding as though he might be trying to growl. "We're in one fine mess. It's like our having a choice between blowing out our brains or letting ourselves being bitten by a cobra."

"The tiger snake of Australia and the green mamba and the boomslange in Africa are far more poisonous," Camellion said facetiously. Rubbing the end of his chin, he appeared to be laundering and pressing any number of thoughts in his mind.

Gerstung emitted a furious snort and glare at the Debrays. "I suppose you also informed your contact about the gold and ODESSA?"

"*Oui,*" Camille said promptly, then turned to the Death Merchant. "Monsieur Kidd, if you turn off the transmitter, the DST agents behind us will realize that something is wrong. There are other agents waiting in Lamballe. They would, no doubt, close in on us."

"And on Jules and Marie," said Georges.

"They could interpret the shut off as a malfunction," said Gerstung savagely.

"It's not very likely," Georges said, "not with a *Beschaffenheit*-type transmitter."

The Death Merchant continued to toy with the tiny .22 five-shot minirevolver. "Naturally the French government would be willing to share the gold with us," he said to the Debrays, his words sliding out on a half-chuckle.

"You know better," Georges said seriously. "We know you have your orders from your government. We also know that the U.S. government is not all that interested in gold. There is another factor to your mission. You are searching for something else. For now, that is no concern of ours. I tell you frankly, we're concerned with far more than finding the bullion and the leaders of the ARC and, eventually, the bosses of the FLB."

"Sure. And I play the tuba in the bathtub," Gerstung said threateningly.

"Let them talk," Camellion said, watching Camille take a drag on her cigarette.

"We want the informer." Georges voice was urgent and strained. "Granted, the two ambushes were bad enough, but there have been other mysterious leaks that have led to various difficulties, going as far back as a year ago."

"Why is finding out the identity of this particular informer so important?" queried Camellion.

"Our superiors are of the opinion that the informer is possibly within the higher echelon of the DST," Georges said. "Either he or she is an FLB sympathizer or a paid informer, paid by either the FLB or, possibly, ODESSA."

"The informer has to be found," Camille said desperately. "There's no way of knowing how much he has learned about DST secrets and to whom he's sold those secrets."

"You're afraid of foreign Intelligence," Camellion said. "How does the SDECE fit into the overall picture."

"We—Georges and I—don't know," Camille said. "French Intelligence looks down its nose at the DST. There's a lot of rivalry between the two organizations. It's only logical to work on the premise that the SDECE has agents within the FLB and the ARC. They want the leaders as much as does the DST."

"It couldn't have been the SDECE that was responsible for the attack on our apartment, or the ambush a little while ago," Camille said hurriedly. "With us and you dead, they'd never get to Yves Gelee and the others."

"Messieurs, it is possible for all of us to work together," Georges suggested. This time he was almost pleading. "I'm sure something can be worked out."

"We're getting closer and closer to Lamballe, Kidd." Gerstung's tone was wearily ironical.

"We're only 48 kilometers away," called out Jordan.

The Death Merchant's face—he looked like a man approaching sixty—did not betray his thoughts. There wasn't any way that he could be positive that Georges and Camille Debray were telling the truth. He didn't have the main ingredient: time, time for several days of intensive interrogation, with the aid of a polygraph and a voice-stress analyzer. Without any kind of evidence to prove that the Debrays weren't lying—*Those two could be anybody!* They could be agents of SDECE. Or they could be secretly working for the FLB. They could even be working for ODESSA. There was only one obvious conclusion.

Finally the Death Merchant spoke. "This is about as bad as trying to plow a potato field with a dull-bladed plow!"

"It's worse," Gerstung said. "You can't get iced plowing a field."

"Gerstung, do you speak German?"

"Ya, ich sprechen Deutsch."

"Verstehen Sie Nazi slang?"

Gerstung looked surprised. *"Sehr gut!"*

"Zum Verheizen!"

CHAPTER EIGHT

"The action you took was the only course possible," said Yves Gelee, speaking French. "But it was still very dangerous. I suppose it's as broad as it's long, since you were so close to Lamballe."

Michel La Bigne disagreed. "They should not have come

here under the conditions that prevailed. It was too much of a chance, too much of a risk."

In the shadows created by the flickering flames of the four candles in the iron ratchet-type chandelier hanging from the low ceiling, La Bigne's thin, dark face had a sinister appearance—an illusion, since he was a balding man of spare frame, whose face always seemed to wear a painted smile whenever he spoke. He was 47 years old, an ex-stone cutter.

"*Mon chef*, the decision was also mine," Jules Laroche said to La Bigne, proving that he was a man of honor and responsibility. "As I explained when we first arrived, after Monsieurs Kidd and Gerstung discovered that Georges and Camille Debray were agents of the *Direction de la Surveillance du Territoire,* we held a conference by walkie-talkie. Monsieur Kidd hit upon the idea to place the transmitter in the Audi and leave the car parked at the edge of Laballe. All of us would then come here in the van. We calculated that we had at least a twenty-minute lead over the DST agents trailing us, and our plan worked." Laroche turned slightly and looked in the direction of Richard Camellion, who was sitting on a box across from Yves Gelee and Michel La Bigne.

The Death Merchant was on cue. "My own analysis of the situation was that we could be here by the time the DST got wise to how we had tricked them. Since Madame Debray had already informed them that our destination was Laballe, we weren't endangering you any more than you were already threatened."

A low bitter, laugh came from Gelee. With his rather coppery-colored skin, planed cheekbones, thick black hair and hawklike nose, the council member of the ARC leadership reminded the Death Merchant of an American Indian, except that American Indians don't have blue-gray eyes and, on their right cheek, a large keloid, an overgrowth of a scar that did not heal properly. From the scant information that Camelilon had acquired from Laroche, had gathered that Gelee—*He can't be over thirty*—was, more or less, the guiding spirit of the infamous *Action pour la Renaissance de la Corse.* He was clever. It had been Gelee who had decided that Marc Lavest, the third member of the Council, should remain in Corsica. That way, Lavest would remain in control of the ARC if anything happened to Gelee and La Bigne in France.

"It's a waste of time to discuss all these pros and cons," Gelee said realistically. "What is done, is done. You're here. We have lookouts posted. If the worst comes, we'll escape through the old coal-mine tunnel that runs underneath the house."

"As Intelligence agents, you gentlemen have surmised that we are prepared for any eventuality," La Bigne said. "Not only do we have to worry about the DST and SDECE, but we're in the heart of Bretagne. I should think that within a radius of forty kilometers, there must be three to four hundred members of the FLB, perhaps even Charles Henri Fauvet himself and his top people. How I would like to see that swine blind and with his arms and legs broken."

"We're all sitting on a time bomb," Camellion said. He leaned forward, both hands around a mug, his elbows on his knees. "We can be certain that the *gendarmerie* and the DST will increase their forces in this area."

"We're going to have a problem moving about," Jordan said with characteristic bluntness."

"Not as much as you might think," La Bigne said. "The police are always around, but they keep a low profile so as not to alarm the tourists. In this area it's the FLB that concerns the flics."

"Maybe so," Camellion said. "But if we're stopped because we appear suspicious, it won't make any difference whether we're FLB, ARC or PDQ!"

"PDQ?" Yves Gelee's eyes went up.

"American slang—'pretty damned quick,'" Camellion explained.

Gelee wasn't amused, but Michel La Bigne laughed and motioned toward the corked ceramic jug on the wooden box in front of him. "Let's have more to drink, *mes amis.* One thing these Bretons can do is make good cider. Hold out your mugs. I'll pour."

The flies have walked into the parlor of the spider! Camellion thought, as he and the other men leaned forward and held out their mugs. To the Death Merchant, the real danger was the ARC—*Once we find the gold, and I doubt if we do.* The FLB and the police were also a threat. And how safe was the farm?

He recalled the events of the last few hours, probing for flaws. The van and the Audi had gone right through the heart of Laballe, a town of less than six thousand people, a town out of the past. Many of the buildings in the business section still retained their pointed medieval towers. On the sidewalks numerous people had been dressed in colorful costumes of the old Bretons, folk clothes that were the most distinctive in all France, especially those of the women, who were justly proud of the beautiful heirloom lace on the white caps, called coifs. Good needlewomen also liked to show their skill on the dark dress material as well.

Once out of Laballe and west of the town, the Audi and the Simca van had pulled under a clump of chestnut trees. Camellion had put the *Beschaffenheit* in the small trunk of the Audi and locked the trunk; Jules Laroche and Marie Morlande had gotten in the van, Morlande blanching slightly when she saw the dead bodies of Georges and Camille Debray. The corpses were an ugly sight. Gerstung had shot Georges in the mouth and Camille in the chest, and there was a lot of blood on the floor.

Laroche had taken over the driving of the van and had driven over rutted, dusty roads straight to the Resnais farm, four miles northwest of Laballe.

By no means was the farm, formerly a winery, picturesque. A gigantic yard, a lot of ancient oaks and maples, their leaf-laden branches twisting toward the cloudy sky. A two-story stone house with a slate roof. A stone barn, smaller outbuildings of wood, the original paint only a memory. Connected to the east side of the barn was the winery, also constructed of stone.

Laroche had parked the van in the rear of the barn, next to four other cars. Just as quickly, Benoit Fachon and Claude Capeau had appeared and had led Camellion and the others through a door in the barn into the winery, muttering that the corpses of the Debrays would be disposed of by other members of the ARC.

"How?" Gerstung had had the gall to ask.

"They'll be buried," Fachon, a hard-faced red-haired man, had said. "Where is no concern of yours."

Fachon and Capeau had led then down the center of the winery that had obviously not been in operation for years. Partially covered with some kind of gray-white mold, the four fermentation vats rested forlornly on their foundations. Wine presses and bottling-and-corking machinery were rusted and covered with dust and cobwebs.

The Death Merchant and the rest of the men had seen

acres of vineyards to the west of the farm. Walking behind Capeau and Fachon, they had soon seen how the grapes were being used. The two ARC terrorists had led them into another section of the winery. In this area were long, wide tables, each covered with grapes being turned into raisins.

The small group had gone to the northwest corner of the building. Capeau had stood on a table, reached up and pulled down on a rusted-iron candle holder fastened to the wall. Without a sound, a pile of boxes on the stone floor in the corner, began to rise and tilt forward, their movement revealing a square opening in the thick-stone floor, an opening through which dim light filtered.

"*Venir, ce façon,*" Benoit Fachon said gruffly and waved toward the opening.

With a feeling akin to being led to their own execution, Camellion, Jordan and Gerstung had followed Capeau down the wooden steps. There, sitting on boxes in the secret room, were Yves Gelee and Michel La Bigne, two of the leaders of the *Action pour la Renaissance de la Corse.*

The Death Merchant evaluated the overall situation as La Bigne filled his mug to the brim with hard cider. To his left was Ralph Gerstung, who seemed to be ready to spring. Jordan was to his right. Across from them and the box that served as a table, were Gelee and La Bigne. At the left end of the rectangle sat Laroche, facing Claude Capeau and Benoit Fachon at the right end. Marie Morlande was not present. After getting out of the van, she had gone to the house.

In case of sudden trouble, three against five weren't bad odds. *But getting to the van and escaping from the farm is another matter!* Camellion was miserable. *Anyhow, where would we go? Damn Grojean!*

Filling his own mug last, La Bigne didn't look at Camellion and the two Company men as he posed the vital question, "How can we trust you *Américains*? What assurance do we have that you will keep your part of the bargain and pay the five million francs after you have the gold?"

He glanced then at Camellion, Jordan and Gerstung, moved backward a few steps and resumed his seat. "We cannot trust you anymore than you can trust us. Is that not so, *mes amis*?"

Yves Gelee didn't give Camellion or Jordan or Gerstung a chance to answer. "We Europeans have even less respect for the American voter," he intoned solemnly. "In their punchy patriotism, they have closed ranks behind a president who is a paragon of ineptitude. Intellectual Europeans have concluded that the American people must have a death wish and are afraid and unwilling to face the future."

"The United States is a disgrace," Fachon said bluntly, his face, in the shadows, appearing even more threatening than La Bigne's. "One of the biggest countries in the world, yet it is a paper tiger . . . a lion that roars, but a lion without claws or fangs."

"Cuba's the biggest country in the world," Camellion said nonchalantly. He let the Corsicans have the punch line as they stared increduously at him. "It's government is in Moscow, its armed forces in Africa, and its people in the U.S."

Even the dour and grumpy Fachon laughed heartily. At length, Jules Laroche said, "I am reminded of the latest joke making the rounds about the American leader. All of us here understand English. I have to tell the joke in English because of idiom." Still half-laughing, he looked in the direction of Gerstung, Camellion and Jordan. "Do you know why the American leader always takes the bottom position on the bed when he and his madame make love."

Jordan and Gerstung shook their heads.

"No," Camellion said.

"Because he can only fuck up!"

There was a great deal of laughter, Camellion and his two men guffawing louder than the Corsicans.

"Tch, tch, for an ex-priest to tell such a joke!" Claude Capeau said with mock reprimand. "Surely you will go to that hell you formerly believed in."

Flabbergasted, Ralph Gerstung turned to Laroche. "You, an ex-priest?"

Amused, Laroche nodded. "As of three years ago." He became very serious. "It was a matter of conscience, *mon ami américain*. I became disgusted with a church that preached social justice, yet allied itself with money and the status quo." Then he snickered. "Besides, I wasn't enjoying myself. My parishioners had all the fun. They'd go out and get drunk, screw, and then come to confession and tell me what I had missed."

After the laughter subsided—Gelee was laughing so hard he spilled some of his cider—the Death Merchant got down to the nitty-gritty of the business at hand. There were times that demanded total honesty. This was one of those times.

"Monsieurs Gelee and La Bigne, we can ask the same question? On the assumption that we find the gold, what guarantee do we have that you won't keep the gold for yourselves and kill us in the process? We have not made the mistake of assuming that you're ignorant. We know that you know the value of the gold on today's market."

"About seven-hundred-million American dollars," Gelee said.

"Yeah," pitched in Jordan, "why settle for horse meat when you can have steak? Why dine in the gutter when you can have *la cuisine française?*"

Yves Gelee stroked one side of his long mustache. "Gold is only worthless metal, until converted to cash. How could we sell the gold on the world market without drawing a lot of unwanted attention to ourselves?"

"*Oui, oui!* We could not do it!" said Claude Capeau.

"The Palestine Liberation Organization has the know-how," Camellion countered, "and we know that the ARC maintains contact with the PLO, just as you have contacts with the Irish IRA and some factions of the Italian Red Army. You can understand why we must take a defensive position."

"How do we know that you aren't planning to sell the gold to the highest bidder?" offered Jordan, a cigarette dangling from one side of his mouth.

"We are both asking the impossible, Monsieur Kidd," Gelee said wearily. "But surely your CIA—"

"We didn't say we were CIA!" jumped in Jordan.

"*Non,* you didn't," La Bigne said, a stormy note in his voice. "But the first contact that came to Bastia in Corsica did. Let us stop playing these games."

"The CIA knows that we are not revolutionaries similar to the PLO and the other terrorist groups," Gelee stated impatiently. "We detest the stupid Marxists—those fools who think they can reshape civilization and create a brave new world for the so-called 'masses.' We'd like to see every communist in hell, at least out of France."

"I'll admit that's the truth," Camellion said with a small laugh. He thought of the July in 1980 when three members of the ARC tossed TNT bombs at the office of the French-Socialist Movement building. On the same day, more bombs were thrown at the Soviet Embassy. In September of 1980 another explosion demolished the office of *France-USSR* magazine, and another caused severe damage to the Soviet Commercial Bank of Europe. Four other bombs were discovered, and defused in time, at the Paris offices of *Tass* and Aeroflot.

"How would we be paid the five million francs?" La Bigne surveyed Camellion and the two CIA men with thoughtful eyes, then took a sip of cider.

Jordan made an angry face. "We don't even have the gold and you're worried about payment," he said ponderously.

"The money is closer than you might think," Camellion said smugly, "let's say 160 kilometers west of here . . . in the same submarine that will transport the gold back to the United States."

There were inhalations of surprise from the five Corsicans, and Camellion was pleased with the effect his words had had. He didn't have to guess what Jordan and Gerstung were thinking. They knew he had lied; they knew there wasn't any five million francs aboard *Scorpion II*.

Camellion, Jordan and Gerstung then got their own surprise from Michel La Bigne, who said, "The gold might be closer than any of us might suspect."

Jordan frowned and thrust out his jaw. Gerstung also concealed his surprise effectively, by blowing smoke at the four candles burning over the box on which rested the jug of cider.

The Death Merchant deliberately by-passed asking La Bigne for an explanation. *Why appear overly anxiously?*

"We didn't make much progress with General Patton's numerous officers," he said slowly, "those over the rank of captain. Some are still in service. Others have retired or have died from natural causes."

"The investigation had to be carried out very secretively," offered Gerstung. "I think it was all a waste of time myself."

Camellion, looking at Yves Gelee and Michel La Bigne, continued, "I presume you know about the three Americans who died in an auto accident last spring in Paris? All three were the sons of officers who had been in Patton's Twelfth Corps."

"You are saying?" asked Gelee anxiously.

"We think that their fathers might have told them where

the gold is hidden and that the sons came to France on a scouting expedition."

"The fathers were investigated?" Gelee fingered the keloid on his cheek.

"We didn't get anywhere with the fathers. All three were retired. CIA experts questioned them about the stolen Nazi gold. All three denied any knowledge of the theft."

Claude Capeau shifted on the box, his body language indicating boredom and impatience. "None of it makes sense to me. To go to all the trouble of stealing the gold, then not coming back for it. Oh, to be sure, there can be only one answer. They had the opportunity to steal the gold and stole it. By some means they managed to get it to northern France. After the war, they did not have the means to come back to France and get the gold. Ha! How those men must have cursed fate. All those millions and they couldn't touch a single bar! Ironic!"

"No more ironic than a submarine sitting out there!" Laroche looked at the circle of faces before him. Finally he focused on the Death Merchant. "Why there's almost nine hundred kilometers of coastline in northern France. Due west of here is the Atlantic. To the north, the Gulf of Saint-Malo and the English Channel."

Claude Capeau was insistent. "How do you intend to get the boxes of gold to the beach? That must be your plan—truck the gold to the beach and then have it taken to the sub, either by motorboats, or else you will use a cabin cruiser that will rendezvous with the sub. How do you think all of that can be accomplished?"

The Death Merchant smiled wryly. "The CIA didn't come to the ARC out of friendship. Like La Bigne said, let's stop playing games. The ARC is getting five million francs. We expect your help in transporting the gold." He turned and fixed his gaze on Laroche. "Tell me about the coastline of Brittany."

The French-Corsicans straightened up, their interest intense.

"Do you have evidence that the gold is in Bretagne?" Yves Gelee's voice was as stinging as a whiplash.

"The northern and the western coastlines of Bretagne." Camellion was adamant. "Tell me, Jules."

Laroche was too startled to refuse. "In the south are smooth beaches and gentle inlets. There are quite a few resorts. Some parts of the north coast are broken up and rocky; yet there, too, are smooth beaches. A long boat or a motor craft could come ashore, if that's what you want to hear. Most of the west coast is a mess—high cliffs, big rocks. There are places, though, where a boat could come ashore."

Gelee's voice was lower this time, but more commanding. "Monsieur Kidd, you are intimating that the gold is somewhere in Bretagne. You have asked for our help. I suggest you give us all the facts."

The Death Merchant's face glowed with triumph. His perseverance had paid off. The French-Corsicans were becoming impatient.

"Correct. I did. A little while ago, La Bigne suggested the same thing." He turned his head and stared at the ARC leader. "What did you mean?"

"We think we have located one of the men who helped the Americans hide the boxes of gold," Michel La Bigne said sourly. "I'll give you the details after you tell us what you know."

The Death Merchant took a sip of cider, leaned forward and put the mug on the box between him and Gelee and La Bigne.

"We have a hunch that the gold is either in Saint-Brieuc or buried somewhere in the area of Saint-Brieuc." Speaking rapidly, he explained about the twenty-three commandos who had been found, their bodies lying in a field a mile south of Saint-Brieuc, emphasizing that the commandos had no practical reason for being in Brittany, that there wasn't any record of their having performed any mission in the area, and that the evidence indicated they had been murdered unexpectedly.

"How can anyone tell if any group of men didn't expect to be shot?" Benoit Fachon asked, mystified.

"They were all shot in the back," Camellion said. "And from the location of the bullet holes in each man's back, the bullet holes were at about the same height in each man. This means they didn't suspect they were about to be killed as they walked away, with their backs to whomever sprayed them with .45 slugs. The caliber of the slugs also indicates they were killed with an American machine gun, either the Thompson or one of our standard grease guns, say the M3 or the M3A1."

"But they weren't killed in the vicinity of where they buried the gold," interjected La Bigne slowly. "What must have happened is that they placed the gold in one area, then were lured to the field and killed. It all ties in with the man we've located in Bordeaux. He insists he was one of the Frenchmen who helped hide the boxes."

Jordan and Gerstung's mouths half-opened in shock, the expression on their faces was like that of a man who has just been told that he has won the grand prize in the Irish Sweepstakes. All of the French police were looking for such a man. So were the FLB and ODESSA! Yet the ARC was claiming to have the prize. Incredible.

The Death Merchant's eyes raked the self-satisfied faces of the Corsicans. If they did have such a man, one of the Frenchmen who had helped hide the hundred boxes of gold, then they held all the high cards—*And knew it!*

"What leads you to believe that the man is telling the truth?" Gerstung was polite, his tone subdued.

Time again for truth and to harvest the fruit while it's ripe! "I'm amazed that the ARC was able to locate this person," remarked Camellion lightly. "The DST, French Intelligence and the FLB working with ODESSA are looking for such a man, yet the ARC just happens to locate him."

"Are you calling us liars?" Benoit Fachon glared at the Death Merchant, his hands knotting into fists.

Thanks to La Bigne, Camellion didn't have time to answer. La Bigne turned to Fachon, held up both hands, palms outward, and waggled them back and forth.

"A diplomat you will never be, Benoit, and one day that terrible temper of yours will place you on a path of total destruction. Naturally they are skeptical of our claim." He turned and smiled at Camellion and the two Company men. "If our positions were reversed, we, too, would be suspicious."

"A lie requires a lot of words, the truth very few," said Camellion, deriving considerable relief from La Bigne's conciliatory gesture.

"You are to be congratulated for your cleverness," Jordan said, genuine respect in his voice.

"Not really." La Bigne sounded as if he had a feeling of regret. "You see, *mes amis*, we didn't find Philippe Castile. He found us."

Speaking slowly, La Bigne gave Camellion and Jordan and Gerstung the story. Even before André Sovey and the other World War II partisans had been murdered, the

ARC had guessed correctly that the men who had helped the Americans stash the gold had been members of the French Resistance movement.

"We knew that the men had to belong to the Maquis," said La Bigne. "The American army had passed through France and had liberated Bretagne, true, but it was the French Resistance that kept the peace and order, that controlled the countryside. It would have been impossible for the commandos to have done anything in Bretagne without the Marquis knowing about it, even if the operation did involve only two or three trucks."

But the ARC had not been able to locate any of the men who had helped the Americans hide the gold. An impossible job. The ARC didn't even have a name.

"It was only eight days ago," La Bigne continued, "that we received word from one of our cells in Bordeaux. The six members had accidentally stumbled onto one of the men. His name is Philippe Castile."

In his late sixties and the owner of a small jewelry store, Castile had been one of the eighteen Frenchmen who had assisted the Americans. After Sovey and the three other former Resistance fighters had been mysteriously murdered, Castile realized that the Americans, who had originally stolen the gold, were trying to silence all the men who had helped the commandos. Over a quarter of a century earlier, Castile and the other seventeen Frenchmen had realized that whoever had stolen the gold from the SS had murdered the commandos. After the commandos had been found, newspapers all over France had carried the story.

For thirty-six years, Castile and the other seventeen men had lived in fear, but gradually they were beginning to relax—until Sovey and the three other men had been murdered. The more Castile thought about the murders, the more concerned he became for his own safety. Taking his best friend, Marcel Galliau, into his confidence, Castile told him the full story, without telling him—for Galliau's own protection—where the gold was hidden. At the time, Castile did not know that Galliau, whom he had known for twenty-eight years, ever since he had left Bretagne, was a member of the ARC; nor did he suspect that Galliau, and five other members of the ARC cell in Bordeaux, had been notified to search for one of the men who had knowledge of the gold.

Each man possessed a very dangerous secret: Castile, his knowledge of the gold; Galliau, his membership in the ARC. Now, out of mutual need, they confided in each other, both knowing that neither could betray the other.

With Galliau's help, Castile went into hiding, staying at the home of Micheline Perrier, one of the ARC members of the Bordeaux organization. Without realizing it, Castile had become, for all practical purposes, a prisoner of the ARC.

"Has Castile revealed where the gold is hidden?" Camellion asked, trying hard to keep a lid on his excitement.

"*Non.* Galliau and the others have asked him over and over to—"

La Bigne stopped talking and, with the other men, turned and looked toward the steps. The trap door was open, and Pierre Thiais was standing on the wooden steps, an expression of extreme distress on his bearded face.

"Get out," he shouted hoarsely. "The police have been sighted!"

"Balls," Gerstung said in disgust.

CHAPTER NINE

A variety of weapons in their hands, the men ran up the steps, their hearts pounding from tension, adrenalin flowing.

"How close are the flics?" Yves Gelee asked once the group had reached the upstairs and was racing down the center aisle.

"Several miles down the road," panted Pierre Thiais, who was in the lead. "And Henri and Louis called down that the flics are moving in from the woods and from each side."

"How certain are they?" called out Jordan.

"As certain as they can get," yelled Thiais. "They're up

in the attic. They can see in all directions for several kilometers."

"Our only hope is to reach the old mine tunnel," La Bigne said.

They rushed past tables of raisins, hurried into the other section of the winery, rushed by wine presses, corking-and-bottling machinery and fermentation vats, and were soon moving through the door into the barn whose stalls were empty, whose only animals were rats.

Claude Capeau had closed the door between the barn and the winery and was putting a wooden bar into place when the sound of automatic weapons came from the farmhouse. Instantly the police in the woods to the rear and in the vineyards to the west answered with automatic rifles and machine guns.

La Bigne and Fachon ran to one of the empty stalls, dug down into a feed trough and began pulling out Erma MP-59 submachine guns and spare magazines. Yves Gelee, by another trough, jerked out a bag of fragmentation grenades. Laroche and Capeau ran to the small windows in the rear double doors of the barn and looked out. Just in time they jerked to one side to avoid a tornado of slugs that first shattered the dirty glass, then buried themselves in square wooden posts supporting the hayloft.

"You should never have listened to the Americans," Capeau snarled at Laroche. "Your stupid plan has led the flics to our doorstep."

"*Fous le camp!*" ("Go to hell!") Laroche spit back. "We did what we thought best at the time."

The muscles in his jaws twitching, Jordan nudged Camellion's arm with his elbow. "Listen, the house is a hundred and fifty feet west of the barn," he growled. "We'll never make it, not lugging your two cases and the other two cases of special equipment."

Overhearing Jordan, Benoit Fachon said savagely, "*Merde!* Forget your damned cases. We can't afford to be slowed down by anything, certainly not your damned luggage."

"Like hell we'll forget it," Jordan said in a cold voice. "Those cases go where we go! Get that through your head, Frenchie." He glanced brutally at Michel La Bigne, who had come over to him and Camellion.

"Benoit is right, *mes amis*," La Bigne said condescendingly, as if speaking to a child. "The cases must be heavy.

Carrying them, we couldn't possibly make a run for the house. Monsieur Kidd, surely you understand?"

"We don't have to carry the cases and we don't have to run to the house," Camellion said genially. "We'll use the van."

"Impossible!" Capeau almost shouted. With his long hair and full beard, he was the classic picture of the revolutionary. "The flics would riddle us. Those are high-velocity slugs those *cochons* are using."

Ralph Gerstung snickered. "What the hell do you think the flics will do to us if we try to run the distance to the house? Even without the cases, half of us wouldn't make it."

The Death Merchant shoved the MAB pistol in his right hand into the left shoulder holster under his white shirt jacket. "The sides of the van are armored and the glass is bulletproof. The odds are with us." He paused, then spoke in a tone that sounded as though he considered himself in total command. "Fachon, remove the wooden bar from the rear doors, but don't push the doors open. The rest of you get in the van."

Startled that Camellion should bark orders at him like a drill sergeant, Fachon looked at Yves Gelee and Michel La Bigne for confirmation. From the house, and from the west, north and south areas surrounding the house came the roaring of gunfire.

"Do as he says, Benoit," La Bigne said, absent-mindedly stroking his short untrimmed beard. "Kidd's plan is a good one."

With a crestfallen look, Fachon turned and started toward the van parked between a Le Car and a Fiat Wagon. By the time Fachon had removed the three-by-five-inch wooden bar from the doors, Camellion and the men were crouched down inside the vehicle, and Jordan, in the driver's seat, had started the engine. Fachon climbed into the van through the front-right door and closed it. Jordan, racing the engine, called out, "Everyone set?"

"Head for the back porch," Camellion said. "Judge the distance, so that you can turn around and place the right side opposite the back door. Do it."

"Here we go, first class all the way!" Jordan yelled, his foot pressing down on the gas pedal.

The van moved forward, at first just fast enough to push the doors a third of the way open. Once the van was past the doors and free of the barn, Jordan fed the engine more gas, speeded up, and began the turn to the left that would take the vehicle to the farmhouse.

Zing! Zing! Zing! Zing! Assault-rifle and machine-gun slugs struck the right side of the van, first cutting through the thin metal side, then glancing from the armor plate.

Ping! Ping! Ping! Ping! More projectiles struck the bulletproof glass[1] of the windshield, the right-side door and the bubble window on the middle right of the van. Within seconds the glass was decorated with spider webs whose depth was one-tenth the thickness of the glass. If the van had not been moving, a sustained rain of slugs would have broken through the glass.

The van was halfway to the farmhouse when the *gendarmes* and the DST agents firing from the woods, a few hundred feet north of the rear of the farm, got smart and began firing at the tires. *Bang!* The right-rear tire blew. The van lurched. Another *Bang!* The right-front tire went flat. Sweat dripping from his mustache and beard, the fierce-faced Jordan fought the wheel, fed more gas to the engine, and ignored the *ping*, *ping*, *ping*s striking the windshield. His head moved up and down and from left to right, the bobbing movement necessary in order for him to see through the windshield through the patterns of spider webs that were becoming more numerous. He hoped that he could make the turn and park in front of the back door before the constant splattering of copper-covered lead demolished the windshield.

Lurching from side to side, the van shot past the northeast corner of the porch, and Jordan began to turn the wheel to his left. *Clang! Zinggggg!* Two slugs hit the engine, and for a moment the pistons missed a stroke or two.

Jordan swung the van around and almost lost control of the vehicle when slugs flatted both tires on the left side. More projectiles hit the engine and killed it. But the van

[1]There is no such thing as "bulletproof" glass. There is "bullet resistant glass." Freon sprays will weaken the glass, making it susceptible to shotgun blasts or ax and sledgehammer blows. This glass is actually a laminate of glass and plastic, somewhat like standard windshield glass. However, sustained firing by pistols or whatever will eventually penetrate the glass. The trick is to direct the fire at the moulding and to penetrate the nonresistant weather strip.

had enough momentum so that it kept going, to the extent that Jordan had to brake the vehicle. The van came to a dead stop. Jordan threw himself from the driver's seat and yelled, "Stay down! The windshield is about to give!"

By this time the police to the east had come around the sides of the winery and the barn and were firing a stream of projectiles at the windshield. The windshield fell inward as the Death Merchant and Ralph Gerstung were pulling the four black cases from the compartment in the floor. Two of the metal cases were slightly larger than an attaché case. The other two were the size of a three-suiter suitcase.

More deadly slugs began cutting the air over Camellion and the other men when the left bubble window finally fell apart under a shower of projectiles.

From the rear of the house Étienne Fouqut was firing an HK G3 SG1 sniper rifle, and Philibert Chambord was using an HK G3A3 automatic rifle, directing a stream of fire from the kitchen window.

"Run for it!" shouted Chambord. "We'll cover you."

"We'll need more cover than what they can supply," Gerstung said loudly. He ducked instinctively as a 9-mm projectile struck the wood paneling on the right side of the van, passed through the wood and the thin metal inside, and zinged loudly against the armor plate.

Yves Gelee surprised even the Death Merchant when he said, "Monsieur Kidd. You and Monsieur take the cases and run for the kitchen door. Don't make a run for it until we begin firing."

"Ralph, take one of the large cases," Jordan said, new hope in his voice. "These larger cases weigh at least a hundred pounds."

"Claude, Benoit," spoke Gelee, "you two rear up and fire through the windshield when I give the word. Jules, you and Michel take the windows in the rear doors. Pierre, you and I will take the side window. Monsieur Kidd, tell me when you and your two *amis* are ready."

"We're ready now," said Camellion. He prepared to jump up, his hands going around the handles of the two smaller cases. "But wait until there's a slack in the firing."

The slack came and as a unit, Gelee and his five men reared up and opened fire with their Erma submachine guns. The roaring of the six automatic weapons were a thunderous wall of sound, punctuated by the clanking of empty cartridge cases that, thrown out by the submachine guns, were falling to the floor.

Camellion, Jordan and Gerstung jumped up and, bending over as far as possible, moved through the door of the van and started across the porch to the back door that Étienne Fouqut had thrown open. Bullets from the *gendarmes* and the DST buzzed all around them. One slug cut across the Death Merchant's back, only half a centimeter from the material of his white jacket. Another clipped rubber from the heel of Gerstung's right foot, putting him off balance slightly. Half a dozen other slugs came very close to all three men. In a few more moments, Camellion and Jordan were through the door and in the kitchen, Gerstung right behind them.

"Ohhhhh!" yelled Gerstung. A bullet had cut so close to the back of his neck that it left a blood line on his skin.

One by one, Yves Gelee and his men retreated from the van, Claude Capeau and Benoit Fachon being the first to reach the kitchen. The others followed, police bullets punching holes in the air all around them. All succeeded in reaching the safety of the kitchen; all except Pierre Thiais, who was halfway to the kitchen door when a bullet hit him in the left temple. Killed instantly, he toppled sideways and lay still.

"The police will close in within the next ten minutes," Laroche said frantically. "We've got to get to the cellar." He glanced at Fouqut and Chambord, both of whom were firing from the window and the door, then down at the Death Merchant, who had opened one of the larger cases and taken out a hundred-foot length of nylon rope.

Yves Gelee went to telephone on the wall. The phone was part of the communications system within the house.

La Bigne snapped an order at Benoit Fachon. "Get the others from the front of the house. We must hurry."

In the cellar, reached by means of a door in the large pantry, Camellion and the two Company men attached the nylon rope securely to the handles of the four equipment cases, while Laroche and Claude Capeau, with the help of Jacques Philber, one of the ARC men who had been in the front of the house, pried open the heavy trap door covering the top of the square fifty-foot-deep shaft that led to the mine tunnel beneath the house.

Nearby stood Yves Gelee, a walkie-talkie in his hand.

The Death Merchant and the two Company men had no illusions about the dedication and determination of Gelee, La Bigne and the other members of the *Action pour la Renaissance de la Corse*. They were definitely willing to die when cornered—and so were Philip Resnais and his wife Jeanne, the owners of the farm. Madame Resnais was 72 years old and bedridden, crippled with rheumatoid arthritis. Monsieur Resnais was 76 years old and so weakened by emphysema that merely walking across the room caused him to pant for air.

Two old people preferred death to capture. They would remain upstairs in their bedroom, and on word from Gelee would press the button of the remote-control detonator that would touch off the explosives previously buried all around the foundation of the large stone farmhouse. As Gelee had calmly said, "the entire house will come tumbling down on the flics."

"Hurry, with those cases," La Bigne said, shining the bright beam of his quartz Halogen spotlight into the mouth of the shaft. "The flics will be in the house any moment."

"We're ready," Camellion said. He motioned to Laroche, Fouqut, Philber and Chambord. "Hold the rope while we lower the cases. Play it out as fast as possible over one side. The rest of us can start crawling down before the cases reach the bottom. Once the cases are down, toss the rest of the rope down the shaft."

La Bigne stabbed a finger at Fachon and a tight-faced Marie Morlande. "Start on down the ladder."

The minutes ticked away slowly. By the time the French police were cautiously stepping onto the front and back porches, and peering through shot-out windows on the east and west sides of the two-story stone house, Yves Gelee was standing at the top of the ladder in the square shaft and speaking into the walkie-talkie, "Philip, do you hear me?"

"Oui, chaque mot," the old man's voice floated weakly from the walkie-talkie.

"Count slowly to twenty-five, then push the button. *Au revoir*, dear friend."

"God go with you."

Gelee shut off the walkie-talkie, shoved it into his back pocket and started climbing down the ladder as fast as he could. To be on the ladder, below the opening above, when the house blew up could mean death from falling stones and other wreckage.

The French revolutionary leader jumped from the sixth step from the bottom of the ladder and, guided by half a dozen beams of light, was running toward the rest of the group when the twelve packages of dynamite exploded with such a thunderous crash that a wall of sound rippled down the shaft and ripped at the ears of the group. The stone house literally fell in on itself; the noise of destruction mingled with the screams of trapped police. Any number of stones from the cellar ceiling fell into the shaft, smashing the ladder into kindling, while the rock roof of the mine tunnel trembled with violent vibrations; and when the stones had stopped falling, the tunnel was completely blocked, the shaft no longer existing. It would be days, if not weeks, before the authorities discovered the tunnel—if ever.

Other than the Death Merchant, Jordan and Gerstung, there were Gelee, La Bigne, and nine other members of the ARC, all armed, all carrying Halogen spotlights that had been stored in the cellar, the batteries strapped around their waists.

With Gelee, Camellion and La Bigne in front, the group of fourteen moved slowly and cautiously through the tunnel whose walls dripped with moisture and whose air was stale and smelled of memories and things long dead. Only seven and a half feet high, the tunnel, cut through rock and hard earth, was fifteen feet wide. In many places, ancient support timbers, black with age, were rotting away. Yet here and there were fairly new support beams, for the ARC had planned well, knowing that sooner or later the tunnel might mean the difference between life and death. On either side of the passage were "rooms" where coal had once been dug from the "face." Now the rooms were black, many filled with collapsed ceilings. And there was the quiet, except for the dripping of water. There was no frightened scampering of rats. There were no rats. Long ago, men had abandoned the mine and, since there wasn't anything to eat, so had the rodents.

The group proceeded through the blackness that dissolved before the beams of the Halogen lights, La Bigne explaining to Camellion that this particular tunnel twisted and turned for almost eight kilometers, but that "We will go only three kilometers to the northwest, to the cellar of a farmhouse that burned down. As far back as four months ago, we hid weapons, change of clothing, water and canned goods below the cellar."

"We even had *cartes d'identité* forged," Gelee said proudly. "They, too, will be waiting for us."

The Death Merchant realized there had to be more to the escape plan than a change of clothing and new identity cards. Yet he didn't want to push and demand explanations.

"I know we're not going to leave the farm by walking down the road," he said. "And we'd look rather *stupide* on bicycles."

Yves Gelee's laugh was low and pleased. "A school bus, *mon ami.* We have one in the barn, hidden behind a false wall. We will shave off our beards and mustaches, put on Roman collars and black suits and—"

"Leave after dark," Camellion cut in, his low voice filled with self-satisfaction. "We'll hit the main road and drive west to Saint-Brieuc. That's the plan, is it not?"

Gelee and La Bigne were so surprised that they almost broke stride.

"*Oui,* to Saint-Brieuc," Gelee admitted, after some hesitation. "How did you know?"

"It's vacation time. What else would priests from Paris be doing in this area of Brittany, if not to visit the shrine of Saint James Brieuc, the patron saint of French farmers?"

"Your logic is excellent, *mon ami,*" Gelee said with reluctant admiration.

"*Merci.* So is your escape plan. But you never did finish telling me about Philippe Castile?"

"It is as I explained," La Bigne said. "The last we heard, Galliau and the others have not succeeded in prying the secret out of him. We might have the answer by the time we get to our destination in Saint-Brieuc."

"Your people there are in contact with the ARC cell in Bordeaux?"

"Not in the way you intimate," Gelee said. "Marcel Galliau and two other members of the Bordeaux *cellule* are bringing Castile to Saint-Brieuc."

The Death Merchant shifted the case to his other hand. *I was right: They also suspect that the gold is in the Saint-*

Brieuc area. Now, how far is the Gulf of Saint-Malo and the English Channel from the gold? At the most, not more than twenty miles. . . .

"That could be a dangerous journey for all four," Camellion said, taking a deep breath. "May I ask how it was done—and I am assuming that Castile and your men from Bordeaux will have arrived in Saint-Brieuc by the time we get there!"

La Bigne did not fumble and hesitate with the explanation. "Castile was first heavily sedated. The four then flew in a private plane from Bordeaux to Rennes. Rennes is only one hundred and seventy kilometers southeast of Saint-Brieuc, an easy day's drive for 'Monsieur and Madame Galliau,' their daughter and the befuddled 'grandfather.' You are not the only man who is adept in the use of cosmetic changing of features."

Somewhat startled but not showing it, Camellion said mildly, "I was wondering when you would mention that my voice doesn't seem to match my face."

Yves Gelee's slow snickering laugh caught Camellion off guard.

"You are also wondering—what is your American expression?—what 'our game' is. In your own mind, you are convinced that we're lying, that Castile has already revealed where the American officers, their commandos and the French helpers hid the gold."

Camellion weighed the odds. *If Castile has not talked and Gelee and La Bigne intend to terminate me and Jordan and Gerstung, why then haven't they tried it? Why keep us alive? And if Castile has talked, the same question needs answering. Why does the ARC need us? Well, let's see if I can lure them into it. . . .*

"*Convinced* is not the right word," Camellion said. "But let's say you're almost correct, that I do believe that Castile has revealed the hiding place. Why do you need me and the other two?"

"Predicated on the premise that we have, shall I say, confused loyalties? That from your point of view, we intend to kill you!"

The Death Merchant laughed within himself—*They did!*

He glanced around and saw, with some surprise, that Laroche and Jacques Philber had relieved Jordan and Gerstung of the two heavy cases. Philibert Chambord was carrying the second smaller case—*My make-up kit.*

Camellion turned back to Gelee and La Bigne, both of whom were probing the darkness ahead with the spotlights. "It does seem rather incongruous that the ARC should be willing to settle for only five million francs when it could have more than half a billion in gold. But could you trust Arafat and his PLO to filter the gold onto the world market? I wouldn't exactly call Arafat a man of honor. He and the PLO are nothing more than cowardly baby murderers. I have more respect for lice on the body of a diseased sow than I have for an Arab with his crap about 'the Prophet!' "

"We, too, have considered Arafat and his PLO trash," La Bigne said smoothly. "*Non, mon ami,* Kidd. We do not intend to play a double game with American Intelligence. It would not be to our advantage to kill you and the others. We have enough enemies without your CIA wanting its revenge."

"And you expect me to believe you?"

"*Non,* we do not," Gelee said seriously. "But what choice do you and the others have?"

He said a mouthful that time! And it's the truth. We don't have a choice. . . .

"I'm thinking of an old Russian proverb," Camellion said. "If you are afraid of the wolf, don't go into the forest.' "

"If it will make you feel any better, let me say that we want something more than the five million francs," La Bigne said. He paused, turned, and looked at the Death Merchant. "*Non,* not more money. A favor . . . a favor from your CIA." He turned and continued his forward movement.

Camellion didn't beat around the bush. "What kind of favor?"

"We'll tell you after we reach Saint-Brieuc," La Bigne said, lowering his voice, "provided that Castile and the others have arrived and that Castile has revealed the hiding place of the gold. If he hasn't, we shall have to use firm methods of persuasion."

The Death Merchant did not reply. He didn't like the way the situation was developing. In a sense, La Bigne was saying that the ARC's helping them obtain the gold was contingent not only on a payment of the five million Swiss francs—which the CIA had no intention of paying!—but also on a favor!

What kind of favor? Damn it! It's an "either-or" situation! And Jordan and Gerstung and I are right smack in the middle of it. . . .

CHAPTER TEN

Heinz Ludwig Wallesch's discomfort had not had its origin in the hot, humid weather. Not only was the Jetta Volkswagen air-conditioned, but with its front-wheel drive the vehicle was very easy to handle. Already they had covered half the distance from Paris to Saint-Brieuc. The new-Nazi's annoyance was generated by the absence of SS-*Gruppenführer* Ernst Rudolf Müller and SS-*Standartenführer* Karl Scherhorn. They had flown off to Turkey. Too many years were on their shoulders for them to undertake a venture in which physical combat might become a reality.

In another way, Wallesch felt proud that the two high-ranking officials of ODESSA were entrusting him with this important mission. *Ya*, he had full authority, even over such old pros as Glucks and Berger.

Lightly gripping the steering wheel, Wallesch stole a glance at André Jaffe, sitting in the front seat next to him, and thought of Jean Duchemin and Charles Fauvet, the other two leaders of the *Front de Libération de la Bretagne*, who were travelling in a Volvo several miles behind the Jetta.

Again the damnable thought stung Wallesch, who was traveling under the name of Jimenez Cuença. If the gold was there, and if the FLB did try a double-cross, he would be one of the first to know it. *And one of the first to die!* he thought bitterly. Damn these French pigs. The only consolation was that there would also be twenty-one trusted Germans in the area—against how many members of the FLB? Neither Fauvet nor Duchemin nor Jaffe had said. In their cleverness, the Germans had not asked.

André Jaffe interrupted Wallesch's thoughts. "We should be in Saint-Brieuc before dark," Jaffe said. "After we have dinner, we should still have plenty of time to contact Jean and Charles."

"I don't like the idea of it taking several days for you leaders to organize your men in the area," commented Wallesch. "although such a delay is understandable considering the circumstances."

A big, sullen-faced man whose casual manner and bulbous nose disguised a very agile mind, Jaffe despised everything German. For that reason he disliked intensely Jimenez Cuenca, not only because he was convinced the man was a Boche, but because of Cuenca's good looks.

"What do you expect our people to do?" growled Jaffee, again twisting his mouth. "Meet us in the public square? Some of our members are farmers. Many others have various occupations. We must be very careful. Not only are the French police in the area, but we must assume that the ARC and the Americans will be close by." He laughed deliberately. "If any group should know the need for caution, it should be you Nazis!" Again he faked a laugh. "But *pardonnez-moi*, Monsieur Cuença. I forgot that you and the other two are Brazilians."

Secretly, Jaffe became angry when he saw that Wallesch was letting the insult slide by.

"There isn't any need to tell me about caution," Wallesch said with an air of superiority. "My people will not come marching down the street either—nor arrive like *jeunes filles en fleur* straight from a finishing school!"

"Or singing 'Deutschland über Alles'!" Jaffe said wryly.

"No more than your people will be singing 'La Marseillaise,' " Wallesch said promptly. He slowed the car when the stream of traffic ahead thickened. "But we'll all be singing funeral hymns should we make any mistakes. In case you don't realize it, this operation is extremely dangerous."

"We can't afford to think of failure," Jaffe said, his voice less sullen. "We do have a lot on our side, mainly the season. This is the time of the year when people from all over France go to Bretagne to worship at the shrine of Saint James Brieuc. The police can't possible check all the thousands of tourists who will be in and around the town."

"Where do all those people stay? Saint-Brieuc can't have too many hotels."

"Two hotels," André Jaffe said. "But there are numerous campgrounds in the area. People come in trailers, campers, motor homes, and some, who stay only a day or so, live in their cars. Religion makes *imbéciles* of otherwise intelligent people. Most of the people who go to Saint-Brieuc will do anything to get to the church in the center of town. The half-wits believe that one of the fingers of the saint is buried beneath the altar."

"That is all very interesting," Wallesch said after a moment's reflection. "There should be a lot of traffic going in and out of town. We'll only be specks of sand on the beach."

"Especially since the church is open twenty-four hours a day."

Wallesch sounded pleased with himself. "There are no campgrounds around the mine?"

"*Non.*" Jaffe rolled down the window and let the wind carry away his half-smoked cigarette. "The closest campground is nine kilometers south of the mine. The mine itself is eleven kilometers northwest of the town. It will not be difficult for us to filter out from several of the campgrounds and assemble in an area close to the mine. Those and other details will have to be worked out after we get to the greenhouse."

Heinz Wallesch adjusted his amber sunglasses and did some fast thinking. Müller and Scherhorn had been very accurate in their assessment of the FLB, especially of the organization's three leaders. Wallesch's thin lips formed a thin, sinister smile. Scherhorn, more so than Müller, was as precise and exacting as a Prussian. He was a positive genius at weeding out the morally uncommitted and those who were psychologically undependable. *Ya* . . . Jaffe, Fauvet, Duchemin and their terrorists were very intelligent men, but still they lacked the finer subtleties of minds truly gifted with natural deviousness.

Jaffe had not told Wallesch a single thing that the German-South American had not already known. Furthermore, there were other facts that only Wallesch and his people possessed, information that would have sent the FLB into a blind rage.

It had been a miscalculation on the part of Werner Gnheinst-Strop and his men from Stuttgart. They had not been trying to kill the sons of the Americans who had been officers in General Patton's Twelfth Corps. Gnheinst-Strop and his boys had been trying to kidnap them. The *Amerikaners,* however, had spotted the trap, and in the chase that followed, their car had rolled over and burned.

The *Europäisch Sektion* of ODESSA had not blamed Gnheinst-Strop for the failure to capture the *Amerikaners. Verdammt!* Everyone knew why. Gnheinst-Strop had powerful relatives within ODESSA. Although his father was dead, he had an uncle who had been a *Sturmbannführer* in the *Totenkopfverbände,* or "Death's Head Detachments," the SS units that had operated the concentration camps and the extermination camps. Another uncle had been an official in the SS state security section, the *Reichssicherheitshauptamt*, or RSHA.

Gott! Suppose Gnheinst-Strop and his experts failed at the abandoned mine? The thought wasn't pleasant to contemplate. There was still another possibility, a very slim one, but yet it existed. Roger Ledoux could be lying. *Nein,* Heinz told himself. Ledoux had all the facts; his story fit; it all hung together. But he could have lied about the location of the gold! *Nein!* FLB men in Paris were holding him captive. Ledoux knew that any false information would result in his dying a slow, horrible death.

The FLB had been half-clever in finding Ledoux, the elderly man who had formerly been in the French Resistance, only half because it had been ODESSA money that had bribed the woman clerk in the file department of the *Service de Documentation Extérieure et de Contre-espionnage.*

Pouring over the old files from the SDECE, the ex-Nazi experts had come across *Opération Tableau Noir* ("Operation Blackboard".) The mission had taken place in Brittany and had involved eighteen Resistance fighters who had helped American commandos search for SS men who might still be hiding in the area of Saint-Brieuc.

Some of the men on the list had died of natural causes over the years. The factor that made the FLB and ODESSA positive that they were on the right track was that André Sovey and the three other murdered Frenchmen were on the list.

The FLB first looked for Raoul Derain. They found him in a mental hospital, hopelessly senile. He couldn't even remember his own name. They searched for Paul Gevrey and soon found that he was in prison—two murders, a life sentence. Their third choice had been Philippe Castile. He had disappeared. The remainder of the men on the list were either dead or in hiding, including Roger Ledoux. He had been hiding out in Marseille. The FLB had traced him through contacts in the Marseille underworld.

The FLB had given Ledoux a choice between talking, or watching and feeling the skin of his face melt away from acid. Ledoux's story, told haltingly, had made sense. And when Müller and the other Germans had asked him why he and the other French Resistance fighters had not returned to the mine and grabbed the gold for themselves, the old man had explained that Tunnel Six had been booby-trapped with plastic explosives in waterproof, rust-proof containers, the entire area surrounding the gold wired to a combination on a relay switch that could be plugged into a battery. If anyone tried to enter without first deactivating the relay switch—*Blooie!* Six hundred pounds of TNT would explode. On the chance that some foolish people—say, speleologists who like to explore caves—might come across the mine that had been abandoned during the beginning of World War II, the commandos and the Frenchmen had erected a wooden wall toward the end of the tunnel, in front of the section in which the boxes of gold had been stored. They had then concealed the wall with a couple of tons of rock.

Roger Ledoux had drawn a diagram of the mine, a map that showed the exact location of the wall and, just beyond, the combination for the relay, which could disarm the explosives surrounding the gold.

Could Ledoux be wrong? He was 74 years old. His memory could be faulty. Wallesch's hands gripped the wheel until the whites of his knuckles showed. *Verdammt!* There were so many dangers. The worst was that the demolition expert, coming along with Gnheinst-Strop, would make a mistake. If the man made one mistake, he could kill all of them—bury them all alive. . . .

"Slow down, damn it!" Andre Jaffe glanced oddly at Wallesch. "What are you trying to do? Set a speed record, or get us killed?"

Wallesch slowed the car, thinking that in a few more days he'd have the pleasure of seeing Jaffe and the rest of

Ya—Zum Verheizen!

the FLB die.

CHAPTER ELEVEN

Richard Camellion had never thought that he would be grateful to Julius Caesar, who extended Roman rule to the whole of Gaul. During those days, two thousand years ago, France was known as Gaul, and the peninsula that is now Brittany was Armorica Letavia.

Roman culture had spread gradually to all classes, and Latin slowly took the place of the Celtic languages. Place names and personal names were Latinized. There are today many French place names that are derived from Roman family names—for instance, Savignac, Savigné, and Savigny are all from *Sabinus*.

Master builders, the Romans erected numerous buildings all over Gaul, and at strategic locales built enormous *castelli*. One of these forts was in Armorica Letavia. Many, many, many centuries later, the center of Saint-Brieuc would stand over where this fort had stood.

But all the Roman forts and garrisons could not stop the flood of Germanic barbarians who gradually overran the Western Roman empire. Many of the *castelli* were torn down, and the stones used for other purposes and buildings. In most cases, however, the stones in the underground dungeons and armories of the forts were left intact, since removing them would have required too much backbreaking labor on the part of the new conquerers. Over the slow passage of the years, some of these large underground areas were filled in with dirt and other refuse, or new buildings constructed over the Roman ruins. In other cases, when the underground areas of the forts were of sufficient depth, the upper portions were used for cellars under new buildings, and the lower parts sealed off.

The Death Merchant was thankful that part of the underground of the Roman fort in Brittany was under the cellar of Armand Fronde's shop and living quarters on Rue de Jaures, the "Main Street" of Saint-Brieuc. Seventy feet below the street level of Rue de Jaures, the ruins extended far beyond the dimensions of Fronde's small cellar. This hidden area, reached by a dozen wooden ladders nailed together, was actually a triangle, the base 45 meters long and each side 32 meters in length—a giant tomb with a low ceiling composed of massive squared stones supported by rough-cut pillars of granite.

It was this ancient Roman ruin in which the Death Merchant, the two CIA agents with him, and the terrorists of the ARC had taken refuge. But now the number had increased by three, now including Philippe Castile and the two persons who had brought the elderly Resistance fighter to Saint-Brieuc, Marcel Galliau and Micheline Perrier, who had posed as Madame Galliau.

The Death Merchant felt sorry for Castile, a thin, age-battered man, who was sitting miserably on a cot next to a pillar whose stones were black with age. The sedatives had worn off, and Castile had regained the use of his faculties. He sat there on the cot, squeezing his hands, unsure of his surroundings and afraid that sooner or later his captors would kill him.

At a rickety table with Jules Laroche and Ralph Gerstung, Camellion concentrated on the map before him, one part of his computerlike mind going over the escape from the Resnais farm in the Laballe area. Could he and Gelee and Labigne and the others have made any mistakes that would enable the French police to trace them to Saint-Brieuc?

In the cellar of the burned farmhouse, the entire group had washed with water taken from ten-gallon-capacity bottles, and changed into the white suits that many priests in France wore during the summer months, complete with a Roman collar and a white bib that was worn over the front of the shirt and underneath the coat. Shoes and hats were black.

The problem had been Marie Morlande. A nun's outfit had not been included in the hidden boxes of clothing, and for one woman to be traveling with a busload of priests would not only be ridiculous, but would draw attention to the group. The only solution was to try to disguise the plump, homely faced woman as a priest. She had bound her breasts tightly, but had protested violently when Camellion had Gelee had insisted that she cut her glistening black hair. Yet she knew there wasn't any other way. There was too much hair to fit under a hat. When the job was completed and she had changed into the largest suit available, she could have passed for a man in very dim light. Camellion could have completely changed her features with his make-up kit, if he had had the time, but without specially tailored clothing and proper padding, there wasn't any way he could reshape her figure into a man's.

With La Bigne driving, they had left in the bus after dark. La Bigne turned on the headlights only after they had reached the dirt road. The bus was only three-fourths of a kilometer from the highway when it was stopped by three police cars filled with uniformed *gendarmes*; there were also three men in civilian clothes—DST agents.

While two *gendarmes* stood on the other side of the patrol cars and kept HK MP 5K submachine guns trained on the bus, two DST agents stepped inside the bus and, from the front of the vehicle, very briefly raked the faces of the "priests" with flashlights. Many of the priests appeared to be asleep, including Marie Morlande who was in a seat toward the rear, leaning against a window. At the time, the danger had been that the DST agents would search the bus and discover the four metal cases stashed under the last four seats in the back. However, the agents had only asked La Bigne what he and a busload of priests were doing off the main road, to which "Father Abboise Noyon" had explained that he and the other priests were on their way to Saint-Brieuc to visit the shrine of Saint James Brieuc, and somehow had taken a wrong turn.

One of the agents had politely asked Father Noyon to produce his *carte d'identité*. Another agent had slowly walked to the center of the bus and, at random, chose Louis Duvaier and Jacques Philber.

"Votre cartes d'identité, s'il vous plaît," the agent had said.

"Father René Feyder" and "Father Clement Cayatte" had promptly produced their identity cards, proving that they, too, were members of the religious society that administered at Notre-Dame Cathedral in Paris.

After gruffly warning Father Noyon to be more careful ("There are terrorists in the area!") the two DST agents had left the bus. With a sigh of relief, La Bigne drove the bus to the highway. The three police cars, red lights flashing, continued down the dirt road.

It took La Bigne only a short time to cover the thirty-two kilometers to Saint-Brieuc and park the bus on a side street only seven blocks from Armand Fronde's shop on Rue de Jaures. The hour was only ten, and the street was ablaze with light and numerous men, women and children. The sidewalk cafés were doing a thriving business. Many of the people were simply killing time while they waited for Midnight Mass in the large church of Saint James Brieuc. For the next two weeks the church would be open day and night and Mass celebrated five times a day. At the noon and the Midnight Masses, a relic of Saint James Brieuc would be displayed—a sliver of wood contained in a glass case. The chip was reputed to have been part of the staff that the saint had carried with him on his travels. It was said that many seriously ill people had been cured instantly after looking at the tiny piece of wood.

Not only were the bistros open on Rue de Jaures, but also the tourist traps, the souvenir shops, including the shop of Armand Fronde. A large, fifty-five-year-old shambling man who laughed easily and was noted for his humor and even temper, Armand was a master woodcarver, who sold religious carvings to tourists and to *spécialité* shops in Paris. Emmanuèle, his wife, and Catherine, his daughter, helped him in the shop during the busy season. Armand's maternal grandfather had been a Corsican, which was one of the reasons why the woodcarver was a member of the ARC. But the main reason was that Armand, as a Breton, hated the French; he hated the *Front de Libération de la Bretagne* even more because of its Marxist leanings.

Singly and in pairs (and in the case of Marie Morlande, in a trio, since two other "priests" were with her), the Death Merchant, the two Company men, and the ARC members strolled along, and somehow, just happened to wander into Armand Fronde's Maison d' Art de Religion. Within an hour and a half, each member of the group had slipped into a back room, and Catherine Fronde had led them to the cellar and to the trapdoor underneath a massive flatbottom dowry chest.

Unlike her mother who wore a traditional Breton costume, nineteen-year-old Catherine wore a pair of jeans and a T-shirt, on the front of which was written in French,

"Musicians Use the Rhythm Method—which was rather difficult to read at first glance, because of the way her breasts poked the letters out of shape. The cynical Gerstung, going down the ladder with Camellion, had remarked that "She is probably the Miss Hourglass of this cluck town. All her sand is in the right places."

That descent had been fourteen hours ago. The group had eaten. They had slept, some on cots, others on blankets on the cold stone floor. Now it was twelve o'clock, noon, although one wouldn't have known the time from the conditions that prevailed in the large underground chamber, where it was always night, where the only light came from seven propane-gas lanterns. Add to the black shadows stale air that clogged the nostrils with the specific kind of smell that indicates a lost antiquity and makes a person feel burdened with guilt, as though he were an intruder, as though he were violating the sanctity of some ancient but sacred crypt.

Tired of playing cards, Jules Laroche placed the deck on the table and considered Camellion with eyes that were piercing in their keenness. "Whatever plan you might concoct, Gelee and La Bigne will have to approve it," he said.

The Death Merchant looked up from the map. Laroche had not spoken menacingly; at the same time, Camellion—and Gerstung, too—was aware of a miasma of hostility in his manner. Camellion had never liked Laroche, and as far as he was concerned the sinewy terrorist had been reared to be rotten.

Without even a hint of a smile, Camellion stared directly into Laroche's eyes. Suddenly afraid without knowing why, Laroche drew back.

"They'll approve," Camellion said levelly. "There's only one way this project can be pulled off. And no matter how we do it, the risks will be tremendous."

Gerstung who, like the others, had changed clothes and was now wearing a seedy suit too small for him, gave a throaty chuckle. "Hell, we're even taking a chance believing Castile. But I have to admit that his story hangs together. And what better place to bury a hundred boxes of gold than at the bottom of an old shaft mine? Who could snoop around the bottom?"

"Not just the bottom," Camellion said grimly, with an off-center smile. "We have to go back five hundred feet through one of the tunnels, remove a couple of tons of rock, take apart a wooden wall and then disarm the explosives."

Laroche put into workds what Gerstung was thinking. "All in one night. We're kidding ourselves. We don't have the time. Even if all this were legal and we could work in the daytime, how do we know that the tunnel hasn't caved in? *Mon Dieu!* It's been over forty years since the mine has closed down. It's a wonder that the shaft hasn't been filled, and the tipple torn down." He blinked rapidly at the Death Merchant. "Just in case the tunnel has collapsed, then what do we do?"

"We pack our toothbrushes and go home." Camellion laughed. "What else could we do?"

Gerstung's speculative look clearly telegraphed—What about General Patton? We're supposed to find out if he was murdered!

"Gelee and the others should be back shortly," Laroche said shortly. "We should have figured out some way we could have kept the bus. I doubt if they're going to find any trucks for rent, much less sixty meters of rope." He frowned, then continued to stare across the area at Marie Morlande who, with scissors and a propped-up mirror, was trying to trim her already bobbed hair.

"You've heard of the Six Million Dollar Man," Gerstung said. "There sits the Two Dollar Broad."

"That was a cheap shot," Camellion said frostily. "One can't blame her being sad. She had beautiful hair, and it was her best asset."

"Don't climb on me," Gerstung growled. "We're cut from the same slab. Neither of us will leave so much as a tombstone behind, and no one will shed a tear."

Deliberately he looked away from the Death Merchant and let his suspicious eyes wonder over the other people in the chamber. Some were relaxing on cots; others were cleaning weapons. Marcel Galliau and Micheline Perrier were close to Philippe Castile, trying to reassure Castile that they would eventually take him back to Bordeaux.

Well into his sixties, Galliau was paunchy and had a halo of blond hair framing a bald head. By instinct, the Death Merchant knew that Galliau was a man who enjoyed good food, good liquor and bad women.

Whether Micheline Perrier was a bad woman was a moot question, but she was certainly a good-looking woman. Just past 30, she had an attractive face and figure to match—a body that had been weaned on riding and tennis, a body used to moving gracefully through drawing rooms. The way she moved, the way she spoke, the way she conducted herself told Camellion that she was from the *classe supérieure.*

"A perfect bed companion, if one is to judge only from the outside," Laroche said, seeing that the Death Merchant's eyes were on the woman and deducing his thoughts.

"Shame on you," joked Camellion. "Such licentious talk—and from an ex-priest at that."

"Take a look. They're back," interjected Gerstung.

Camellion swung around and looked toward the point of the triangular-shaped chamber. Yves Gelee was just stepping off the ladder onto the stone floor. Behind him came Michel La Bigne, Bernard Jordan and Claude Capeau.

"I hope they didn't forget the food," Gerstung said. "My stomach is beginning to get the feeling that my throat's been cut."

Gelee, Jordan and La Bigne started toward Camellion and the two other men at the table. Gelee and the other two men wore shirts and slacks. That morning Camellion, by means of the "magic" in his make-up kit, had worked for an hour on each man's face, changing each man's features. At the end of four hours, he had been exhausted. But he had been satisfied with the job he had done. A mustache here, a beard there, and the disguises were complete—coupled with phony papers, forged driver's licenses and *cartes d'identité.*

Capeau, similarly dressed, waited by the ladder and looked up the shaft. "I'm ready," he called out. "Lower away." He glanced at Henry Monet and Philibert Chambord who had been sitting on a blanket on the floor playing dominoes. "Come on over here and help me."

Watching the three men approach the table, Camellion remembered the risk they had taken with the four cases the night before. He had carried the make-up kit. La Bigne had carried the case with the Auto Mags and ammo for the twin .44 magnum AMPs, Étienne Fouqut and Jacques Philber had lugged the larger cases filled with special weapons, the radio and the explosives. If the DST agent had stopped one of the men carrying one of the cases—*But we made it.* Nor was it only luck. There were also other people on the streets with packages and suitcases—*And we weren't the only "priests."*

Gelee, La Bigne and Jordan pulled up chairs and sat down close to the table, Jordan wiping his face with his handkerchief.

"Did you get the truck and the rope?" asked Gerstung, staring at the two Bretons who appeared tense and nervous. Bernie Jordan wasn't exactly icy cool.

"Oui, oui, et non," sighed Michel Gelee.

"What is that supposed to mean—yes, yes, and no?" Puzzlement clouded Gerstung's eyes.

"You were gone almost four hours," Laroche said. "We were getting worried."

La Bigne supplied the answers. "We bought the rope from the local *quincailler*—ninety meters, in case we need more. The hardwareman asked why we needed so much rope. We told him that we were buying it for a friend in Paris, that rope is so much cheaper in the country than in the city. He seemed to believe us."

"Three hundred feet should be more than enough," commented the Death Merchant. "Where is the rope? I know you didn't carry it down Rue de Jaures."

Gerstung put his elbows on the table and rested his chin on his folded hands. "No matter what we do, it's a chance. We're pretending that the impossible is possible." Glancing toward the ladder, he saw that Capeau, Monet and Chambord were unfastening ropes from a large jug of water and two portable coolers filled with food.

"We had the hardwareman put the rope in the trunk of the car we rented," Gelee said hesitantly. We parked the car half a block down the street from Armand's shop. The only thing we can do is wait until dark and then bring the rope in through the back door."

"Another risk," Gerstung chimed in glumly. "But I don't see any other way." He made a face at Gelee. "What's the second 'yes' and the 'no' mean?"

"We found a large truck, a moving truck. Dual wheels in the back," Gelee said slowly. "It belongs to a friend of Armand Fronde. Armand phoned him and said he needed the truck to send a shipment of wooden statues to Paris. Claude and Michel went over and picked it up from the man, a baker. Claude and Michel gave the impression they were buyers from Paris."

"The 'no' part is that the truck won't be available until tomorrow afternoon," spoke up Jordan. "But that's only half the problem. The other half is a real stinger."

"I don't think it's all that bad," La Bigne demurred.

Camellion opened his mouth, but Gerstung jumped right in, his face and voice full of rage. "And what happens if something goes haywire and the truck gets shot full of holes? Fronde and his whole family will be in one big mess and have the flics pounding on their door!"

"We know that," Gelee angrily. "So does Armand. But you haven't heard the full story."

"Let's have the good news," Camellion said to Jordan.

Jordan's smile was gentle. "The Frondes want to leave France on the sub. They want to go to the U.S. I've already agreed. There wasn't any other way."

"Crap twice over! Wait until you report that request to"—Gerstung glanced furtively at Gelee and La Bigne, then stared at Jordan—" to you-know-who! They'll never approve."

"Bernie, don't report the request," Camellion said to Jordan. Seeing Gerstung make a face of disapproval, he spoke rapidly. "In the field, I have full authority, and if I say that the two Frondes and their daughter go aboard the sub, then aboard the sub they go. I say they're going. Case settled. Period. As—"

"Yeah? Suppose the skipper—"

"Ralph, zipper your mouth," Camellion said pleasantly. "You're always running your mouth when your brain's in neutral." He let his eyes roam over the rest of the group. "The captain of the boat has been informed that the authority of the agent in charge of Pink Slipper 5 supercedes his, except on the high seas, in regard to the operation of the boat. Like I said, case settled. Double period."

Silent in his rage, Gerstung leaned back, hooked his hands on the collar of his open shirt and did a slow burn.

La Bigne made a helpless gesture with his hands. "Getting to the mine, going down the shaft . . . those are the problems that confront us. Those and many more."

"God damn it! Let's face it," Jordan said flatly. "It's impossible. It will take the better part of the night just to get to the mine, go down the shaft, remove the rock and tear down the wall." He poked a finger at Camellion. "And if you make one mistake with that relay switch—all on the assumption that Castile is telling the truth"—he smiled and shrugged—"we'd have only a few seconds to know about it, wouldn't we?"

"The mine is approximately eleven kilometers northwest of Saint-Brieuc," the Death Merchant said. "Or we can say that the mine is half the distance from Saint Brieuc to the village of Guingamp. What matters is that from the mine to the coast the distance is five miles, or, to you Europeans, eight kilometers." Pausing, the Death Merchant's strange blue eyes stabbed directly into the dark orbs of Michel La Bigne. "It's truth time, *mon ami.* How many ARC men have infiltrated Saint-Brieuc?"

"Ten men and eight women from Paris," admitted La Bigne. "They're at one of the campgrounds, supposedly all strangers to each other. We can get word to them through one of their number who's always at the Bleu Bouteille bistro."

Gerstung spoke spontaneously. "The way to get to the mine is to walk out of town with all the rest of the rubes. We head toward one of the campsites and keep going." He looked at La Bigne. "The camp your people are at, how far is it from the mine?"

"Nine kilometers south of the mine."

"Six miles isn't all that far," Camellion said. "The way I see it, we can leave the rope in the car and park the car several kilometers north of the campground. There are thirteen of us that can work. We'll leave town when the people who attend Midnight Mass start going back to the various campsites. With the other ten men, we'll be twenty-three in number. More than enough manpower."

Jordan made a vague gesture. "DST agents and maybe SDECE boys are in town. We spotted a 'gonio' van parked six blocks from here. It was disguised as a regular van, but they couldn't hide the loop. They're either going to try some of their radiogoniometry on us or else hoping to triangulate some FLB transmission. Anyhow, what difference does it make?"

"You mean because of the con-box on our own transmitter," the Death Merchant said.

"I mean the time factor," Jordan said reprovingly. "Whether we have twenty-three men or twenty-three hundred, the time is all wrong. It seems to me, you keep ignoring the time factor."

"How about the truck?" asked Gelee. "We can't pick it

up until late tomorrow afternoon. How do we get it to the mine and make sure we're not seen?"

"Let me finish," Jordan said impatiently, his intense gaze on Camellion. "Damn it, it will take us almost until dawn to get to the mine and get down into ths shaft. We'll have to either slide down or use the steps by the side of the shaft. Only God knows what condition those steps are in. How do you think we can—?"

Suddenly, Jordan stopped speaking, and his face froze, as if for a few seconds he had entered into a state of suspended animation. The quick-freeze look changed abruptly to one of amazement, then to one of total comprehension.

"Ah-ha! So that's it! You know we can't do the job in one night! What's the real plan?"

The Death Merchant didn't answer, his thoughts on those who would shortly die. During the long hours that he and the other people had been hidden in the chamber of the Roman ruins, he had seen many individual auras blacken, then vanish altogether.

Including Gelee's and La Bigne's.

And Jordan's has just turned dead black!

CHAPTER TWELVE

Accompanied by Bernie Jordan, the Death Merchant was only another devout worshiper lost in the enormous crowd that had just left the church. With several hundred other people, he and Jordan began walking toward the campground nine kilometers south of the mine. With the same group, going to the same camp, were Yves Gelee, Michel La Bigne and thirteen of their ARC organization. The remainder of the ARC people would come to the mine the following night, using cars that the ten ARC men had driven from Paris.

Jordan and Camellion, as well as the other men in their

group, knew that they wouldn't have to walk the entire mile and a half to the camp. Cars always stopped and picked up those who had to walk. A couple in a Volkswagen, the women still wearing her wimple that she had used to cover her head in church, stopped and gave them a lift at the edge of town.

The Honda Accord LX was also inconspicuous. It was only another automobile, one among dozens. It was certainly, beyond doubt, one of a kind. Not only did it carry the three hundred feet of rope, but also the four vital cases and the Halogen spotlights. Should anything happen to the Honda, the equipment it carried or its occupants, Pink 5 would turn into a total disaster. In the front seat were Ralph Gerstung doing the driving, and Jules LaRoche. In the back sat a terrified Philippe Castile and Marcel Galliau. The Honda would proceed along a dirt road, then cut off on a side road and with lights out, head for the mine.

The camping area was filled with tents, vans, campers, and a variety of vehicles, and people. Camellion, Jordan and the rest of their group wandered around the camp, each man acting as if he belonged and knew where he was going. Several hundred feet to the north, just beyond the camp, was a patch of woods. How to reach those woods was a problem that had been foreseen and solved by the Death Merchant, who very soon found what he wanted—a Fiat station wagon parked toward the south side of the camp. He tossed a fountain-pen-type incendiary underneath the empty vehicle and calmly walked away. He had rejoined Jordan, and the two were walking leisurely toward the north when the incendiary exploded with a loud bang. A few seconds more and the intense heat of the thermate ignited the gas tank. The flames and explosion that followed made everyone in camp jerk his or head toward the burning junk scattered over a wide area.

There were shouts of of fear and alarm, and many men and women began running toward the area of destruction—all except the Death Merchant, Jordan and the ARC men. They hurried the few hundred feet across the grassy flatland and were soon in the dark woods, moving slightly northwest, cursing as twigs, bushes and other growths tore at their clothes. Through the trees, they could see only the diamond white-blue of the stars and the yellow sliver of a quarter moon.

* * *

By the time Camellion and the other men reached and scouted the mine, dawn was only an hour away. There stood the tipple, three stories high, outlined against the night sky, dark, brooding and ominous. When the mine had been in operation, it had been in the vast tipple that the bituminous coal had been washed and sorted by size, the different sizes dropping into different bins. Next to the tipple was the steel framework, a tall framework of girders that carried the miners to the bottom of the shaft in an open elevator. On the other side of the framework, there was another elevator that raised the coal cars whose contents were dumped into the hopper of the tipple. At the very top of the girder-tower were two wheels, eight feet in diameter. At one time, steel cables had lain in the grooves of the wheels, the end of one cable fastened to the elevator that raised and lowered the miners, the end of the other cable attached to the platform that raised and lowered the coal cars. The other ends of the cables were attached to two drums in the motor house a short distance from the tipple. Other tin-sided buildings were in the immediate area—the mine office, the shower and locker rooms, repair and storage sheds, etc.

The Death Merchant took out a penlight with a red filter and flashed HERE WE ARE in a special code, based on Morse code, that had been worked out between him and Gerstung. Twice more he flashed HERE WE ARE. A red flash came back from the mine—COME AHEAD. Three times in succession.

Gerstung had parked the Honda Accord LX in a long, low building that had been a garage. With conversation at a minimum, the Death Merchant and his crew went to work—in the dark. Their eyes had become accustomed to the darkness and they didn't dare risk having anyone see lights moving about the surface of the mine. The ninety meters of rope, the four cases, the lights, food and water were carried close to the shaft, and the Honda's top and sides covered with rusted pieces of corrugated iron that were lying loose on the ground.

Camellion, Jordan and La Bigne searched for, and soon found, the escape steps that had been built in a room-sized recess to one side of the elevator framework. Built of thick wood planks, the steps had been erected in a series of twenty-foot lengths that angled first to the left, then to the right, a landing at the end of each length. However, the framework to which the steps were bolted was of iron.

"Keep away from the center of the steps," warned Camellion who was first to descend. "Walk toward the sides, and don't trust the railing too much either."

Camellion snapped on a large flashlight and directed the beam downward on the first section of steps. They looked solid, but looks could be very deceiving.

Very slowly, testing each step, Camellion, Jordan and La Bigne moved downward. Finally they reached the bottom, having found only a dozen steps that were dangerous and partially rotted through. Camellion and La Bigne made the return trip to the surface, then, with the help of some of the other men, securely attached rope to the handles of the four cases and carefully lowered the precious equipment down the dark shaft. When the cases reached the bottom, Jordan untied the rope and gave a signal with a flashlight. The rope was quickly pulled up. Food and jugs of water were then lowered. Again Jordan untied the rope, and it was hoisted to the surface. This time the rope was taken to one of the storage sheds and concealed behind a stack of empty, rusted gasoline drums.

The entire group, led by the Death Merchant and La Bigne, very slowly started down the steps. There were two exceptions—Henri Monet and Étienne Fouqut. Each with a jug of water and half a dozen cans of tinned beef, they had made their way to the top of the tipple, to positions that would give them a view of the entire countryside. Monet and Fouqut would keep in contact with the group in the mine by means of an AN/PRC-6T transceiver.

Marcel Galliau, Claude Capeau and Jacques Philber were very careful with Philippe Castile, making sure that the elderly man didn't stumble or step on one of the dangerous steps. There were, however, no accidents. Everyone reached the bottom of the shaft without mishap. By now, dawn was a reality, and light could be seen in the square top of the shaft two hundred feet overhead.

The Death Merchant hoped that, if Castile had had a faulty recall of the past, his being in the same surroundings would rectify any former mistakes. Yet now the elderly man still insisted that the tunnel he had drawn on the diagram was the correct one.

There were six tunnels that led inward from the bottom of the shaft. Castile pointed to one of the tunnels that led south. "That one," he said in a weak voice. "The sixth tunnel. We carried the gold into that tunnel."

The Death Merchant, Gerstung and Laroche led the way, the three bright white beams of their Halogen spotlights dissipating the inky darkness ahead. Any number of thoughts rolled around in Camellion's mind. *"A favor from your CIA," La Bigne said. Well, we've reached Saint-Brieuc, and La Bigne hasn't said a word. I think I smell a frog in a bottle . . . somewhere along the line. And we haven't learned a single thing about General Patton.*

Camellion and the others played their lights over the walls, ceiling and floor of the wide tunnel. On the ground were two sets of rusted rails over which cars filled with coal had once moved. Support posts were still in place, although in some places rock had fallen from the ceiling and blocked the way, thereby forcing the group to go around or crawl over rock. On each side of the tunnel were the wide entrances of the "rooms" where coal had once been taken from the "face." First the coal had been blasted free with explosives. Machines then scooped up the coal and dumped it into electric-powered "buggies," which, in turn, took it to the cars that would be hoisted to the hopper of the tipple.

At the end of 150 meters, they came to a pile of rock, large and small chunks of limestone, that completely blocked the way.

"I said the rock would be there," cackled Castile with a half-giggle. "There it is. Behind the rock is the first wall."

Startled eyes swung toward Castile, the stares alarmed and furious.

"The first wall!" Camellion exclaimed sharply. "Old man, you said a wall. Now you say the first wall. I think the termites of time have eaten at your brain! How many walls are there?"

Castile paused, the rusty wheels of his memory creaking slowly.

"*Oui,* I said a wall. I didn't remember the second wall until we got to this cursed place. Behind the rock is the first wall. Then there is a space of several meters. The second wall has the box with the relay switch and the combination. It is in the center of the second wall. I am positive. Behind the second wall are the boxes of gold. In that chamber, the walls and ceiling are lined with explosives. I know; I am certain. They made sure we saw the explosives."

"They?" asked Camellion.

"The five American officers with the American commandos."

"A hell of a fine mess!" grumbled Gerstung.

"Let's get to work," Camellion said dogmatically. "We'll pull away enough rock to give us room to get at the wall. He pulled a pair of heavy work gloves from his coat pocket. "Let's get started."

With the illumination from only two flashlights—all the Halogen lights had been turned off to conserve their power—the Death Merchant and half a dozen other men began attacking the hill of rock.

By 4:00 P.M. they had succeeded in clearing a five-foot-wide space through the eight-foot-thick wall of rock and had chopped a ragged doorway through the wooden wall with axes. Seven feet back was the second wooden wall and, just as Castile had said, the box containing the relay switch and a combination circuit. The deadly box was mounted in the center of the wall, five feet from the rock floor.

Gerstung and Jordan let the beams of their flashlights rest on the box, which looked like a foot-square cube. La Bigne, Laroche and Gelee watched anxiously, looking as though they were holding their breath.

Noises came from Gerstung's throat, sounds that could have been cynical chuckling. "Well, in another hour we'll either see the gold or be scattered all over this tunnel."

"One or the other. There can't be any 'Mr. Inbetween,' " Camellion said. He pulled a folded leather kit from an inside coat pocket, placed the kit on the stone floor, opened it, took out a screwdriver and removed the front panel of the box. Inside the box was a maze of colored wiring attached to a pulse transformer and a series of wheels, slightly larger than those found in the bottom of the better-type combination lock. The pulse transformer and the combination assembly were connected by nine wires to the vital relay.

"How can you be sure that your modern disarming devices will be able to figure out the correct combination?" Gelee whispered.

"I can't," Camellion said laconically. "I'm counting on

the fact that science has taken a lot of long-distance strides in the past thirty-five years, especially in the area of electricity."

La Bigne commented, "*Nous avons de la chance.* We are most fortunate that you brought the necessary equipment."

"Luck didn't have anything to do with it." Camellion unscrewed the aluminum cover of the pulse transformer. "I only considered all the possibilities and brought everything and anything I thought I might need. That's why those cases were so vital."

"By the time—"

"Quiet, Bernie. All of you shut up and let me concentrate."

The Death Merchant placed the cover on the floor and saw that the transformer was standard—ferrite cores and epoxy encapsulation. The relay was standard, the winding set in a U-shaped frame. But the steel spring holding back the armature plate from the top of the winding was heavier than standard. The fixed upper contact and the fixed lower contact were mounted on the right of the U-frame. Under ordinary circumstances, he could have inserted a small piece of wood between the two contact points, and that would have ended the danger.

But the expert who put this gismo together was damned good. He was, no doubt, a commando demolition expert. He's used a resistance-bridge pickup, and it's connected to the combination, the relay and a transducer. Put a piece of wood between the gaps and attack the walls, and the whole mess will explode.

To cut the wires would also result in an explosion.

Below the nine brass wheels of the combination were two tiny bulbs, one red, the other green. Below the bulbs was the plug-in for the battery connection that would activate the entire mechanism.

The Death Merchant, who had paused long enough at the bottom of the shaft to open one of the large cases and stuff the necessary equipment into his pockets, reached into a coat pocket and took out a Cadmite battery pack with a six-foot-long cord, which had a dozen different kinds of plugs branching off from the end. Camellion took one with two prongs, pushed the prongs into the slots of the plug-in and turned on the battery pack. The red light started to glow. Next he took out from another pocket a device that resembled a stethoscope. He put the ear plug into his ears and placed the magnetized end against the pulse transformer, more than a little amused at the awed stares from La Bigne, Laroche and Gelee. Jordan and Gerstung regarded him calmly. They didn't know exactly how he was doing the job, but they had an idea that he would synchronize the numbered combination wheels with the surge of electricity in the pulse transformer.

To the Death Merchant, the process was simple. All he had to do was listen with the potentiometer and detect the difference in impulse potential of the voltage that existed between two points, detect the voltage drop across an impedance from one end to the other, in this case from the transformer to the relay.

Camellion began turning the first combination wheel which, like the other eight wheels, was numbered from one to twelve. When he reached number nine he heard the loud buzzing of the transformer through the potentiometer. Within seventeen minutes, he found the correct numbers on seven more wheels. One more wheel to go. But Camellion didn't go on to turn the ninth wheel. Instead he removed the plugs of the listening device from his ears, let the potentiometer dangle from the transformer, then turned to face the men gathered around him in a semicircle.

"Is that it?" asked La Bigne.

"The green light isn't on." Gerstung sounded edgy.

"Why didn't you touch the last wheel of the combination set?" Gelee asked.

"Maybe for the same reason that La Bigne has never told me what it is the ARC wants from the Company," Camellion said, turning to La Bigne. "The favor you mentioned, *mon ami.*"

"Good point," Jordan intoned. "We've come past Saint-Brieuc."

Michel La Bigne nodded. "We refrained from mentioning it because we were afraid it might interfere with what we all must do . . . the job ahead of us."

"Now's the time to put out all your cards, face up." Camellion was firm.

"We want the CIA to give us five hundred kilograms of high explosives—in five-kilo blocks—and five hundred detonators that are remote-controlled."

Gerstung laughed loudly. "The high guys in the Pickle Factory," he said, using a rare nickname for the CIA, "aren't about to give you guys more than a thousand pounds of high-boom stuff. You birds are a lot short on the smarts."

"*Vous espérez trop*," Jordan said softly.

"We expect consideration for the help we are giving," Yves Gelee snapped back. "Without us, you Americans would not even have been able to find the gold, much less reach the mine."

"Will you put in the request for the explosives and the detonators, Monsieur Kidd?" La Bigne stepped closer to Camellion, a sly glint in his dark eyes. "In return we will reveal information we are positive will be of interest to your government."

"Sure, I'll put in the request, but that's all I can do. Now's the time for the information. No more of this 'later' business."

La Bigne brooded in silence for a few moments. "Philippe Castile and two other Resistance fighters—two of the four who were murdered—shared another secret in common. The three were standing on one side of the truck, right here at the mine, and overheard three American officers talking. The three officers were on the other side of the truck that had brought the gold to the mine."

"Get to the point," demanded Camellion.

"The American officers were discussing the best way to murder General Patton should anything occur that might make him suspect his own people of stealing the gold from the SS."

Jordan and Gerstung perked up with renewed interest. Camellion retained his pose of nonchalance.

"Did Castile and the others hear the officers mention any names?"

"Only one—'Masters.' "

"Interesting," Camellion said, scratching his left cheek. "We'll have to remember that name."

"We'll also have to have a long discussion with Castile," Jordan said, his smile broadening. "We'll have plenty of time once we're aboard the submarine."

The faces of Gelee, La Bigne and Laroche became framed in amazement.

"Castile . . . *un sous-marin?*" La Bigne said, stepping back.

Jordan explained in a breezy manner. "Yesterday afternoon, when I made radio contact with the sub, I told them that the three Frondes and Castile would be coming aboard."

"The Frondes, *oui*," murmured Gelee. "But Philippe Castile?"

The Death Merchant smiled. "To keep the ARC from putting him to sleep forever. That was your intention, was it not?"

Pursing his lips, Gelee glanced at La Bigne, whose eyes narrowed. But, like Gelee, he remained silent. Nor did Laroche make any comment. Finally, Gelee made a motion with one hand. "Very well. Take him. It is no concern of ours."

No longer smiling, the Death Merchant returned his attention to the relay box and inserted the ear plugs of the potentiometer into his ears. He thought of how sheer good fortune would have to play a large role in the successful operation of getting the gold from the mine to the beach, and from the beach to the submarine. Suppose the commandos from *Scorpion II* didn't reach the beach in time—*Or hit the wrong section of the beach? If the cabin cruiser doesn't leave Plymouth on time? But first—the gold . . .*

Slowly he turned the last wheel in the combination set—one . . . two . . . three . . . The buzzing from the transformer came when he reached number eleven.

The green light glowed.

The combination was 9-4-8-6-6-9-3-1-11.

He stepped to one side, thinking that so far the gas detector in his pocket had not buzzed. The mine was free of methane gas.

He motioned to Laroche and Jordan, both of whom were holding axes. "Go ahead. Chop a doorway."

The wall was made of unpainted pine boards that, after 35 years of stale air, were as dry as Sahara sand and as brittle as glass. A dozen blows from each ax, and a ragged opening appeared. Then several more blows from each man knocked off the giant splinters.

Jules Laroche was the first to go through the makeshift doorway. The others followed, moving the beams of their flashlights around the chamber. In front of them, ten feet away, were the boxes of gold bars—five stacks, each stack composed of two layers, nine boxes in each layer. The sixth stack contained ten boxes, five boxes in each layer.

The chamber was in reality the "face" of a "room." While the ceiling and the left wall were of rock, the right and rear wall were solid coal. By each wall were five cylinders, each cylinder two feet high. From the top of each cylinder protruded a heavy-duty cable, the other ends of the fifteen cables terminating in a metal box mounted on the wooden wall—the rear of the relay box. From one side of the box stretched exposed copper wires, each wire half the thickness of a steel clothesline wire. Six wires that had been stretched across the wall had been chopped through.

"I'll be damned!" muttered Jordan, staring at the stacks of boxes, the words coming out in a kind of croak.

Yves Gelee, playing the beam of his flash over the walls and ceiling, murmured. "But is it safe to move the boxes to the bottom of the shaft?"

"Huh? Of course it is," snorted Jordan. "See how those wires by the door have been broken?" He paused while Gelee turned and swept his flash over the floor by the doorway. "If Kidd had failed in disarming the box, we'd now be splattered all over these walls."

Camellion glanced at his watch: 6:00 A.M.

"It's six o'clock," he said. "We'll go back to the others, get something into our stomachs and sleep for four hours. Then we'll go to work."

"Bon." La Bigne nodded with satisfaction. "It's going to be brute labor carrying those boxes to the shaft. "But we have almost all of the day and half of the night. The three explosions will go off in Saint-Brieuc at exactly midnight. By then the truck and the cars will be here."

The Death Merchant headed for the chopped doorway. "I gather that your people won't place the Composition C-4 where it will harm innocent people?"

"There's an old warehouse at the south end of town," La Bigne said. Emile and Vincent will blow up the warehouse. No one will be harmed."

"I don't think there'll be any trouble tonight," LaRoche said enthusiastically. "Everything has gone well so far."

The Death Merchant moved through the opening in the wall. *Yes . . . well so far. But there will be trouble, plenty of trouble. . . .*

Not only could he see Death—many in the group had black auras[1] or no auras at all—but he could smell Old

[1]The human aura can be seen with a photomultiplier tube under certain conditions. Psychics can see the human aura with the "mind's eye." So can men and women who have lived very close to death.

Grimy Bones. Each time he inhaled, the inside of his nose seemed to freeze, and there was that kind of sweet-sour smell. He had smelled it many times before—the stink of the Cosmic Lord of Death.

Camellion felt neither joy nor sadness. He did think of the paradox in which man's highly developed brain had placed him. The "lower" animals had automatic responses and reflexes that protected them from a premature end of life. Yet man was the only animal who knew that, at some future date, Death would be inescapable.

Therein lay the paradox, for ironically, man's every accomplishment was the result of the direct consequence of the challenge of Death. The very essence of man was the constant awareness of his own mortality. Death was the prime motivation in all creativity, in all forms of scientific and artistic endeavor. If man knew that his tomorrows would stretch into infinity, his only struggle would be for immediate creature comforts and bodily satisfaction. His awareness of time would end and he would be reduced to the level of a moron, to the level of an animal. The struggle would end. Without struggle there could be no satisfaction, no awareness of accomplishment.

The real tragedy was that man didn't realize that the only real "death" was "life" in the present three-dimensional continuum. To be confined in a body, to be imprisoned in a tiny dungeon of flesh that was subject to all kinds of ailments—*It's spirit incarcerated in solitary confinement. . . .*

The Death Merchant felt a kind of envy for the people around him, for those with black auras, and for those without auras. They were lucky.

They will soon be dead!

They will soon be free!

CHAPTER THIRTEEN

The thought of moving the hundred boxes of gold bars from the end of the tunnel to the top of the shaft made the Death Merchant think of an old Russian proverb, Pray to God, but keep rowing to the shore. Only the Death Merchant and ten other men could carry the boxes. Philippe Castile was too old, Marcel Galliau had a heart condition, and Henri Monet and Étienne Fouqut were in the tipple, acting as lookouts.

Claude Capeau was the first man to be stationed at the opening of the tunnel, an AN/PRC-6T in his hand, serving as tunnel lookout and contact between Monet and Fouqut in the tipple. Camellion, Capeau, and the other nine men rotated on tunnel watch. After each man would put down his box of gold close to the shaft, he would walk over to the man on watch, take the transceiver from his hand and wait until the next man in line had set down his box. In this manner, the workers got a brief rest between trips to the rear of the 500-foot-long tunnel.

Carrying a box filled with gold ingots was not an easy task. Not only was it the weight—45 kilograms (or 100 pounds), but the size of each box—20″ long, 10″ wide, and 10″ deep. Too small for two men to carry comfortably. All a man could do was pick up a box by the handles at each end, then huff and puff along the tunnel, his way illuminated by the Halogen lights attached to his belt.

At the start there had been two further difficulties: two masses of rock that had tumbled from the ceiling. To climb over these two obstructions, while carrying one-hundred-pound box, would have been impossible. So Camellion and nine men had moved some of the rock, just enough rock to permit a man to pass through with comfort.

During the day there was some cause for worry. Late in

the morning a car stopped and a man, a woman and a teenage boy got out and started looking over the mine—tourists obviously, since the woman kept warning the boy not to go beyond the fence enclosing the mouth of the shaft, and the man kept snapping pictures of the old buildings and the tipple.

Late in the afternoon, three young fellows on motorcycles roared in and started to poke around inside several of the buildings, but not the buildings in which the rope and the Honda Accord LX were hidden. After twenty minutes or so, the three men climbed over the fence and peered down into the darkness of the shaft. Then they climbed back over the fence, got on their machines and roared off. Without knowing, they had saved their lives by not going down the steps to the bottom of the shaft.

By 8:15 P.M. the last box of gold was stacked ten feet from the mouth of the tunnel that opened into the shaft. Now, in the main, there wasn't anything to do but wait and worry and hope that all went as planned in Saint-Brieuc.

A red-orange sunset, and twilight gradually turned into darkness. Henri Monet and Étienne Fouqut were replaced in the tipple by Benoit Fachon and Jacques Philber. The rope was removed from behind the empty drums and the four cases hauled to the surface. While Yves Gelee, Michel La Bigne and the other ARC members put together submachine guns and assault rifles that had been concealed in the Honda Accord, the Death Merchant, Jordan and Gerstung opened two of the metal cases and removed their special weapons. Camellion strapped two .44 magnum Alaskan Auto Mags around his waist and fastened a case containing ten spare magazines to the front of his belt.

Bernard Jordan preferred black-leather, spring-type shoulder holsters, each filled with a Safari Arms "Match Master" .45 autoloader. Gerstung also used shoulder holsters and two Safari Arms SF .45 auto-pistols, only his were stainless steel, that is, stainless-steel slides on an aluminum frame[1].

"There's no sense in getting out the shotguns and other stuff until we're ready to go," Camellion said. "We still

[1]Safari Arms, of Phoenix, Arizona, is the only company in the U.S. that manufactures a .45 auto-pistol with a steel slide on an aluminum frame.

have to hoist the boxes from the bottom of the shaft and load them onto the truck."

"Yeah, but let's not leave this stuff out in the open," Jordan said, glancing up at the black sky dotted with blue-white stars. He pointed to a long shed for storing parts, spare cable and other pieces of equipment for the steam-powered winch that had raised and lowered the two elevators in the shaft.

"Let's take the cases in there," Jordan suggested. "Then I'll contact Plymouth on the radio. If that damned boat and specially built barge aren't on time, we're sunk—and I don't mean that as a pun either."

Ralph Gerstung glanced at Laroche and La Bigne who were passing.

"I don't trust any of those French bastards," he said with unaccustomed gravity after the two men were out of hearing range. He closed the lid of one large case and snapped the latches. "And I like this damned mine even less. It reminds me of an unkept graveyard."

"We have to trust them," Camellion said in a practical tone of voice. "I'm not too concerned about their double-crossing us. They could have killed us after we reached the gold, or anytime during the day."

"Yeah, and they do want you to ask the Company for explosives," Jordan said, "provided they were serious and not trying to put us on the wrong track."

"Let's get these cases out of here," Gerstung said.

He and Jordan each carried one of the larger cases, and Camellion carried the two smaller cases, one in each hand, to the parts-storage shed. They placed all four cases in one corner, after which Jordan took out the high performance *Geheimschreiber* with its con-box and timer. It took him ten minutes to speak the message, but less than half a second to "squirt" it into the air.

The group in Plymouth, England, sent a return message. By the light of a flashlight, held by Camellion, Jordan pulled the tape from the *Geheimschreiber*, stretched it out, and the three men read, ALL READY IN PLYMOUTH. BOAT AND BARGE WILL BE WAITING BEYOND LEGAL LIMIT. WILL APPROACH BEACH ON YOUR SIGNAL, EITHER RADIO OR THREE FLARE. KDCT-BXBTO-FGVB-GHRTTT-T-Y-IUTB-VV-B-5-EBGASDR.

"What the hell does the last line mean?" growled Gerstung. "It's not any of the regular emergency codes."

"The machine is in perferct working order," said Jordan, mystified.

"I know what it means," Camellion said, stone-faced. "It's for me and it's personal." He paused, then said to Jordan, "Put the radio away. We'll put the four cases in the truck that carries the gold."

"I'll believe it when I see it," Gerstung said heavily.

"We should hear it before we see it," the Death Merchant said. "When that warehouse blows sky high."

Camellion was wrong. At 11:50 P.M., Fachon and Philber, high in the tipple, called down on the AN/PRC-6T and reported a string of lights on the dirt road that led to the mine.

"The cars are several miles away," Fachon said. "Eight or nine pairs of headlights. We can't be sure."

"*Bien, merci,* Benoit," Michel La Bigne said. "We'll be ready." He shut off the walkie-talkie, and motioned to the men around him. "Hide yourselves and be prepared for anything. The cars must contain our people, but we can't be certain until they get here, until they give the proper signal."

In the darkness, the Death Merchant could see La Bigne's eyes jump to him. "Monsieur Kidd, you and your two men can go anyplace you want. I think that experts like yourselves know what to do."

"Oh, don't worry about us," Camellion said reassuringly. His concluding remark made even Gerstung feel uneasy. "The Great Marching Dead always knows its own."

He turned and headed for the shed where the four cases were stored.

Camellion, Jordan, and Gerstung crouched down in the doorway in the southwest corner of the shed. From their position they would be able to see the cars turning in from the road to the west and to watch Gelee give the reply signal to the lead vehicle. Gelee, La Bigne and LaRoche made themselves small behind the large steel girders supporting the section of the tipple that stuck out over the rusted railroad tracks.

Its lights out, the first vehicle was slowly turning into the mine area when Camellion, the two Company men and everyone else heard the double explosion from the southeast . . . rolling thunder from the direction of Saint-Brieuc.

"Scratch one warehouse," Gerstung muttered.

The first car stopped. The man next to the driver got out and, with a small flashlight, blinked out a terse message in morse code: *LES FLEURS VONT ÊTRE ARROSÉES.*

With his own flashlight, Yves Gelee returned the signal to "The flowers are going to be watered,": COME AHEAD.

The first car turned on its headlights and started forward. Seven other cars followed; then came the truck, a three-axle truck with a two-axle full trailer.

The cars very quickly parked by the sides of the various dilapidated buildings to the right of the drivers. The driver of the truck pulled up past the shaft, then, with Gelee, La Bigne and several other men directing him by hand signals, began backing up to the shaft. He stopped when the rear of the trailer was only a dozen feet from the fence on the east side of the shaft, got out of the cab and walked over to Gelee, La Bigne, and half a dozen other ARC men. Men and women got out of the seven cars, doors slamming in rhythm.

"My God, there's enough people here to start a revolution," Gerstung groaned as he, Jordan and Camellion hurried toward La Bigne and Gelee and the other men crowding around the two leaders of the *Action pour la Renaissance de la Corse.*

"There should be thirty-eight," the Death Merchant said, "which means that a lot of us will have to ride in the truck with the gold."

"Five tons of gold," Jordan said, "and say a dozen people. That's a lot of weight, even if it is only ten kilometers to the beach. On the other hand, trucks will easily carry more than they are rated to carry. And that truck looks like an eight-ton job to me. It should be able to carry up to twelve tons."

"And then some," Camellion said. He spotted Armand Fronde and his wife and daughter. Not far behind the Frondes were Marie Morlande, Micheline Perrier and three of the eight women who had accompanied the ten ARC gunmen from Paris. Some of the women wore shorts; others were dressed in slacks. Morlande and Perrier and several of the other women carried submachine guns.

Getting close to La Bigne and Gelee, Camellion and the two CIA men were in time to hear Emile Herbillón say, "I'm positive that the whole east side of the church was blown to bits. Vincent and I planted more than enough *plastique* to do the job." A brawny, heavily bearded man, wearing a beret, Herbillón rubbed his hands together in satisfaction. "Fifty to a hundred people must have been killed. Ha, *mon chef,* let the *Front de Libération de la Bretagne* explain that!"

Gelee and La Bigne, knowing that Camellion and the two Company men overheard Herbillón, faced the Death Merchant and his two companions without any embarrassment over their treachery.

"A church is not a warehouse, *mon ami,*" Camellion said, a lilt to his voice. "I take it you meant the Church of Saint James Brieuc?"

Emile Herbillón and Paul Piegts, the driver of the truck, turned and stared at Camellion, hostility in their eyes; Piegts's dark face was twisted in a sneer. Every bit as tough as he looked, Piegts had been a noncom in the French Foreign Legion and was very high on the wanted list of the DST, not only as a terrorist in the ARC, but because he had once belonged to the OAS.[2]

La Bigne explained, "These are the three American agents.

Piegts put his hands on his hips and laughed amiably. "Ah, so it is your three who are responsible for this *fantastique* scheme! Tell me, 'Mr. American,' after we get the gold to the beach, how are you going to make it float on water?"

Gelee thrust in, "We won't know the arrangements until we reach the beach."

"Don't worry about it," Camellion said. "The gold will float. It's a secret I learned from Jesus Christ, back in my fourth incarnation. I was a Palestinian back in those days."

"If I wanted to talk to a fruitcake, I could have gone to a bakery!" Piegts studied Camellion, as if measuring him. He was debating whether to test Camellion by starting an argument when Yves Gelee, guessing his intention, edged in between the two men.

"We didn't tell you that we were going to blow up the

[2]*Organisation Armée Secrète* ("Secret Armed Organization") was the group that, headed by General Raoul Salan, attempted to ferment a revolution within the French army and prevent France from granting independence to Algeria. Salan was sentenced to life imprisonment on May 23, 1962.)

church, because we didn't think you'd approve of killing people you might consider innocent."

"We are at war," La Bigne said, "and consider the Bretons the enemy. Who knows how many of them belong to the FLB."

"Why should you *Américains* care?" Jules Laroche was completely on the defensive. "France is not your nation. Your only concern should be getting the gold aboard your submarine."

The Death Merchant faked a sneer. "I don't give a damn if you skin alive every man, woman and child in Saint-Brieuc," he lied. "My only concern is the gold."

"For all we care you can blow up all of paris," Gerstung said with a slight laugh. "It might be an improvement."

"Let's get to bringing up the boxes from the bottom," the Death Merchant said to Gelee and La Bigne. He looked behind him and saw that although the lights of the cars had been turned off, dozens of people were out in the open, most bunched up into groups. "And have those people get in the buildings," he said, turning back and facing the two ARC leaders. "They're grouped up as though they were waiting for a sideshow to open."

"This *Américain!* He gives orders?" Piegts sounded on the verge of being enraged.

"Enough of your nonsense, Paul," Gelee said harshly. "There is a difference between dictatorial commands and intelligent suggestions." He said to L'aroche, "Jules, have those men and women get inside the buildings, and tell them to be on constant guard."

Hearing noise from the rear of the trailer, the Death Merchant jerked a thumb toward the parts-storage shed. "Listen Laroche, tell whoever goes into that long shed to leave those four cases alone. They could blow themselves to the moon and back."

La Bigne nodded his permission at Laroche, who left the group, hurried over to the men and women and started barking orders like a drill sergeant.

Yves Gelee motioned to Camellion, Jordan and Gerstung. "They should be about ready in the truck. I've sent some men to get the rope."

They moved to the rear of the trailer, where several men had opened the doors, had jumped up inside and were removing the cock-pins of a nine-geared winch. At the front of the trailer, while one man held a flashlight, two other men were moving a fifteen-foot-long iron bar with a large grooved wheel in the center. One of the men also had a length of coiled wire over his shoulder.

"That winch is a godsend," the Death Merchant said, directing his words to Paul Piegts and Emile Herbillón. "Was it on the truck? If not, where did you get it?"

"Armand Fronde borrowed it from the local miller," Piegts explained irritably. "He gave the excuse that he needed it to go to the coast and lift some heavy rocks. He said that he was going to start carving in stone."

Jordan said, "A reasonable explanation, but what gave you the idea that a winch would come in handy?" He moved back with the others to make room for the men who had jumped from the back of the trailer and were pulling out the iron bar and the wheel. To the left of the truck, two men were approaching with the coiled length of rope that had been hidden in a shed behind empty gasoline drums.

"There's no mystery about our having the winch," Emile Herbillón said without hesitation. "We knew that a mine was involved. What better place to hide a treasure than in a mine. Jacques over there"—with a jerk of his head he indicated one of the men carrying the bar with the wheel—"used to be an engineer. He suggested a winch would come in handy. Once we got it, it was easy to bolt the winch to the bed of the trailer."

"Then he's the man to take charge," Camellion said and touched Gelee on the arm. "Let's go have a talk with him."

They walked over to the southeast corner of the shaft, to where Jacques Pleven and Blaise Cogny had taken the rod and the wheel.

Gelee made the introductions, then Camellion said, "Monsieur Pleven. You're an engineer. You're the man to boss this job."

"Down below are one hundred boxes," Gelee said. "Each weighs about forty-five kilos."

Pleven sniffed. Thirty-four years old, he was a small, coiled spring of a man, who seemed powered by unlimited energy. "What is the size of each box?" Gelee told him. All the time, Pleven kept nodding his head, like a bird pecking for seed.

"It will be an easy job, but time consuming," Pleven said. He stabbed a long finger at the bar and the wheel on the ground. "We'll place the bar diagonally across the east and south ends of the protective fence, wire the ends to the pipe, attach the rope to the winch and run the rope over the wheel. How many meters of rope do you have?"

"Ninety meters," Camellion said. "The shaft is sixty meters deep. The rope won't take more than three hundred pounds, which is one hundred and thirty-six kilograms."

"I concur, Monsieur Kidd," Pleven said. He had a nervous tic, so that when he blinked it seemed that his left eye was almost winking. "Three boxes each times means thirty-three trips, then one more for the single box."

"We have to be on the beach no later than dawn," Camellion said. "In your opinion, do you think we can do it."

"Monsieur, after we leave here, what might happen is out of my hands," Pleven said. "But it will take at least two and a half to three hours to load the gold from the mine into the truck."

Bernard Jordan mused. "We'd be pulling out of here at three-thirty "And it's eleven kilometers to the beach. Close, but we should make it."

"All right, take over the show," Camellion said to Pleven. "The sooner we get started, the faster we can get out of here."

Five men at the end of the tunnel carried the boxes of gold to the center of the shaft. Claude Capeau and Jules Laroche would place three boxes within three rings of rope, tie the three sections to the rope dangling down the shaft, then signal with a flashlight. The man peering down into the shaft would signal to the man at the winch, who would then hoist the three boxes to the top of the shaft. Several men would pull the boxes over the corners of the two protective railings, using long poles with makeshift hooks at the ends. As the man at the winch carefully let out the rope, the other men would pull the three boxes to the ground, free them from the ropes and toss the three lines back down the shaft. The man at the winch would pull a cock-pin and the rope would fall rapidly to the bottom of the shaft, the wheel on the rod spinning. Men on the surface would then lift the three cases into the trailer, where other ARC terrorists were stacking the boxes in rows, starting at the rear of the trailer. The entire process would then be repeated, the men working as rapidly as possible. Every now and then the men would take turns at the winch, although, because of how the gears were arranged, a ten-year-old boy could have turned the main wheel with ease.

The night was very quiet. There was almost no breeze. To the north of the mine there was a large, long mound of slack—the finest screenings of coal produced at a mine can be used as fuel when cleaned, coal that had once burned internally and had glowed red in the night—which now stood like a gigantic shadow.

The work continued, the men sweating from the efforts of their labors.

2:30 A.M. More than half the boxes had been brought to the surface and stored in the trailer. All this time, the Death Merchant, Jordan and Gerstung had been doing some serious revaluation of some of their plans.

Jean-Baptise Rollet, one of the ARC men from Paris, had reported that he had heard on the radio that the French CRS and the *Gendarmes Mobiles* were on maneuvers not far from Lamballe. It was a sure bet that the Campagnie Républicaine de Sécurité, riot-control troops and the *Gendarmes Mobiles,* motorized units of the *gendarmarie*, mostly small armored cars and troop carriers, would roar into Saint-Brieuc once they heard about the explosions at St. James Brieuc Church.

"The three of us are not going to ride in the trailer," Camellion announced to Jordan and Gerstung. "It's too dangerous."

Jordan looked up at the star-studded sky and the yellow sliver of moon. "I don't believe they intend to cross us, or we'd be cold cuts by now." He lowered his head and turned toward Camellion. "Or do you have another reason?"

"I'm thinking of how fast the three of us can escape should the CRS or the *gendarmes* show up. With all that weight, the truck and trailer won't be able to win any races."

"That makes sense," Jordan said. "If the French police got their hands on us, we'd be older than Methuselah by the time we got out."

The very practical Gerstung inquired. "So what car do we use, and how do we go about getting one?"

"Let's have a talk with Gelee and La Bigne," Camellion said.

"Have you picked out a car?" said Jordan.

The Death Merchant nodded. "A Datsun 280-ZX. I like its T-bar roof that's open to the heavens."

Fifteen minutes later, as a result of Camellion's insisting that he and Jordan and Gerstung could do a better job outside of the trailer, La Bigne was ordering Laurent Zédé to turn over the keys of his Datsun to the Death Merchant.

A young man who was built as solid as a tractor, Zédé was furious.

"Why should I?" he cried angrily, sizing up Camellion. "I went to a lot of trouble to steal that car." A sly glint rose in his eyes and he shook the keys in Camellion's face. "I'll give you the keys, *Américain,* if you're man enough to—"

No one, especially Zédé, saw Camellion's right hand move, his fingers positioned in a vicious Nukite spear-hand thrust, fingers that stabbed into Zédé's solar plexus, with just enough force to shock his nervous system and force the big man to sink to his knees, gasping for breath.

Four other terrorists muttered angrily and stepped closer to the Death Merchant. They stopped as La Bigne said sharply. "Enough! The *Américain* was man enough. You all saw it."

Camellion, who had bent down and pulled the key's from Zédé's hand, motioned for several of the men to help the stricken man to his feet. "He'll be all right," he said. "But he'll ache for a few days."

"How did you do that?" one of the men asked. "The blow didn't seem to have much force."

"Force had nothing to do with it," Camellion said. "It was the type of blow and how it was delivered.

La Bigne placed a hand on the Death Merchant's shoulder. "I'll go with you while you put your cases in the car. Some of our people might cause difficulty."

"Bon," said Camellion.

The four men started toward the Datsun parked to the east, Camellion knowing that he was walking with men who were more dead than alive.

I doubt if they see the full sunrise. . . .

CHAPTER FOURTEEN

If uncertainty were congenerous to a state of grace, Heinz Wallesch, the leaders of the *Front de libération de la Bretagne* and the other terrorists would have been living saints. Rupert Gnheinst-Strop and the group of Germans with him, suffering from the same brand of insecurity, would also have been candidates for "sainthood."

Everything had gone well the previous day. Until midnight . . .

Car by car, van by van, the entire force had driven into Saint-Brieuc and had gone to the campground nine kilometers south of the old Michelet mine. By 10:30 P.M. the last vehicle had arrived, a large truck with four rear wheels on the trailer.

Any number of people at the camp had expressed a mixture of amusement and amazement over a couple's using a moving van to come to the shrine of Saint James Brieuc. But as François Tournoux, the driver of the truck explained, he and his good wife did not have any other means of transportation, "And we had to come to the shrine. We promised God that we would. Because of my work, we will have to leave right after Midnight Mass. The trip was worth it. We'll get to see a relic of the staff carried by Saint Brieuc."

Likable people were Monsieur and Madame Tournoux . . . he a jolly man with a double chin and laughter in his eyes; she, younger than he by twenty years, a pretty but slightly overweight brunette.

In keeping with their act of being deeply religious, François Tournoux and Gabrielle Incoe, who was posing as his wife, went to Midnight Mass with hundreds of other people.

A few minutes before midnight, Gabrielle was dead, her

body squashed by large stones from the east wall of the church that had been blown to bits. François Tournoux was dying, although he was still conscious. A huge block had broken his right shoulder and right arm, crushed his chest and made mush of his insides. Pinned to the floor by the block, his spine fractured by the padded kneeling rail between the pews, he could feel the blood pouring from his mouth and hear the screams and groans of the injured and the dying all around him. But he was in shock, his mind in limbo. He didn't even realize that he had only a few more minutes to live.

Back at the campground, a disgusted Heinz Wallesch and the three leaders of the FLB guessed what had happened. Furious and frustrated, the four further deduced that since the ARC had blown up the church, the enemy was either on its way to the mine or was already there and loading the gold.

"The ARC and those *Américains* have outsmarted us," Charles Henri Fauvet spoke with effort. "God damn their souls to hell." Standing next to the broad-shouldered Jean Duchemin, the bantam-sized Fauvet looked as small as a child.

"We can't be positive that anyone is at the mine," said André Jaffe, who was even more brawny than Duchemin. "The ARC doesn't blow up churches. Why should—?" He stopped abruptly, thought for a moment, and a look of pure rage exploded over his face. "Those dirty sons of whores! They intend to blame us for the destruction. *Dieu!* All of France will hate us. We'll lose thousands of sympathizers here in Bretagne. But how could the ARC have arrived ahead of us? How could they have learned the location of the gold?"

"The same way we did," Duchemin said bitterly. "They managed to find one of the old freedom fighters."

Standing next to the van with the three terrorist leaders, Heinz Wallesch and Rupert Gnheinst-Strop exchanged worried looks. Three years older than Wallesch, Gnheinst-Strop did not have Wallesch's good looks. But in other ways the two men were very similar. Both were convinced they were members of a superior race and were supremely arrogant; both had been brainwashed since infancy into believing that the New Nazism would eventually unite East and West Germany and create a Fourth Reich. Articulate in German, French, Spanish and Portuguese to the point of glibness, Wallesch and Gnheinst-Strop were motivated by only one creed—Germany Today! Tomorrow the World!

"We have to go to the mine," Wallesch said without any preamble.

Fauvet, Jaffe and Duchemin stared at him and preserved a stunned silence, their severe expressions indicating disapproval.

"We can't remain here," Wallesch said with firmness. "Within an hour those CRS troops and the *gendarmes* around Lamballe will be in this area. They won't fan out over the countryside until daybreak. By then, we'll have had more than enough time to reach the mine and grab the gold. We'll still have time to repaint the trailer and push the five crates of refrigerators in front of the gold. By the time the police get to the mine, we'll be well on our way back to Paris.

"Nonsense," Fauvet said scornfully. "We can't approach the mine without being seen. They are sure to have lookouts posted in the tipple and around the perimeter. They could see our lights miles away!"

"Where's your imagination?" snapped Wallesch. "We have a dozen infrared devices. The men next to the drivers can watch the road ahead."

"There is some moonlight," Gnheinst-Strop said persuasively. "The drivers won't have all that much difficulty once their eyes are conditioned. They will have to drive very slowly."

Duchemin dropped his cigarette and crushed it on the ground with the heel of his shoe. "Keep talking, *Allemand*."

"Let's go inside the van and consult the map," Wallesch said.

By 3:00 A.M., Wallesch, Gnheinst-Strop and their force of Germans, and the FLB leaders and their men, had driven very slowly to within a half mile of the mine, parking their cars and the truck to the southeast. Armed with Heckler and Koch G3A3 automatic rifles and HK MP 5A3 submachine guns and aided by night-vision devices, the force had crept stealthily forward and now surrounded the mine on three sides.

Charles Fauvet was with FLB killers to the south, Duchemin heading the group that would come in from the east. André Jaffe would lead the terrorists from the north. With

Duchemin and his group were Karl Glucks and a handful of Neo-Nazis, all tough young men who despised even their French allies. To the west, Alfred Berger and other Nazis were concealed in trees fifteen liters to the west of the road that ran from north to south past the mine.

Heinz Wallesch and Rupert Gnheinst-Strop and thirteen more Nazis climbed the north side of the slack hill north of the mine, most of the Germans cursing as their feet sank a foot into the crunchy, cinderlike material. They were even more disgusted when they had to lie down on the gritty slack when they reached the top of the hill.

"*Ya,* we have them," Wallesch said happily, staring through a night-vision device. "I can see men loading boxes onto the trailer. They have some kind of wheel rigged at one corner of the shaft. They must have a winch inside the trailer."

"The others must be inside the buildings. See all those cars?" His face shining with sweat, Gnheinst-Strop also surveyed the mine site through a night-sight instrument. "Taking them will not be easy."

Wallesch gave a remote smile. "The stupid swine are doing our work for us. Losing a few men will be a cheap price to pay."

"I was thinking the same thing," rejoined Gnheinst-Strop. "It's a break for us that we can use their truck. We won't have the time to transfer the gold from their trailer to ours." He pushed off the safety of his automatic rifle, then paused as if remembering something. "But how do we know how many boxes they've brought up?"

"I think they got here just before, or immediately after, the explosion," Wallesch said smugly. "It's almost three-thirty. By now they should have most of the boxes in the trailer." He pushed the safety of his AR off and shoved the firing lever to full automatic. His mouth twisted into a sneer. "Let's give it to them."

CHAPTER FIFTEEN

The explosions of high-velocity cartridges did not come as a total surprise to the Death Merchant and the people with him. Sooner or later, he and the French had expected trouble. They hadn't, however, anticipated a total ambush at the mine site, in that they had depended on Benoit Fachon and Jacques Philber in the tipple, to warn them of any approaching vehicles.

Camellion, Jordan and Gerstung had unpacked two of the cases, putting the weapons and other equipment on the floor behind the front seats of the Datsun, and had walked to the area where the gold was being hoisted from the shaft, when the clashing roar of automatic weapons—the firing from the south, the east and the north—shattered the stillness of the early-morning hours.

Riddled instantly with 9-mm Parabellum projectiles were Emile Herbillón, Vincent Saussier and Pierre Lafitte, the three men who had been taking the boxes of gold from the rope slings and lifting the boxes onto the trailer. All three were cold cuts by the time they hit the hard ground.

Blaise Cogny, who had been working the winch, threw himself backward and reached for the Belgian FN Nato rifle leaning against the wall. Adolphi Dominé and Edmond Gerdes, also inside the trailer, dropped behind the boxes and grabbed Czech M-25 submachine guns.

With slugs burning the air around them, many zinging off the steel girders supporting the tipple, the Death Merchant and the rest of the group jumped to the side of the trailer, then crawled underneath the small boxcar on wheels.

"Balls! It's either the FLB or the damned flics," Gerstung spit out, pulling his two SA .45 Match Masters. "All we can do now is run to the beach." He glanced at Yves

Gelee, who had turned on the AN/PRC-6T walkie-talkie and was telling Jules Laroche and the other men in the mine that the surface was under attack and that they should come to the surface as quickly as possible. "Watch yourselves on the steps," shouted Gelee into the mouthpiece. He shut off the transceiver and turned to the Death Merchant, who had a .44 Alaskan Auto Mag in each hand and whose face was expressionless. In that flash of an instant, Gelee wondered how any normal man could fire such huge weapons—one-handed—with any kind of accuracy. Yet, he knew why. Days ago, Gelee had guessed that the man called "Kidd" was an expert in matters of violence.

Before Gelee could speak, La Bigne cried out, "They have to be waiting for us to the west. They know that the road to the west is the only way out of here."

"Damn it, we had only four more boxes to bring up," said Jordan with a calmness that was frightening.

"We'll go to the east," Camellion declared. "Piegts, drive straight east. You can make a swing around the slack hill, then move northwest to the road. It's all open country for half a kilometer to the north."

Piegts's tough, leathery face shone with disbelief. "You must have a death wish!" he said hoarsely. "Those are not *poules mouillées* out there. They'll still blow us apart."

"I know they're not milksops," Camellion assured the Frenchman. "But my way is the lesser of two evils, and we'll be riding shotgun for you."

"In more ways than one," Gerstung said sinisterly, thinking of the three deadly Manville 12-gauge shotguns, each of which had twenty-four shells in the drum and with each round could spew out twenty-seven, number-four buckshot pellets, each pellet measuring 0.24 inch (6.1 millimeters) in diameter and weighing 19 grains (1.2 grams). All twenty-four shells could be fired as fast as one could pull the trigger.

"We can't abandon Laroche and the other men in the mine," La Bigne said firecely. "We—"

"I didn't intend to!" the Death Merchant savagely cut him off. "You hear our own people firing? They will prevent the enemy from making a charge. As soon as Laroche and the others get to the top, have the men inside the trailer set up a cover fire. The rest of you can pile in the trailer and close the doors. Then Piegts can start up and head east."

"Who's going to ride up front with me?" asked Paul Piegts anxiously.

"I will!" Jacques Pleven said angrily. "I want the chance to toss slugs at those *bâtards*."

"Get going, *Américains*," La Bigne said. "Tell the others we're going to take the east as an escape route."

"Piegts, blink your lights twice when you're all set to roll," the Death Merchant said. "Once we head out, we'll keep in front of the truck."

Camellion, Jordan and Gerstung moved out from underneath the trailer. To the screaming of ricocheting projectiles, they left the protection of the truck and, running a pretzel-crooked course, raced the 38 meters (or 125 feet) that would take them to the Datsun Z. All around them the world consisted of automatic rifles and submachine guns firing. ARC people, mostly women, were firing from the garage and the shower building, sending streams of slugs toward the south. In the repair shop, office building and cable-storage house, other ARC women were firing toward the east and the north.

Camellion and the two CIA men didn't run to the Datsun. To do so would have brought concentrated fire from the enemy. Better to head for the car when the other six vehicles were getting ready to move. Anyhow, no one was going anywhere until Jules Laroche and the other men were on the surface, and until Piegts was ready to start the truck and trailer.

Panting, the Death Merchant and the two Company men darted through the doorway of the shed in which they had stashed the four cases. Although the room was dark, they could still make out the forms of Armand and Emmanuèle Fronde, and their daughter, Catherine, who were lying flat on the dirty wooden floor; Madame Fronde was praying frantically to Saint Brieuc, the Virgin Mary, and to dozens of other saints. Camille Rousset was firing an MAT sub-gun from a northside window, short three-round bursts toward the top of the slack hill in the distance. Belda Bakovy was throwing lead from a low window on the east side of the building. From a window to the right of the doorway, Laurent Zédé was positioned with a Belgian Vigneron SMG.

And none of them have an aura, none except Gerstung. He's a born survivor!

Jordan and Gerstung hurried to a window in the southwest corner of the old building, several of the rotting floorboards cracking under their weight. Camellion quickly briefed Zédé, who regarded Camellion with a gaze that was half awe, half envy.

Camellion finished with, "How does your stomach feel?"

"It hurts," admitted Zédé, who then gave Camellion half a smile. "It was fair. I don't hold it against you. But tell me, American—could you have killed me as easily with the same blow?"

"As easily as spitting on the sidewalk."

They both spun at the sound of furious firing to the north—the deep coughing of an FN Nato assault rifle and the higher snarling of Czech chatter boxes. Jules Laroche and the other men had reached the surface, and everyone was getting into the trailer. From one of the buildings on the south side of the mine, a woman screamed.

Shortly, the headlights of the truck went on, then off, then on, and off again.

"That's it!" Gerstung said. "Time to put wheels on our feet."

The Death Merchant called out in French to the Frondes and the two ARC women, "all of you, listen! We're getting out. Run to the cars you came in. We're going to drive east, cross the tracks, then turn and head northwest to the dirt road. As Zédé and the two ARC women turned and ran for the door, Camellion yelled angrily at the three Frondes, "Hurry! Hurry! Your lives depend on speed!"

Camellion felt a hand on his arm. It was Jordan. "It's now, Kidd. Now! We can't wait for anyone."

"Yeah, you're right. Ralph." With a last look at the Frondes—Catherine was trying to hurry her mother and father along—Camellion followed Jordan and Gerstung out the door and, with the two men, zigzagged to the Datsun 280-ZX, only a short distance away.

All around them, weapons were firing, some of the ARC people setting up a cover of projectiles for others either running to cars or starting up engines. The Death Merchant and the two CIA men crawled into the Datsun, and Gerstung turned the key in the ignition. All around them was Death. Marie Morlande was running from the first-aid shack to a Saab hatchback when several 9-mm HK slugs struck her, one in the side and one in the back.

A rain of projectiles shattered the windshield and the windows of a Toyota Corolla that was just starting to move. The blast of heavy-jacketed, hard-core lead chopped into Francine Toulon, Camille Rousset and Belda Bakovy, the savage impact forcing their bodies to do a Mexican-jumping-bean act for a few moments. Several blinks of an eye, and the three bodies slumped, their blood splattered all over the interior of the car.

Ralph Gerstung, his mouth fixed in a death's-head grin, switched on the lights and stepped on the gas. The Datsun shot forward. Several 9-mm slugs ricocheted loudly from some portion of the vehicle on the right, but Gerstung only increased speed, cursing the FLB under his breath.

The Death Merchant, in the front seat, turned and yelled at Jordan, who, in the rear, was feeding a cartridge into the firing chamber of a Model 10 Ingram SMG. The small machine gun had an extralong magazine that contained fifty-seven 9-mm cartridges with explosive bullets, each bullet having a recessed impact fuse and an explosive charge under the fuse. These cartridges would not explode when dropped accidentally, but when they did explode, would not exit from the body of the target.

"Hand me the twenty-two chopper," yelled Camellion.

Jordan reached down, picked up the machine gun and handed it to Camellion. The weapon was an American Model AM 180, known as the "short hand" because it had only a stubby barrel and no stock. Only eighteen inches long, the chatter box had a drum fixed to the top, the round magazine containing 177 .22 Long Rifle cartridges that could be fired from one round at a time to as much as a full 177 rounds in less than five seconds.

Gerstung, hunched over the steering wheel, put on speed. Sixty feet behind the Datsun was the truck and its trailer full of gold and the main body of the ARC force. One rear door of the trailer had been secured, the other door left open so that the men could fire through the space. The only trouble was that the door kept banging back and forth. In the cab, Paul Piegts and Jacques Pleven pretended to ignore the carnage exploding in front of them.

Eenemy slugs had found the gas tank of one car, a VW Squareback, and the vehicle had exploded and was burning, the red-orange flames creating thousands of flickering shadows that slid in silence over the tipple and the other old buildings. Fortunately, no one had been in the vehicle when it exploded.

Death tapped Armand Fronde and his wife as they were getting into an Opel sedan, behind the wheel of which was Barbara Bouget, one of the eight young women who had come from Paris. The left side of Armand's head exploded from several 9-mm bullets, and he fell into the back of the car—most of his body wedged between the front and rear seats, his legs dangling outside, his feet sideways on the ground.

Madame Fronde, as she was getting into the back seat of the Opel from the opposite side, was the recipient of several bullets in the back and a slug through her right cheek. She fell to the accompanying screams of her daughter, Catherine, who was getting in next to Barbara Bouget, her chin striking the side of the open door.

Bouget didn't hesitate. Her face a mask of fear, she stepped on the gas. The Opel jumped ahead, the sudden movement throwing Catherine against the padded dash and forcing the two open doors in the rear to swing back and forth like metal sails in the wind, the door on the left side impeded by Armand Fronde's dangling legs.

Marcel Galliau didn't even get the chance to make the race for life. He had had a heart attack in the old office building and was unconscious and dying.

Micheline Perrier grabbed an MAT machine gun, paused and looked at Philippe Castile, who looking pitifully at her. She knew he could not make the run. He was too old, too slow. If he remained in the shack the police would find him, and he would talk. The whole world would then know that it had been the *Action pour la Renaissance de la Corse* that had blown up the church in Saint-Brieuc. Dedicated to the Cause, Perrier did what she felt she had to do. She fired a short burst of slugs that ripped open Castile's chest and kicked him instantly into the next world.

With a final look at the dead Castile, Perrier turned, ran out the door and raced toward an Audi that Madeleine Vaudrey was just starting up, yelling at Vaudrey to wait for her. Vaudry wouldn't have waited for the president of France! She fed gas to the car and it jumped forward. Not that it really mattered. A few seconds after Perrier had yelled, three 9-mm slugs slammed into her right side, ripped through her lungs, chopped through her heart and took their exit from her body via her left side. Blood bubbling from her mouth, Perrier dropped the MAT and melted to the ground.

"Who knows?" snarled Ralph Gerstung. "We might even come out of this alive!"

Ahead of the Datsun 280-ZX was Christine Chollet in a VW Dasher wagon, and Laurent Zédé and Rosemarie Canrobert in a Renault. Far to the right of the Datsun and slightly behind it was Madeleine Vaudrey in the Audi. Between the Datsun and the truck/trailer were Barbara Bouget and Catherine Fronde in the gray Opel, with Armand Fronde's legs waving grotesquely from the rear left of the car.

With slugs stinging all around her, Christine Chollet took the VW Dasher across the tracks and began to negotiate the short curve that would take her to the north side of the long, slack hill. Close behind her was the Renault, Zédé increasing speed after he crossed the railroad tracks, to the extent that the rear of the car almost skidded to the right as he went into the steep curve.

Ralph Gerstung was going even faster, but the Company "Q-Man" had iron control of his nerves and was a far better driver than Zédé. The Datsun didn't skid.

Fifteen Heckler and Koch automatic weapons roared from the top of the slack hill, several hundred projectiles popping all over the Dasher wagon. Chollet's head exploded, her hair, parts of her skull, blobs of brain matter and tiny patches of her blouse splattering over the seat and the dash. Out of control, the VW Dasher turned sharply to its left and plowed into the middle north side of the slack hill.

By this time, Zédé and Canrobert in the Renault were north of the slack pile and in fatal trouble. So were the FLB terrorists to the east. A split second after Heinz Wallesch, Rupert Gnheinst-Strop and the other thirteen Nazis on top of the hill opened fired on the Renault, the Death Merchant, in the Datsun going around the curve, cut loose with the M-AM 180 "short hand" submachine gun. With experienced motions he sprayed the trees and bushes east of the curve with the full magazine of 177 rounds, his reward numerous cries and yells of pain. Instantly, Jordan handed Camellion another drum. The Death Merchant tossed the empty drum out the window, attached the full magazine to the weapon and pulled back on the cocking knob, the first .22 Long Rifle cartridge sliding slickly into the firing chamber.

Laurent Zédé and Rosemarie Canrobert died too quickly to feel pain. Scores of projectiles ripped into the Renault. Glass shattered. Ricochets screamed. Two spitzer-shaped projectiles stabbed into Zédé's neck. Three more ice picked him between the shoulder blades, going in at such a steep angle that they emerged through his stomach and hit the floor. Blood pouring out of his mouth, and his head rolling from side to side, Zédé slumped over the wheel. Next to him, Rosemarie Canrobert jumped and jerked in a sitting-down tango of death before the impact of slugs that ripped through the roof scattered her head and most of her slim neck all over the dash, the side of the right door, and on her lap.

The left-front tire blew. The blasted Renault wobbled crazily for a moment, then flipped, rolled over on its left side and exploded, red fire, tinged with black oily smoke leaping skyward.

Elated by their success, Wallesch, Gnheinst-Strop, and the rest of the New Nazi brotherhood were getting ready to swing their hot barrels toward the Datsun-ZX, which Gerstung had taken around the short curve and which now was headed west, seventy meters to the north of the slack hill—far enough away so that Camellion and Jordan could see the top of the slack pile.

It was then that the Nazis got the shock of the early morning. Bernie Jordan thrust the Ingram through the left-rear window, in union with the Death Merchant who stood up in the front seat and reared upward through the right opening in the T-bar roof, the M-AM 180 short-hand machine gun in his hands. Before the Nazis could fire, the top of the slack hill began exploding from the impact of Jordan's special 9-mm M-10 Ingram cartridges. Equally as destructive were the .22 Long Rifle slugs that ripped across the top and found cloth and flesh.

"Mein Gott!" yelled one of the Germans. Reacting instinctively, he rolled over to the other side of the hill with some of the other Nazis. In so doing, he and the other members of the new "Master Race" exposed themselves to the weapons of La Bigne, Gelee and the ARC men in the trailer that Paul Piegts was taking around the curve past the railroad tracks. While two ARC men held the door

open, Blaise Cogny, Edmond Gerdes and Henri Monet raked the south top of the slack hill. At the same time, Jacques Pleven poked an MAT chatter box through the right window of the truck and raked the trees and bushes to the east.

On the hillside, four Nazis, with no place to hide, jerked and died together. More yelled and some screamed as .22 Long Rifle slugs stabbed into their bodies, or 9-mm projectiles struck some portion of their bodies and exploded.

Just as quickly the firing was over. Eight Nazis were dead. Three more were dying, including Rupert Gnheinst-Strop. A 9-mm Ingram bullet had exploded in his right thigh, and he was bleeding to death. Only a terrified Heinz Wallesch and three other trembling Nazis were alive and untouched.

The Datsun raced northwest, the Death Merchant and Jordan reloading their weapons. Behind the Datsun and slightly to its left was Madeleine Vaudrey in the Audi. Behind her, to her right, was the Opel with Barbara Bouget and Catherine Fronde, the latter of whom had become hysterical over Bouget's jerking the car from side to side to dislodge the corpse of Catherine's father. The movements had worked. The dead man was no longer wedged between the front and rear seats.

The last vehicle was the truck and its trailer full of gold bars and ARC members, Piegts driving at a top speed forty miles per hour.

Just before the Datsun reached the road, the Death Merchant and Jordan opened fire, sending streams of .22-caliber and 9-mm projectiles to the west of the road, at the darkness five hundred feet to the southwest.

Alfred Berger and some of the other astonished Germans managed to return the fire, but all the slugs missed—all except one. As Gerstung swung the vehicle onto the dirt road, a 9-mm bullet zipped through the large rear window, missed the tip of Jordan's nose by less than 22.23 millimeters (seven-eighths of an inch), barely grazed the Death Merchant's left shoulder and—*Ping!*—put a neat round hole in the front windshield.

"I say, the chaps seem to be shooting at us!" mocked Gerstung with a fake British accent.

"All right, let's get to the beach," Camellion said. "By the way, that was a good piece of driving back there. You're good."

"Huh! You should see me tap-dance!"

In back, Jordan opened one of the cases on the floor, took out the *Geheimschreiber,* turned on the small, powerful transmitter, extended the antenna and shoved its end through the right open window. He didn't have time to use the con-box. He did use the scrambler.

"This is PS-five . . . PS-five, . . ." he said in French, his mouth only an inch from the mike and its coiled length of wire. "We're slightly less than eight kilometers from the landing area at the beach. That's Grid Four, Section Seven, the same coordinates as in the two previous transmissions. Signal with the YB code when you see our headlights."

The Datsun, followed by the Audi, the Opel, and the truck, moved north on the dirt road that, four miles to the north, would turn northwest and lead to the town of Paimpol near the coast of the English Channel. At the end of the four miles of dirt road, Camellion and Company would leave the road, turn northeast and take the three-quarters-of-a-mile path that led to a section of the beach of the Gulf of Saint-Malo.

Gerstung switched the lights to bright and glanced at the left sideview mirror. "Even if the truck could make better time, it wouldn't make any difference. Thirty-five is top speed on this road."

"Five miles isn't all that long," Camellion said briskly. He leaned back in the seat and watched the road ahead. "My only concern now is how fast the FLB can regroup and follow us. The French police are another worry. It will be daylight by the time we reach the beach, and the CRS and the *Gendarmes Mobiles* will be out in force. We can't fight armored cars and helicopters."

"Make it an hour with the FLB," Jordan said from the rear. "They first have to get to their cars—and they wouldn't have dared to park within half a mile of the mine. And we can't really be sure that they will come after us."

"We have to count on another attack," Camellion said with evident concern. "The FLB knows the direction we're headed, and logic will tell them that we're going to the beach. They know we wouldn't be stupid and drive to Paimpol."

"That's the stone-cold truth," Gerstung said genially. "What we need is a rabbit's foot, but not the kind that was carried by General Custer."

"I hope to God you're wrong, Kidd," Jordan said, turning and then looking out the rear window. The lights of the Audi were sixty feet behind.

"You're not hoping anymore than I am," Camellion declared, thinking that the countryside was perfect for an ambush. In this part of Brittany the land was wild and lonely, a landscape of great old trees set darkly together and many brambles in the tangled mass of underbush . . . and here and there a ruined dwelling abandoned to wind, rain and decay.

The very first streaks of light were in the east, a kind of advance guard for the dawn that would follow. Gerstung slowly drove the Datsun over the flat rocky ground, then over rock interspersed with sand. Another 150 feet and the burly radials started to sink in pure white sand. For another hundred feet the beach was all sand, and beyond were gentle breakers that became surf rolling over the beach, then out again, with unvaried regularity. The smooth, sandy part of the beach was several hundred feet wide, and, on each side, were low hills covered with weeds and, where the beach should have been, masses of limestone bunched together in irregular patterns.

A hundred feet to the left of the Datsun was a Juvis camper that had been unhooked from the triangular mount attached to the rear of a white Citroen. The Citroen was to the left of the camper.

Camellion and Jordan got out of the Datsun and walked around to the other side of the car, where Gerstung was standing. The three glanced briefly at the camper and Citroen, and the Death Merchant said, "Bernie, you guide the others in. Have the two cars park next to us, and tell Piegts he has the room to turn around and back the trailer toward the beach. Tell him to move in until the trailer's wheels sink into the sand. The closer he can get to the water, the faster we can get the boxes onto the barge. Ralph and I will go tell the people in the camper to get lost."

"They're called 'innocent bystanders,'" Gerstung said with a slight laugh.

Jordan nodded, turned and strode heavily through the sand toward the Audi. Madeleine Vaudrey had switched the lights to dim and was driving forward very slowly.

Their feet digging into the fine sand, Camellion and

Gerstung were almost to the rear of the camper when an overweight young man in his early twenties stuck his head out the door and blinked sleepily at the two men. His eyes widened and his mouth half-opened when he saw the big auto-pistols buckled around Camellion's and Gerstung's waists.

A woman called out wearily from inside the camper, "Who is it, dear?"

By then, Camellion and Gerstung were at the rear of the camper. "We're the *Direction de la Surveillance du Territoire,*" Camellion said in an authoritative voice. "Your name, Monsieur?"

"F-Felix . . . Felix Le Tac. My wife, Claudine, is inside." The young man's voice shook with apprehension. "We haven't done anything. We are only camping here by the sea. We—"

"Ne vous inquiétez pas, Monsieur," Camellion said soothingly. "You have not broken any laws. But it is necessary that you and Madame Le Tac leave immediately. It's a matter of national security. You can return for your camper after ten this morning. Now, get in your car and leave."

By now, Felix Le Tac's eyes were as wide as saucers.

"One more thing, Monsieur Le Tac," Camellion said. "When you come to the dirt road, continue on to Paimpol. Do not go south or you might be killed by terrorists. When you reach Paimpol, do not tell anyone that you have seen us, or you will be imprisoned. Now hurry."

"May w-we get d-dressed first?"

"Oui. But you must be out of this area within the next ten minutes."

As they hurried away from the camper, Gerstung whispered angrily, "Why didn't you tell them to go south, damn it? They might have run into the FLB and slowed them down!"

"The FLB would have killed them," Camellion said harshly. "What would we have gained? Not a damn thing."

They saw that the Audi and the Opel were parked to the left of the Datsun and that Jordan, farther back, was talking to Piegts in the truck.

"Come on," Camellion said. "We'll stand on top of the Opel and signal the *Moonstone.*"

They went back to the Datsun and took an IRSS signal lamp, a pair of IRSS goggles and a long-range Javelin M-

222 night-viewing device from the two larger cases. They then hurried to the Opel. In front of the car, Madeleine Vaudrey and Barbara Bouget were doing their best to calm Catherine Fronde who was sobbing uncontrollably. Vaudrey and Bouget glanced nervously at Camellion and Gerstung as the two men climbed onto the hood, then onto the roof of the Opel.

To the left, the Le Tacs were backing out in their white Citroen. To the south, Michel La Bigne, Yves Gelee and the other ARC terrorists had jumped from the trailer, and Paul Piegts was slowly turning the truck and trailer around, in preparation to backing the trailer as close to the water as he could.

On the roof of the Opel, the Death Merchant put on the goggles with the thick infrared G-lens and turned on the Infrared Signal Systems lamp. Standing next to him, Gerstung adjusted the J-M-222 night-viewing device, put the wide-viewing plate to his face and looked toward the sea.

"I don't see a damn thing," Gerstung muttered. He reached up and adjusted the device for longer and wider focus.

Camellion, staring out toward the calm water of the Gulf of Saint-Malo, held the IRSS lamp above his head with his left hand and, with his right, began tapping the button on the small box attached to the lamp by a long, thick cord of rubber-wrapped wire. Five times he sent the message in YB code: WE'RE HERE AND READY. PLEASE REPLY.

There was no reply.

There was only more daylight on the horizon.

"Damn it to hell and Harlem! The *Moonstone* is not there!" Gerstung sounded not only angry but afraid. "Those idiots in Plymouth pulled a master goof. They probably went to the wrong beach."

A dozen more times the Death Merchant sent the message on the IRSS lamp. There was no response.

Bernard Jordan and Michel La Bigne appeared at the side of the car.

"Did they reply?" Jordan asked.

The Death Merchant removed the goggles, lowered the lamp and jumped from the roof of the Opel.

"The boat is not there. And if the boat isn't there, neither is the barge and the commandos from the submarine."

"My God!" Jordan turned and stared at the water, as if

he might see the antisubmarine ship and the barge rear up out of the water. But on the eastern horizon there was only more light. Very soon, the sun would be crawling up over the water.

"C'est impossible! Un désastre!" cried La Bigne.

"Oh, it's possible, and you're right: it is a disaster," said Gerstung, who also had jumped from the roof of the car. "Those morons in England are so dumb they think the Bermuda Triangle is a musical instrument."

He turned to the Death Merchant, who had turned sideways and was watching Paul Piegts slowly back the trailer to the beach. "Well, mastermind, what the hell do we do now?" Gerstung demanded. "Walk on water?"

CHAPTER SIXTEEN

There wasn't anything to do but dig in and expect the worst, not only from the FLB, but eventually from the French police who would, sooner or later, come to the isolated stretch of beach. The Death Merchant knew that they couldn't make a stand around either the Opel, the Datsun, or the Audi; there was too much danger from exploding gas tanks.

"We'll split up into three groups," he told the assembled ARC terrorists. He paused and looked at the hard, dirty faces around him, faces that were anxious but resigned to death. A short distance away were the truck and trailer, the rear wheels of the latter half buried in the sand and still sinking, very slowly. A hundred feet from the open rear end of the trailer, the surf rolled in and out over the beach.

Off to one side, Bernard Jordan was at the *Geheimschreiber* transmitter, every ten seconds sending out: P-S-5 AT DESIGNATED LOCALE. ANSWER. And every time he sent the message, he thought of the DST radiogoniometry trucks in the area. It was almost a certainty that they'd get a cross-fix location.

Camellion turned back to the group. "The wheels of the trailer are still sinking, but the sinking will stop when the bottom edges of the open doors wedge in the sand.

"Who cares about the damned trailer?" Louis Dubaier said irritably. "We're all as good as dead. There can be no surrender!"

Yves Gelee turned on him with fury in his eyes. "Shut up and listen. There is always some hope. We're not dead yet. When—"

"I got them! They answered!"

Everybody turned and looked in the direction of Bernard Jordan, who picked up the transmitter and ran to the group, breathless with excitement. "They didn't get the coordinates mixed up," he explained. "One of the electric engines on the barge wouldn't start. Mr. B. said that the full force is on its way. He said they'll hit the beach in half an hour."

"Who knows? We might make it yet," Camellion said amid a babble of excited voices. He put his hands on the butts of the Auto Mags in the holsters low on his thighs. "Some of us . . . that is. . . ."

"Kidd, you said three groups." La Bigne took a deep breath. His high forehead was dotted with heavy beads of sweat and his slender frame seemed very tired. "I'm guessing that you meant in back of the trailer and in rocks on the hills on each side."

"Correct," said Camellion. "Piegts and Pleven are emptying the truck's tank. There'll be little danger from fire. Not counting Mademoiselle Fronde, there are twenty-one of us. Six will stay behind the trailer. Eight can go the left, and seven to the right. Those that go to the right can take Miss Fronde with them. All we can hope to do is hold them off until our commandos arrive."

Gelee unconsciously rubbed a finger along the ugly keloid on his right cheek and smiled at the Death Merchant. "As you *Américains* would say, 'Let's get with it.' "

The beach was bathed in bright sunlight, and there wasn't a single cloud in the sky. Jordan had destroyed the *Geheimschreibe*r by hammering it into junk with a tire iron. At the suggestion of Jules Laroche, the three cars had been moved far ahead of the truck and spaced widely apart from each other. In case they were set on fire, the flames would not reach the truck and trailer.

Camellion, Jordan and Yves Gelee waited by the side end of the trailer's right door, the bottom edge of which was buried several inches in the fine, white sand. Waiting by the left door were Gerstung, La Bigne and Claude Capeau, each man armed with a submachine gun and a side arm. In addition to his two .45 Match Masters, Gerstung, who had taken off his shoes and socks, had a deadly Manville semiautomatic shotgun, an odd-looking weapon that looked like a stainless-steel drum mounted in the center of a short frame. Stainless-steel tubes for the shells—shoved into each tube horizontally—protruded in the same direction as the foot-long barrel. Five inches in front of the round drum magazine was the forward handle. The rear handle—the trigger in front of the handle—was to the rear of the drum. The weapon was cocked by means of a knob protruding from the center rear of the frame.

"Kidd, you are sure that the five million in Swiss francs is aboard the submarine?" Yves Gelee asked with unabashed candor.

"I said so, didn't I?" Camellion said and glanced at Jordan who smiled ever so slightly, then resumed looking toward the west. Camellion and Jordan knew that Yves Gelee as well as Michel La Bigne were doomed. If FLB slugs or French police bullets didn't terminate the two terrorist leaders, there was only one way they would ever leave *Scorpion II*—and that was stone dead. As in all "Black Operations," the Company could not take any risks—*But first things first! We're no doubt outnumbered. I might be the only survivor . . . I and Gerstung. Today is not our time to die.*

To the left, to the south, 150 feet away, was Jules Laroche and his group. Adolphi Dominé and four men and three women were hidden in the rocks on the low hill to the right. Everyone expected the attack; yet everyone—except Camellion—was, nonetheless, surprised with the suddenness of the assault when it did come. The Death Merchant wouldn't have been amazed if Adolf Hitler had pedaled by on a tricycle. The coordination of the three-pronged attack didn't astonish him either. All along, he and the Company men had suspected that agents of ODESSA were helping the FLB.

There was the loud chattering of automatic weapons to

the west, the north and the south, the staccato snarling accompanied by high screaming ricochets, not only from the front of the truck but from the three cars spread out in front of the truck and trailer.

"Those sneaky no good bastards!" Jordan grumbled. "A forward thrust and a pincers. They've sneaked around and are coming in at our boys from the north and the south. They've guessed our—"

The violent explosion of the Datsun's gas tank cut Jordan short.

Yelled Gelee, "The damn fools are deliberately firing at the cars. They must think some of us are hiding inside."

Several seconds later, both the Opel and the Audi dissolved with big *beroooooms* and giant blossoms of red fire, burning parts of the vehicles flying out over the rock and sand.

The Death Merchant didn't waste the energy explaining to Gelee that the FLB and the ODESSA agents had a systematic method to what the Frenchman considered their stupidity.

No one spoke. The firing from the west was so intense that neither Camellion nor any of the other five men dared stick his head out beyond the edges of the doors. Machine guns and assault rifles continued to roar from the rocks to the north and the south . . . the firing of the enemy, and the return fire of the two besieged groups.

Within several minutes there was a decrease in the roaring of weapons from the north and the south—all normal enough to the Death Merchant, who realized that with each side tossing high-velocity lead from automatic weapons, either victory or defeat would come rapidly. The rate of firing from the west slackened off somewhat, and the enemy cars came in very fast, the drivers getting up speed so that momentum would carry the vehicles through the deep sand. All the while, enemy projectiles continued to glance off certain portions of the truck—first chopping through the thin-metal outside covering of the doors—and to knock splinters from the edge of the door.

To the left, Claude Capeau shouted in a highly nervous voice, "Hear those cars! We've got to get inside the trailer!"

He moved to go, but was pulled up short by Gerstung, who grabbed him by the arm. "*Stupide!* That's exactly what they want—to bottle us up. Stay put!"

In response to Yves Gelee who voiced the same opinion as Capeau, the Death Merchant shook his head. "We'd have no chance at all inside the truck. Those cars won't get far in the sand, and all of them can't hit us from the sides at once. We also have total freedom of movement. The men inside the cars do not."

"You had better be right, *Américain!*"

"I am!"

The Death Merchant was right—and so was Gerstung. Engines racing, enemy cars charged the trailer—a British TR7 and a Volvo to the right, and a Fiat 128 sport coupe to the left. At the same time, Camellion and the other men could hear motors in front of the truck.

Catastrophe was only seconds away.

The Cosmic Lord of Death had already gathered his quota of victims on the low hills to the left and right.

To the south, Jules Laroche and his group had been whittled down by enemy slugs. And so had the force of Germans and French who had attacked. On the long west slope of the hill, five ODESSA agents and eight FLB terrorists lay crumpled with sightless eyes. Fouqut, Chambord, Cogny and Philber were bloody corpses. Unconscious from a bullet in his left shoulder and from one in his right side, Henri Monet was dying. Only Laroche, Benoit Fachon and Louis Dubaier were alive. Afraid that a larger force would be sent against their position on the hill, the three decided to take their chances with the others at the rear of the trailer. Soaked with sweat, they reloaded their weapons and started the dash toward the trailer: Laroche ready with Cogny's FN Nato rifle, Fachon and Dubaier carrying Czech M-25 submachine guns.

On the north hillside, Adolphi Dominé's group had also killed its share of terrorists and had paid dearly for the privilege. Dominé and Barbara Bouget had almost been cut in two by 9-mm Parabellum slugs. Paul Piegts was dying, on his knees, swaying back and forth; the blood leaking out of him from a stomach wound. Next to him lay an almost headless Edmond Gardes.

Jacques Pleven and Jean-Baptise Rollet arrived at the same conclusion as Laroche and his men. Run for it! There was safety in numbers. Pleven and Rollet figured that if they could reach the trailer, they might be able to hang on to life until the American commandos arrived. Nor did they take time to look for Madeleine Vaudrey and Catherine Fronde. Neither woman could be seen, and Rollet and Pleven automatically assumed that the two women were dead somewhere among the rocks.

As it came about, the decision of Rollet and Pleven was as ill-fated as the choice made by Laroche and the two men with him. All five left the hilltops and began the zigzag run to the trailer, half a minute before the cars raced in. The result was that—even before the enemy to the west could swing its guns toward them—the five ARC men, who saw the three cars start up, realized their mistake. They were already halfway to the trailer. They couldn't go forward. They couldn't retreat. The men in the cars would riddle them into nothingness. The five did the only thing they could: They dropped to the sand and opened fire on the three cars.

Camellion, Jordan and Gelee spotted Pleven and Rollet running toward the trailer, just as Gerstung and his two companions saw Laroche and the two men with him racing from the southside hill. There wasn't any way to stop them, no time in which to shout a warning.

Dietrich Boess, the driver of the British TR7, was almost to the end of the trailer when he realized that using the three cars had been a serious miscalculation. In the first place, no one had suspected that the sand was so deep; and now the TR7 was shifting all over the place and stopping ahead of schedule. In the second place, no one had counted on a crossfire. The plan had been to exterminate the ARC men on the flanks.

Neither Raoul Lepage, sitting next to Boess, nor Arthur Wilocay, in the back seat, had a chance to use their Heckler and Koch MP 5A3 submachine guns. Less than fifteen feet to the right of the sliding and slipping TR7, the Death Merchant and Jordan opened fire with their Manville shotguns.

The Volvo was twenty feet to the left of the TR7, and slightly ahead of the British auto. Jean Dupuy, the driver, Erwin Kapp, next to him, and Clement Maudet, in the rear, realized too late that they had driven into a crossfire.

"Stop the skidding! Stop the skidding!" screamed Maudet, who was desperately attempting to sight in his HK 33A3 automatic rifle on two men lying belly prone in the sand to the left of the Volvo. But Dupuy couldn't stop the vehicle from slipping and sliding from side to side in the sand. As much in a panic as Maudet and Kapp, Dupuy didn't have the least idea what to do.

Taking the advantage, Jacques Pleven and Jean Rollet raked the side of the Volvo with streams of 7.62-mm and 9-mm projectiles; Pleven triggering a Madsen light automatic rifle, and Rollet firing an M-X-4 Beretta, their slugs ripping into the car with all the fury of a sledgehammer smashing a crate of eggs. Within a few clicks of time, Dupuy, Kapp and Maudet were ripped apart, and the Volvo, with its cargo of corpses, started to bog down in the sand.

As did the TR7. While Yves Gelee leaned around the edge of the trailer door and fired short bursts with a Hungarian M-AMD assault rifle, the Death Merchant and Jordan continued to pull the triggers of their Manville shotguns—*Beruuuum-beruuuum-beruuuum!*

The twenty-seven number-four buckshot pellets from Camellion's first round erased the face and exploded the head of Arthur Wilocay. Jordan's first shell did an operation on Raoul Lepage, one that scattered his skull and brain all over the inside of the car and against a terrified Dietrich Boess, whose own head, a few seconds later, dissolved into a bloody mess from blasts triggered by both the Death Merchant and Jordan. All its glass shot out and its right side a field of dents from shotgun pellets, the TR7 slowed, then came to a halt when Jordan blasted the engine with two more 12-gauge shells.

To the left, Gerstung Capeau, and La Bigne opened fire on the Fiat 128 coupe. Never was a single vehicle hit by so many slugs and shotgun pellets. Glass shattered. Ricochets screamed an off-key aria of total destruction . . . all out of rhythm with a dozen loud *bangs,* as though a string of large firecrackers were exploding, these miniexplosions caused by La Bigne who was firing Gerstung's Ingram and its explosive 9-mm ammo.

The two FLB terrorists in the Fiat might as well have tried to survive in the center of a ten-ton TNT explosion. Parts and pieces of Gasper Saint-Denoix's body were slammed across the front seat of the vehicle. His right hand was literally blown from the steering wheel, becoming a mess of bloody goo composed of chopped flesh and shattered bone, at the same time that Emile Leroi's face received ten number-four buckshot pellets and his chest and side exploded from four 9-mm Ingram projectiles. Leroi pitched between the seats; blobs of flesh, tiny patches of blue and green from his blood-plastered shirt, along with bits and chips of bone, scattered all over the inside rear of the demolished car. The motor of the Fiat simply stopped running and the car came to a dead stop in the deep sand, streams of blood pouring from underneath the doors.

Eight cars and three vans had pulled up in front of the truck and trailer. These vehicles had gone unnoticed by Camellion and Jordan, who had concentrated their fire on the British TR7. Nor had Gerstung, La Bigne and Capeau seen the cars, nor heard the engines above the roaring of the shotguns and other weapons. But Gelee, who was firing around the edge of the door, had spotted some of the cars to the west and yelled a warning to the Death Merchant and Jordan.

Pleven and Rollet had seen all the enemy vehicles, but they had been so close to the Volvo that they had been forced to fire at the car and ignore the FLB terrorists and ODESSA agents in front of the truck and trailer.

To the south, Laroche, Fachon and Dubaier had also seen the main body of the enemy, and deduced correctly that Gerstung, La Bigne and Capeau could handle the Fiat. Consequently, Laroche and his two companions concentrated on the mass of the enemy in front of the truck, killing nine in less than two minutes.

Now, feeling that the FLB forces were sufficiently disorganized for the time being, Laroche, Dubaier and Fachon struggled up from the sand and made a dash to the rear of the trailer. Pleven and Rollet, their weapons empty, tried the same tactic. Better to try then die, than lay there and be slaughtered like cattle.

The FLB was to have its vengeance. HK automatic weapons roared. Jacques Pleven went down first, a dozen 9-mm projectiles knocking him to the sand. Then it was Rollet's turn to wake up in eternity. He let out a high cry of pain when the first bullet struck him in the right thigh and started to kick him down. A micromoment later his torso got chopped by several dozen more hard-core lead projectiles. Rollet was as dead as he would ever be when the lower part of his jaw went flying away in the breeze and several more 9-mm projectiles drilled tunnels in his head. The bloody corpse, in its slug-shattered clothing, sank to the sand.

"You damn fool!" yelled Ralph Gerstung at Michel La Bigne, who was sprinting from the end of the trailer's door and was charging across the sand toward the front of the bullet-blasted Fiat. "Let's be crazy with him," Gerstung snarled at Claude Capeau, who was also surprised at La Bigne's sudden move. Both Gerstung and Capeau deduced that La Bigne was attempting to give cover fire to Laroche, Dubaier and Fachon.

At the opposite end of the trailer, the Death Merchant stepped out from behind the protection of the door's wood and metal and began pulling the trigger of the Manville shotgun. The range was long, and he knew that the pellets would do little damage—*But what FLB idiot is going to be stupid enough to make a test by standing still to find out?*

Jordan shoved shells into his Manville. Yves Gelee ran to the end of the other door to help Gerstung and Capeau who were both firing from around the door, Gerstung in a crouch, Capeau down on one knee, using a Spanish 9-mm 3R Parinco submachine gun.

La Bigne's move had been so sudden that the FLB and the ODESSA agents, getting ready to gun down Laroche and his two men, didn't see him for four or five seconds. By then it was too late. Before the enemy could concentrate on La Bigne, he had reached the front of the Fiat, ducked down, snapped up the Ingram and had begun firing. He had forty-one cartridges with explosive bullets in the SMG and intended to use every one of them in an effort to save Laroche and the two other ARC veterans.

Dozens of 9-mm slugs exploded all over the sides and fronts of some of the cars and one of the vans. Windshields exploded. Headlights shattered. Four French FLB terrorists were killed within thirty seconds. One man's face exploded when he looked up at the wrong time. The second man lost his left arm at the shoulder and fell screaming, his life spurting away from the stump in thick streams of red. The third man died in a gurgle of blood, a bullet having exploded when it hit his throat. The fourth man caught a bullet in the groin. He cried out and fell with his head between his knees.

ODESSA didn't get off scot-free. Emil Ehrhardt, a good friend of Heinz Wallesch, tried to run from the rear of a van to the side of a Porsche. His timing couldn't have been worse. One of La Bigne's 9-mm explosive bullets went off in his belly and uncoiled his intestines, pieces of which flew outward like gray-white snakes.

La Bigne's crazy-brave action worked. Projectiles burning hot all around them, Jules Laroche and Benoit Fachon managed to reach the front of the Fiat. Louis Dubaier was not as lucky. He was only six feet from the wrecked Fiat when a single 7.62-mm projectile hit him in the left side, just below his belt. The bullet cut through the inferior vena cava (the large vein that carries blood back to the heart from the abdominal organs) and shot out his right side like a rocket. Bleeding to death and losing consciousness, Dubaier crashed to the sand and lay still.

For eleven minutes a worried Heinz Wallesch and an angry Alfred Berger had argued with the three leaders of the FLB. Charles Fauvet and André Jaffe wanted to leave the beach with all possible speed, their logic based on the lack of time. Jean Joseph Duchemin agreed with the two Germans: To Duchemin, retreat in the face of such a small enemy force was unthinkable. An all-out charge was the only way to win a lightning victory over the ARC. The next step? Grab ten to fifteen boxes of gold bars. They alone would be worth millions of francs.

Finally, Wellesch's glib tongue—with the help of Duchemin—persuaded Jaffe and Fauvet that to attack in force was the only solution.

"The loss of manpower will be terrible," Fauvet said. He rubbed his round chin and looked at Wallesch. "Have you thought about that?"

Wallesch had an instant, ready answer. "Let's be practical," he said in a matter-of-fact voice. "As it is, we don't have transportation for the men we have. We've lost too many cars. Let's not lose sight of the fact that this is war and that men die in any war. The value of the gold will more than offset our losses."

In the face of such logic, all Jaffe and Fauvet could do was agree.

The Death Merchant and the men with him had expected and anticipated the FLB charge. Why not? The FLB outnumbered the ARC three to one. There was the gold. The trailer was bogged down in the sand, but even a dozen boxes of the gold was worth millions.

Weapons roaring, the FLB and the ODESSA killers moved in along both sides of the truck and trailer, some even climbing the ladder on the front of the trailer and waiting for their chance to slither along the roof.

"One of you get over here!" the Death Merchant yelled. "I'm almost out of ammo and so is Jordan."

"Correction," Jordan shouted, "I am out."

Claude Capeau ran toward Jordan and the Death Merchant, at the same time shoving the last magazine of 9-mm ammo into the Parinco sub-gun. Jordan, who had been standing next to Camellion, ducked to the protection of the trailer door and tossed down the now useless Manville shotgun. Lightning quick, he pulled the two Safari Arms Match Masters from their black shoulder holsters, thumbed off the safety catches of the twin .45 pistols, dashed back to Camellion and Capeau and began firing.

To the left, while Gerstung and Gelee set up a heavy cover fire, La Bigne, Fachon and Laroche sprinted from the front of the Fiat to the end of the leftside door, all five escaping enemy bullets not only because of Ralph and Yves' accurate fire, but because of the serious tactical error the FLB had made. Instead of spreading out and giving each other enough room in which to run and shoot, they had bunched up, falsely assuming that the closer they stayed to the sides of the trailer the safer they would be, assuming erroneously that the FLB gunmen in the front ranks would quickly gun down the opposition.

The opposite had occurred. On the right side, the Death Merchant and Jordan had not even had to aim their Manville shotguns. All they had to do was point to the west and keep pulling the triggers. The result had been a bloody turkey shoot, with the 6.1-mm pellets of the 12-gauge knocking over terrorists faster than pins being hit by balls in a bowling alley.

The slaughter on the left side had been even more terrible for the FLB and the Neo-Nazis—Gerstung and the five ARC men cutting them to pieces with the Manville and with streams of machine-gun fire. But now, only a few minutes later, the Death Merchant and his group began to run out of ammunition. The remainder of the enemy began to close in, and the Cosmic Lord of Death began to step closer.

"Get back behind the door," Camellion yelled after firing his last 12-gauge. He jerked reflexively when a 9-mm projectile missed his left hand, rapped the fore grip of the Manville and struck the right side of the round magazine, which was the only thing between the bullet and Camellion's stomach. With a high-pitched whine, the bullet glanced off the hard steel of the drum and, at an angle, shot toward the northwest. A second bullet missed the right side of Camellion's head. As he made a dive for the edge of the door, two more full-metal-jacketed bullets narrowly missed his back. It was the same with Jordan and Capeau, slugs buzzing around them like bees enraged with bronchitis. But the luck of the two men held. They, too, succeeded in reaching the safety of the door.

Gelee, La Bigne and Gerstung were already behind the leftside door, pulling side arms from shoulder holsters. Laroche and Fachon fired their last rounds at the FLB terrorists closing in and dived behind the door at the same time that the Death Merchant pulled his two Alaskan Auto Mags and calmly began putting .44-magnum slugs through the roof of the trailer, the 12½-inch-long Mag-Na-Ported barrels driving each 265-grain-jacketed soft-point bullet at 2,000 feet per second. With more than enough power to drive through both shoulders of an Alaskan moose at forty yards, the projectiles tore through the roof of the trailer and into the bodies of the three Frenchmen and two Germans who thought their slow crawl was a state secret.

One man took a .44 bullet through the chest. Another, rolling over got a slug in the left side; the bullet went all the way through his body and headed skyward. Leon Deguild, losing his nerve, tried to get up and run toward the rear of the trailer roof. He almost made it, but not quite. A JSP bullet zipped through the roof at a steep angle, struck him in the base of the spine and went out through the highest part of his chest—an inch below his Adam's apple. Busard Challe was trying to get up when a .44 slug tore through the roof and struck him in the chin, blew apart his mouth and dissolved the back of his head. Then it too shot for the bowl of sky above.

Heinz Wallesch and the ODESSA fighters still alive realized that they had made an extremely serious error in judgment. The three leaders of the FLB and their remaining men werer also forced to acknowledge the mistake, plus the bitter fact that all they could do was go forward and complete the attack. To retreat would make them even greater targets. To make matters worse, neither the Germans nor the French had the time to reload their automatic weapons and now were forced to use their handguns. Wallesch and his men came in from the left, the FLB from the right.

The Death Merchant used his last two .44 bullets to kill three of the Neo-Nazis, one slug going through two men, then stabbing through the shot-out rear windows of the wrecked TR7. Out of ammo, Camellion's only chance now was to use the AMPs as clubs, and he did so with incredible speed, attacking Kurt Schumann, who was so ugly that he would have won first prize in a King Kong look-alike contest. Camellion forced Schumann to drop the Mauser Parabellum Swiss Model autoloader in his right hand by breaking his right wrist with the barrel of one of the AMPs. He used the barrel of the other AMP to crack the German's skull, the bone crunching under the impact of the long Alaskan barrel. Schumann immediately sagged, and began to die.

Karl Glucks was jumping around, trying to sight in his Menz/Bergmann PB Special at Camellion, but the Death Merchant was too fast. Too far from Glucks to attack him eyeball to eyeball, Camellion threw the left AMP, hoping his aim was accurate. It was. The top of the big Auto Mag hit Glucks in the right upper forearm, the pain causing him to drop the autoloader and emit a bellow of rage. He saw the tall, lean man duck to one side and dodge the 9-mm bullet that Heinz Wallesch sent at him from a Walther P-38. Wallesch didn't have time to fire the second shot. Camellion kicked the weapon from his hand and it went flying backward. Nor did the Death Merchant have time to turn all the way around and face Glucks, who had made up his mind to kill Camellion with his bare hands. Launching himself from the balls of his feet, Glucks tackled Camellion and sent him crashing to the ground. Glucks immediately tried to crawl on top of him and get his big hands around the throat of his opponent, who didn't try to break away. Instead, Camellion brought up his left arm and shoved it against Glucks's throat, knowing that when the man shoved his arm out of the way, he would automatically lean to the left.

"Sterbe, du unehelich!" snarled Glucks and, leaning toward the left, pushed down Camellion's arm. The Death Merchant used his right hand to reach the back of his neck and pull the ice pick, with its weighed steel handle, from the special holster strapped to the top of his back. He was pulling out the ice pick just as Wallesch returned with the

P-38 and stepped within range of his right leg. With one quick motion, Camellion kicked up with his right foot, again knocking the P-38 from Wallesch's hand, turned back to Glucks and muttered in German, "You try dying," and stabbed downward with the ice pick, forcing the needle-pointed blade through the back of Glucks's neck. A loud "Ohhhhh!" gurgled from Glucks. His eyes bulged hideously and his mouth welled up with blood as an inch of the ice pick appeared through the front of his throat below his Adam's apple. With a final shudder, Glucks died.

Exerting all his strength and ignoring all the blood splashing over him, Camellion rolled the corpse from the top of his body, then frantically scooted forward on his heels and elbows. He leaned backward, lifted his legs and caught Heinz Wellasch, who was about to bend down and pick up the P-38, in a scissors' hold, his powerful legs tightening around the German's waist. Squeezing tightly, Camellion lifted the surprised Wallesch from the ground, twisted him around and slammed him down hard butt-flat, with such force that the German's coccyx, or tail bone, was crushed. Stunned, agony knifing through his entire rear end and his spinal column, Wallesch was helpless. In a flash, the Death Merchant was up on his feet and upon him, coming in from behind, dropping to his knees and wrapping his arms, in front and in back, of the German's neck. Expertly, Camellion applied a commando neck-break. There was a dull snapping sound, as if sticks had been broken, and Wallesch went limp, his neck broken.

Without even glancing around him, Camellion made a dive for the Walther P-38.

Only a dozen feet away, Ralph Gerstung used a "Scribe"—a small, razor-sharp, three-edged blade attached to the inner top of a fountain pen—to turn into a corpse a man with a thick black mustache and a hawk's beak of a nose. Five times he stabbed Jean Joseph Duchemin, each time driving the short blade in deeply, the last time into the left side of Duchemin's neck.

A minute earlier, Duchemin had used an M92 9-mm Beretta to put three slugs into Calude Capeau, who had used the last two of his MAB pistol cartridges to kill August Bauhaus and Eugen Barmstardt. Capeau had crumpled close to the two ODESSA agents he had killed. Now the dead Duchemin fell less than six feet from the body of Capeau.

The Death Merchant wasn't fast enough to save Bernard Jordan, who had killed a French terrorist and a German with karate stabs and chops and was in the process of breaking the back of Maurice de Nedde. A second after Jordan snapped de Nedde's back with a slam-down over the knee, Alfred Berger twice plunged an eight-inch-blade knife into Jordan's back, between his shoulders. He would have stabbed Jordan a third time if Benoit Fachon had not grabbed his right wrist with both hands, twisted the knife from Berger's hand, half-turned him around, and then kicked him viciously in the groin. Fachon scooped up the knife and, with a swift, experienced motion, shoved the blade into Berger's stomach and ripped upward with the sharp length of steel. With tiny groaning sounds, Berger started to sink to the ground, his mouth twisting, his eyes rolling back in his head.

Berger hadn't even hit the ground when Heinrich Schroeder, using a Mauser HSc pistol, put several 7.65-mm bullets into Fachon's chest. Schroeder then hesitated, trying to decide whether to aim at Jules Laroche who was choking Henri Fauvet to death, or at Yves Gelee, who was struggling with Gilbert Debré. Since Fachon was twice the size of the sawed-off Fauvet and since Debré was holding his own with Gelee, Schroeder chose to fire at Jules Laroche, the two 7.65-mm projectiles boring into Laroche's right side. Consciousness started to flee from Laroche's dying brain; yet he was aware of a happiness approaching ecstacy. With his very own hands he had killed Charles Henri Fauvet.

An elated Schroeder turned the Mauser HSc toward Gelee. He didn't pull the trigger; he didn't get the chance. By then, Camellion had picked up the Walther P-38. Now he snapped off a shot. The weapon cracked, and the 9-mm projectile bored sideways into the left side of Schroeder's head, an inch above the top of his ear. Terminated in an instant, Schroeder dropped to the ground, his corpse tumbling across the legs of a dead FLB terrorist. Nonetheless, Gelee remained in serious trouble, but no one could help him: Once more Camellion sighted in with the P-38 and pulled the trigger, but there was only a ridiculous click—the Walther was empty. Michel La Bigne was slowly losing the battle with André Jaffe. Gerstung, who was locked in combat with John Viallier, was trying to twist the muzzle of a German broomhandle Mauser toward Gerstung's chest.

During the next twenty seconds, while the Death Merchant was pulling up his pants legs, Henry Chasseurs picked up an empty HK 3A3 assault rifle by the end of its stock. Chasseurs rushed up behind of Gelee and, swinging the weapon like a baseball bat, caved in the side of Gelee's head with the barrel. Gelee died instantly without as much as a groan and dropped to the ground. Much to his frustration, the Death Merchant discovered that the two .357 Magnum COPS were gone. The ankle holsters were empty. Due to the intense movement of his legs earlier, the cross straps had worked free and the COPS had been lost. With a lot of hope and confidence, Camellion decided on another tactic and reached into his left pants pocket.

Gilbert Debré, breathing heavily, and Henry Chasseurs surveyed the dead Gelee with satisfaction; then looked around in disbelief, their expressions stunned. They were standing on a beach filled with bodies, corpses twisted in grotesque positions. Except for themselves, the only ones alive on their side were André Jaffe and John Viallier, who were struggling with two of the enemy.

Debré's and Chasseurs' mouths fell open with shock and fear when they turned and saw the Death Merchant. He was the last man on earth the two terrorists ever saw. The NAM minirevolver in Camellion's hand cracked one . . . two . . . three . . . four times. Debré and Chasseurs jerked, jumped, uttered short cries of pain and sank to the sand, each dying with two .22 Long Rifle slugs in his chest.

Camellion was too late to save Michel La Bigne. André Jaffe, far the stronger of the two, had succeeded in getting a headlock on the ARC leader and had pounded in the top of his head with a pair of heavy brass knuckles (only the "brass" was steel). Grinning with victory, Jaffee let the dead La Bigne slide to the ground. Jaffe wasn't aware of it, but his grin was the grin of a death's-head. John Viallier, too, had been tagged by the Cosmic Lord of Death.

Jaffe didn't even have time to spot Camellion and realize he was standing on the brink of eternity. The NAM minirevolver spit again. Jaffe jumped and cried, "Ohhhh-uhhhhhh." Camellion had aimed the tiny revolver very carefully, and the fifth and last .22 projectile had hit Jaffe in the side of the neck. The bullet zipped all the way through his throat, clipping the right internal jugular vein during its quick passage. His arms jerking, drowning in his own blood, Jaffe wilted to the bloody beach. The Death Merchant, jumping over bodies, moved toward Ralph Gerstung, although he was positive that the CIA street man would win—*His aura is a healthy blue. He'll be around for years.*

Camellion was only six feet from Gerstung and Viallier when there was a muffled shot. Survival expert that he was, Gerstung had turned the tables on the FLB terrorist. Twisting Viallier's hands and arms, he had gradually forced the muzzle of the broomhandle Mauser underneath the doomed man's chin. Gerstung had then squeezed Viallier's hand, forcing his finger to push against the trigger. The 7.63-mm bullet tore its way through the floor and the roof of Viallier's mouth, severed his tongue, bored through his brain, and blew off the top of his head.

Gerstung let the corpse sag to the sand. He glanced at the Death Merchant, bent down, picked up the Mauser, then looked around the area. A graveyard! Corpses and vehicles filled with bullet holes! The sun was high and bright. The day promised to be hot and humid. There were other certainties: The *Front de Libération de la Bretagne* was finished. The *Action pour la Renaissance de la Corse* might survive, since one of its leaders was still safe in Corsica. But the Death Merchant doubted it.

Camellion and Gerstung stared toward the water, toward the sound of the engines in the east, shielding their eyes from the sun with their hands.

The special barge and the *Moonstone* were arriving.

Gerstung took a deep breath, pulled a dirty handkerchief from his pocket and wiped his grimy face. "Didn't I tell you that they'd goof it in England, Kidd? They're so damned dense at the London station that the Chief of Station wears prescription underwear. Thirty well-equipped commandos in the barge and another ten on the boat; yet they couldn't get here until the show was over with. Now that's efficiency."

"The big show might only be starting," Camellion said evenly. "The *Gendarmes Mobiles* and the CRS must be out in force by now. No doubt they've heard the racket here on the beach. I'm going after my Auto Mags. I suggest you find your Match Masters."

* * *

Its two white masts gleaming in the sun, *Moonstone* remained a mile from the beach, the bow pointed west, the vessel bobbing gently in the calm water. The Special Forces Amphibious Operation Vehicle moved through the blue water straight for the shore, the top section of its gigantic wheels showing above the waterline.

The Death Merchant and Gerstung watched the SFAOV move through the breakers. As the depth of the water decreased, the height of the wheels increased, and the speed of the vehicle increased in proportion to the craft's leaving the water. Once it was fully on the beach, it was moving at thirty miles per hour.

The SFAOV resembled the DUKW, a U.S. Army two-and-a-half-ton amphibious truck. However, the SFAOV was much larger, its length 48 feet, its width 19.6 feet. The pilot compartment and engines were in the stern. Outside the stern were two large rudders and two three-bladed screws. It was the six enormous tires that made the vessel resemble some weird monster from the deep. Made of solid rubber, the tires, outer flat surface was reinforced with steel-cable lacing; each tire was nine feet tall and six feet four inches wide.

The bodies lying between the water and the back of the trailer did not deter the SFAOV. The big wheels rolled right over the corpses, squashing the bodies the way a steamroller would flatten grapes and plums. When the vehicle stopped, it was only thirty feet from the rear of the trailer, and although its tremendous tires had sunk several feet into the sand, the vehicle would not have any difficulty moving back into the water, even after the boxes of gold were loaded onto it. Not only was each wheel individually driven, but in situations in which the surface of the ground was slippery, a substance that could only be called "instant liquid concrete" could be squirted underneath the tires. The concrete would harden immediately and give the tires the necessary traction.

A ten-foot-wide section of the slanted prow opened outward and fell to the beach; commandos poured out of the vehicle and raced down the tilted platform, each man wearing an Armour of America Tactical Vest with an inset of Bristol Armour. In addition to 5.56-mm CAR-15 carbines or CAR-15 submachine guns, some of the men carried RSAF grenade launchers. Eight commandos at once detached themselves from the main body and spread out in teams, two teams to the south, two to the north. In each team there was an AR-10 7.62-mm light machine gun and a Dragon antitank weapon system. Shoulder launched from a firing tube, the Dragon MAW missle weighed twenty-seven pounds, had a range of 3,280 feet and was guided by electronic pulses sent through wires that accompanied the missile in flight.

Three men walked down the ramp and strode toward Gerstung and the Death Merchant. Two of the men were young, tough-looking and dressed like the other commandos. The third man, squared-jawed and over six feet tall, had a chest like a grizzly bear and arms like oak limbs. He wore combat boots and jet-black coveralls, and had two 9-mm SIG auto-loaders in black holsters on a black cartridge belt strapped around his waist. Two 9-mm Browning pistols were snug in black shoulder holsters.

One of the young men said to Camellion, "Sir, I'm Major Dustin Bogg." He indicated the other officer. "This is Lieutenant Wayne Bryan. And this—"

"He knows me," Vallie West said. One of the few people who knew that Richard Camellion was the Death Merchant, West winked at Camellion. "We've sort of met before, haven't we, Mr. Kidd?" He looked around the beach. "I see you've been rather busy this morning."

"I had help," Camellion said.

"The cargo is in the trailer?" Major Bogg looked at the Death Merchant.

Camellion nodded. "In the trailer—and the sooner you get the boxes in the water buggy and we get out here, the better off we'll be. An armored unit of the *Gendarmes Mobiles* is in the area.

"And don't goof it," added Gerstung. "If you guys had showed up sooner, we'd have been off the beach by now."

"Who are you?" demanded Bogg. "What is your function in regard to this operation?"

"Hell, I don't know," said Gerstung, talking around his identity. "I'm just an English teacher who came along for the ride. I ain't never done nothing like this before. I ain't doing nothing now; and if I get out of this in one piece, I ain't never going to do nothing no more neither."

Bogg, who reminded Camellion of a recruiting-poster American with his fresh-faced, boyish manner, gave Gerstung an odd look, after which he turned and motioned to one of the commandos. At once Sergeant Wilburn and those commandos who were not dragging bodies out of the way moved toward the trailer.

"Val, I take it you're no longer in retirement," Camellion said. He cocked his head to one side, as if listening.

West finished lighting a cigarette. "I'll clue you in on the sub. Yeah, I hear it, too."

Within a few minutes they saw the French spotter helicopter, the craft coming in from the southwest at a low altitude.

"The ship will take care of him," Major Bogg said confidently, staring up at the chopper.

At only five hundred feet, the Muraine-17K eggbeater flew directly overhead, its rotor blades creating a terrific racket. Once the chopper was over the water, it started to swing to the southeast. Up whooshed a slim, six-foot-long Viper sea-to-air missile from *Moonstone*. The Viper made contact ten seconds later. The chopper became a ball of fire, parts of it and its pilot and copilot raining down into the water.

The commandos, each man carrying a box of gold from the trailer to the SFAOV, didn't even bother to look up.

It was the ever-watchful Gerstung who first spotted Catherine Fronde and Madeleine Vaudrey. As if in a trance, the two women were stumbling down the low hillside to the north.

"They were part of your force?" Major Bogg asked the Death Merchant, who, watching the two women, deduced what must have happened. The two women had lain quietly in the rocks and had pretended to be dead. A chance in a million, and it had worked—then . . .

"Major, tell your men to the right to wait until they get closer, then terminate them," Camellion said. "They're excess baggage out of necessity."

Somewhat nervously, Bogg pulled the Rank 203 UHF transceiver from its case on his belt.

EPILOG

It was 1 P.M.

With a shower and a shave behind him and in brand new fatigues, the Death Merchant moved down the narrow corridor, the muffled throbbing of *Scorpion II*'s turbine moving with him, his thoughts reviewing the last phase of Pink Slipper 5. Getting off the beach and into international waters had not been difficult. There had not been a battle. The *Gendarmes Mobiles* had retreated after losing four Charrot armored cars to the deadly Dragon antitank missiles. The French had then tried to use two Muraine-17K gun choppers, one against the SFAOV on the beach, the second against *Moonstone*. Viper sea-to-air missiles had knocked both helicopters from the morning sky.

It had taken the commandos only twenty-six minutes to load the boxes of gold onto the SFAOV, another fifteen to roll off the beach into the water and put out to sea, the *Moonstone* riding shotgun.

Whether the French did not have any patrol boats in that section of the Gulf of Saint-Malo or had not wanted to do battle, was a question that only the French could answer. What did matter was that *Moonstone* and the SFAOV had not encountered any resistance and had proceeded to the "X-Marks-The-Spot," 61.27 kilometers west of Brittany—270 degrees west by magnetic course, 275 degrees by compass course.

At these coordinates the truly tricky part of the operation had been carried out. The commandos transferred to the *Moonstone,* and divers from *Scorpion II* floated up large air tanks to the SFAOV and bolted them to the port and starboard sides of the amphibious vehicle. Other divers attached fifty-foot cables to the four corners of the vessel. Special petcocks in the SFAOV had been opened, and the vessel allowed to submerge very slowly, sinking in proportion to the air released from the tanks, the rate of descend slow enough so that another group of divers, waiting below, had time to attach the ends of the four cables to the bottom hull of the submarine. The task required almost split-second timing, with the divers having to secure the ends of the cables by the time the very slowly descending SFAOV was from forty-five to fifty feet below the portside hull of *Scorpion II*. The several dozen divers had had only six minutes in which to do the job. One loose bolt in any of the clamps holding the cables—after the ends of the cables had been slipped through the "I-Rings" in the hull—and the entire operation would have dissolved in catastrophe. The SFAOV would have tilted sharply and the boxes of gold would have tumbled to the sea floor, 3,000 feet (or 900 meters) below the surface, too deep for divers to recover.

The operation had, however, gone smoothly. Even now, divers were working at the task of taking the boxes of gold from the SFAOV to the lockout chambers of the submarine, a slow process because of the time required to flood and unflood the three diving chambers.

Camellion reached the officers' aft wardroom. He went through the open bulkhead and walked over to a table where several JG's were starting to explain a new board game called "Chap Acquitted" to Vallie West, who was sipping guava nectar laced with brandy.

"It takes at least three to play," Lieutenant Buckmaster was saying. He glanced at Camellion, then turned back to West. "Three to play, and a 'dummy.' It's the dummy that will get in-depth knowledge of the incident. As you can see, the board is a map of Chappaquiddick and has a road running around it."

"What's the object of the game?" asked West with a deep laugh. "Does the winner have to drown a secretary?"

Lieutenants Buckmaster and McDevitt laughed. Camellion smiled.

"Hardly," said Buckmaster. "The object of the game is to complete a drive to cover up the facts by answering questions with evasive answers or wild excuses and, in doing so, to acquire more charisma than the other players."

"Here's the fourth man." Sidney McDevitt looked up at

the Death Merchant, who was standing next to West's chair. "Sit down and join in."

"Thanks, but there are matters that West and I have to discuss," declined Camellion. "Maybe later. We'll be on board for the next few days."

"Ah-ha! You're giving away secrets," joked Ed Buckmaster. "Since we're going straight to the States after the mysterious cargo is aboard, you two spooks are going to be picked up by more spooks in the mid-Atlantic."

"*Spooks?*" V West, with a large grin, pretended ignorance. He pushed back his chair and stood up. "Do you mean ghosts?" He and Camellion both knew that the crew of *Scorpion II* was almost certain that the operation was a CIA deal.

The two officers laughed. "You know damn good and well what I mean," Buckmaster. "But we know how it is. See you both later."

Earlier, Vallie West had told Richard Camellion that he had come out of retirement because he was bored with the business world and ". . . need the action to keep from ending up cutting out paper dolls in some rubber room."

Now in the privacy of a small meeting room, the Death Merchant got the rest of the news from West.

"I know the contents of the message you received from Plymouth, the one you got while you were at the mine." West grinned. "Need I say more, old buddy?"

Camellion bent forward confidentially. "The bottom line is that you're going with me to Austria," he said.

"You got it. I'm going to help you learn the secret of the Devil's Trashcan. . . ."